TOJ

MW01128169

And The

High Space L-Evator

BY

Victor Appleton II

Made in The United States of America

THE NEW TOM SWIFT INVENTION SERIES

Tom Swift And The
High Space L-Evator

By Victor Appleton II

It is something man has talked about and written about for decades, but has been thought to be beyond our reach. A space elevator capable of pulling up or lowering down vast payloads using almost no energy and firmly anchored in absolutely nothing but a gravity balance point.

Now, Tom Swift seeks to construct an even larger space station than his original Outpost in Space. To do it surpasses the capabilities of his fleet of cargo rockets. Even with their conversion from burning fossil fuel to using powerful repelatrons, they would only be able to complete the task in about twenty years.

Tom wants it done in under two.

As he works to perfect first the cables and then the lifting system, he finds that he is being opposed on several fronts, the most surprising of all is his own government. But the worst one is a fanatical faction within a worldwide governing body.

They might claim that having a military presence on the station is "for the good of mankind," but Tom sees an ulterior motive that some people might seize an opportunity to turn his peaceful station into a deadly weapon!

This book is dedicated to Konstantin Tsiolkovsky who, in 1895, suggested building a very tall tower, one up to a geostationary orbit point, with a large elevator in the middle. Others saw the problem with such concentrated weight on a relatively small footprint and soon designs called for a high-strength cable system running up to a heavy anchor that used the rotation of the planet to keep it taunt. No matter how, I applaud the people who conceived of the notion. Now it is up to Tom Swift to see that it gets built. The story is also dedicated to fellow fan author Leo Levesque whose *Flight To The Pleiades* gave me inspiration and a few plot points to set into motion.

The pressure wave hit Bud, tossing him backward and over the edge!
PAGE 161

TABLE OF CONTENTS

CHAPTER   **PAGE**

AUTHOR'S NOTE:

Computers are great. Unfortunately, computer programmers, or probably more specifically the people who manage programmers—the ones with no viable experience in what they manage—seem to fail to understand who and for what purposes their software is used. Case in point, the program I use to write and layout my books.

The most recent updates removed valuable features, features I need and want to use. It is a program running on my Macintosh.

So, it is with disappointment that I thought I would need to set this up using Word. I hate Word! To my horror I also found that my old version of Word no longer works in the new OS. Oh-oh!!!!!

Then it hit me. I still have my older Mac with its glorious fully functional version of Pages. So, with a delay in getting this out of a day, I pulled the old girl back out of the closet and went to work.

The result is just what I wanted. Hurray for outdated technology!

In a perfect world application programmers would not work in a vacuum, they would perform detailed studies of the changes people are asking for. This "take a shot in the dark" approach in not a good one.

Of course, in a perfect world we would actually have a real Tom Swift and his marvellous inventions.

Quality paperbound copies of all of this author's works may be found at the following web address:

http://www.lulu.com/spotlight/tedwardfoxatyahoodotcom

... and on Amazon.com in paperbound and Kindle editions

Tom Swift and the High Space L-Evator

FOREWORD

In modern history there are far too many instances where a man or group of greedy men—greedy for power over those around them—have promoted agendas of hatred, ultra-patriotism, and pay-the-poor-for-votes. None have been good for the masses and most are looked back upon with disgust.

We unfortunately live in a day and age where those we ask to take care of us turn out to be in it only for themselves. Or, have a mean streak that lets them enjoy the suffering of others. Or are so tied up thinking about themselves and how to remain in positions of power that they forget they are just a tiny part of a much larger thing.

I like to call that larger thing... mankind.

I also, in moments of personal weakness, think seriously about how nice it would be for a stray meteor to strike at the buildings housing the rascals who spend more time trying to keep themselves re-elected than in running our nation. One streaking fiery ball going *splat!* and it would be over.

Then, I open my eyes, yawn and realize that it is never a good idea to power down six grilled cheese sandwiches starting at lunch until just before going to sleep.

As a species we have come so far and often so fast that our technology outpaces our common sense. This is something that Tom faces in this new adventure.

Victor Appleton II

CHAPTER 1 /

ANY COLOR YOU WANT AS LONG AS IT IS BLUE

"I GO AWAY with Sandy for two weeks to visit my folks in California and come back to a huge hole in the ground. What gives?" the dark haired twenty-two year old man with the decidedly athletic build asked. "Did someone try to bomb Enterprises? If so, they missed!"

The person he was speaking to was about the same six foot height and a little slimmer with blond, shortish hair—although his wife teased him about it becoming longer and a little "shaggy around the ears" in the past year or so. He was the world famous young inventor and scientist, Tom Swift, and his best friend, Bud Barclay—also recently his brother-in-law after marrying Tom's younger sister—had just walked up to him.

"That hole is the newly excavated area that will be home to a brand new assembly company for Swift Enterprises. It," he swept his right arm from right to left, "will be the home of Swift Motors, our new automobile manufacturing company." He said this with so much pride that Bud felt a small shiver run down his spine.

"Jetz! So, your dad finally made the commitment?"

"Yes. Actually, he made the commitment six months ago but it took this long to get the architectural designs approved by the county and the town. Even though we're a couple miles outside the city limits, dad wanted to make certain that he had the full support of *all* the governments involved, including the state and feds. It all came together the day after you and Sandy left and the equipment rolled in the following morning."

They looked out over a one-mile by one-and-a-half mile tract of land that had formerly been covered with rocks, small hillocks, irregular dips and ruts, scrub grass, springtime wildflowers and several hundred scraggly trees. Even this close to a body of water the size of Lake Carlopa, this area had practically no draining water running through it. In fact it remained so dry that the winter and spring rains, along with the two to three feet of snow that fell in the area around Shopton, New York, barely made the top five inches damp at most times of year.

It was inhospitable to most plants and animals and so it had been very easy to clear any indigenous species and to relocate them a mile or so farther on.

"That site," Tom explained, "will soon hold three buildings. One office building like Enterprises' Administration building, one huge storage and subassembly manufacturing building that will start out inside one of my giant habitat inflatables like we use at the Mars colony, but about fifty percent larger, and the third building will be the assembly hall. That one goes up first along with the inflatable followed by the Admin building and finally the permanent subassembly building."

Bud nodded but Tom could see that he had many questions to ask. He waited for the man who was one of Swift Enterprises' top test pilots to get things in order in his mind.

"Okay. For starters, *what automobile?*"

Tom laughed. He drew in a deep breath and started to explain. "You know all about our Y4 and Y8 engines since you were integral to testing them." He referred to a radically new design for internal combustion engines that placed either four-cylinder or eight-cylinder engines in sets of three arranged in an inverted Y formation. All pistons attached to one central shaft and were timed so that not only was at least one piston just starting on its "firing" cycle at any given time, but everything was so balanced that the engine was under constant power. This meant that it not only ran more smoothly than any other conventional engine, it had an enormous amount of torque—about five times that of any similar displacement engine—and it didn't require a heavy flywheel to keep the engine running, even at idle.

Losing that weight plus all the other refinements lightened the engine and made it so powerful that a pair of the larger engines totaling less that eight liters displacement ran the generators that powered the giant transcontinental freight-carrying bullet trains Tom had created a few years earlier.

"Yeah. Of course I know about them. So, *what* about them?"

"First, you also recall my resonance engine from last year?"

"Sure. What to do when the oil left by dinosaurs goes away. Use sound pressure."

Tom decided not to correct this friend regarding the source of most of the world's petroleum.

"We have fielded dozens of requests from other manufacturers and, at last count two days ago, over one hundred thousand inquiries from the public about when cars featuring our engines would be getting built and going on sale. Car companies want to license the technology and drivers want to sit behind the wheel of a car powered by something so new and different. And powerful."

His eyes showing his appreciation for what Tom had just said, Bud nodded. "And powerful is *right*! So your dad figures that the best way to get them built without making compromises is for Enterprises to do it themselves?"

"Exactly. Except, just as we have what was the original Swift company we now run as the Construction Company and keep all its books and monies separate, this new endeavor will be a totally separate corporation."

Bud was rubbing his hands together. "When do I get to drive the first one off the line... and what will the first one off the line be?"

"To start with, it will be nearly a full year before the first pieces begin assembly. There's a lot to construct, design, and hand-build as our concept proving vehicles before that. But," he added seeing Bud's slightly disappointed face, "there will be ample testing to be done on the first concept cars starting in about seven months. I don't suppose you would be interested in a temporary transfer over to the new company to help with that?"

"You bet! Wow. I can hardly wait to tell Sandy. She'll be jealous as— ohhhh. Right. She'll be *jealous*." He turned to Tom, biting his lower lip. "Is there some way she can have a go at the cars as well?"

Tom had lived with his sister for more than twenty-one years. He definitely knew her and her reaction if she believed she was being slighted on something like this. And, since she had been working at Enterprises for a year there could be no more, "Sorry, but only employees can..." excuses.

"Not to worry, flyboy. She will definitely get a go. We do need a female perspective on the cars after all. Where you and I might just go for the flash and power, I'm certain that there are other refinements that need to be part of the production vehicles so that everyone can enjoy them."

They talked another hour about what would be part of the plant and where on the new property it would sit. Bud was surprised that Tom and his father intended to replant several well-tilled, de-rocked and fertilized areas with the same wildflowers that had been removed. Plans had also been made to divert a small stream mainly containing drainage water from several of the surrounding hills from its current path close to the back wall of Enterprises, and move it underground into a large holding pond on the new premises. It would be filtered and cleaned of any impurities before going into the pond that would act as a storage area for water to be used on all plants, grass and new trees that would be planted around the facility. A study had shown that enough water would be left, even during the dry summer months, to make it safe to stock to the pond with some fish and water plants.

As they turned to leave and go back to Enterprises, Tom

inquired about Bud and Sandy's trip.

"Oh, it was fun. Mom and dad send their love to all things Swift, of course, and my grandmother was there to add a little color and more than a little antagonism to everything."

"Is she still having her nothing good to say about anything attitude?"

Bud sighed and nodded. "It's getting worse. She is now having memory issues and will need to go into an assisted living complex before too long. The folks at the facility have already interviewed her and are fairly sure they can stand her." Bud grinned. "I love the old gal, but she really got to me this time, calling Sandy my 'blonde bimbo.' Sandy took it in stride, but I actually got angry." He sighed again.

"Well, in your absence and my sister being insulted the new plant isn't the only thing that has happened. But, I don't suppose you'd want to hear about that. Probably not nearly as exciting as the whole verbal abuse thing." Tom was looking at his best friend out of the corner of his eyes.

Bud stopped and grabbed Tom's shoulder, also stopping the inventor.

"Give!" he demanded, good-naturedly.

"Okay, but it'll have to wait until we get to the Admin building." Tom soon had to increase his pace so that Bud wouldn't beat him to his car and go rushing off. The inventor had hiked the seven-plus miles around Enterprises to the new site and wanted to take advantage of getting a ride back.

When they got out of Bud's car at the parking lot next to the Administration building, Bud started chanting, "Tell me, tell me, tell me..." like a small child. He was even visibly hopping slightly up and down with excitement.

Tom could only shake his head and smile. "Up the stairs, little Budworth," he commanded. "And no more sugar for you today!"

Bud was only mildly surprised when they walked right past the large office Tom and his father Damon shared and down the hall to Tom's large laboratory. Along with a smaller office/lab/apartment Tom kept down in the underground hangar for the *Sky Queen*—Tom's first large-scale invention and still a pet favorite of his—this large lab provided the inventor with practically all the equipment and testing capabilities anyone could want.

As they entered the room Bud's eyes caught sight of the clear tomasite-enclosed test chamber along the left wall. He immediately could see a difference.

"It's so... shiny! The windows are as clear as they were the first day you opened the door." He turned to Tom. "Is that what you wanted to show me? Replacement windows on the old explode-o-chamber?"

The flyer was making reference to the five or six times something had gone in an unexpected direction leading to whatever was inside exploding. Luckily, Tom hadn't been inside when most of those happened, although he had been inside when a few experiments using sonics or chemicals had gone awry and had come close to a fatal accident.

"Nope!" Tom said. "But I did find a way to polish the inside of those panels. Dad just finished developing a new bonding agent that let me create buffing pads of tomasite and Durastress micro-particles. That, along with a silicon paste and a little elbow grease and they are good as new. I kind of got tired of looking over at them all scratched and cloudy. But, that isn't the thing. *This* is!" he stated pointing at a set of equipment sitting on the largest of his test benches.

They walked over to it all the while with Bud tilting his head one way and then the other.

The device consisted of a base plate, probably five feet wide by eight feet long—in Bud's estimation—that was slightly convex. Surrounding the edges were six arched armatures that rose above the base by nearly five feet. They made the thing look like an upside-down metal and plastic spider.

"Okay. I have to admit I got a bit too much sun on our trip and it may have fried a few of little Bud's brain cells. You're gonna have to tell me what that is."

Tom now pursed his lips. To him it was obvious, and he was a little surprised that Bud didn't see it.

"Think back a couple years," he told his best friend. "Then add Doc Simpson into it. Something I made for him—" he trailed off seeing that Bud's brain was finally wrapping around something.

"Wait! Is that a giant version of the old sonic inside-peeky-at-guts-thingie you built?"

Tom laughed. Bud never used the standard names for any of Tom's inventions. This was no exception. The inventor, in an effort to help Enterprises' young doctor, had designed and built a device that you could lay a patient on and a combination of sonic and other electromagnetic wavelengths were sent down from a trio of arms that could be positioned all around the body. The resulting body scans were then presented in full color as a hologram floating right in front of a surgeon's face. This was possible by the use of one of Tom's earlier inventions, his 3D telejector.

It had come in handy in saving Tom's life on a couple occasions, and now Swift Enterprises was building them for the medical industry where they revolutionized many surgical techniques by allowing the doctor to see exactly what was going on inside, in real time, before a single incision was made. Without x-rays.

"Yes, Bud. It is a new and as you can see, larger version. This one uses all the various wavelengths from our medical version, but I've added very low range and power radio waves. You won't be able to use an AM or FM radio within about fifteen feet of this when it is running."

Giving his head a little scratch, Bud inquired, "What will it be for? Are you expecting that we'll find a race of giants on Saturn or something like that you'll want Doc to examine?"

Tom shook his head. "No. This one is purely for scanning inanimate things. I intend to use it for looking at various metal and synthetic objects to detect fatigue before any other method might find it. I have been hoping to find the time to do this ever since that PanAtlantic passenger jet broke apart over Newfoundland last year. The end result of the Canadian and U.S. investigative boards was metal fatigue hidden so deep inside of the wings that only a complete tear down would ever have located it. It was a terrible loss of life and if there is anything Enterprises can do to keep that from ever happening again..." He left the rest unsaid.

Bud's work life revolved around aircraft and he was one of those who could look at an aircraft design, even when sketched on paper, and tell you what wasn't going to work right and appreciate innovations. He slowly raised his right hand.

"A question. Actually, I have two questions. First, wings on most aircraft are a lot bigger than this. They just won't fit in between the arms. So—"

"Ah. Well this is just the test unit. The final version will be about four times larger and the armatures will be both flexible and extendible so the thing will work on even the largest of the super jumbo jets' wings. And, for the body there will be a second unit that will be in two parts, one outside and one inside. It will require that seats and overhead bins be removed but it will be autonomous and move around inside on treads with the outside unit being held in place by a special Attractatron unit inside that will only hold onto the outer plate and not the hull of the aircraft."

Bud whistled. He truly marveled at what Tom was capable of and understood the importance of a complete metal and carbon fiber scan device such as this.

"Isn't it going to freak out some technicians when they see a curved metal plate roaming all over their aircraft?"

Tom grinned and nodded. "Yes, except it isn't going to be metal. You recall how we excavated an area on the Moon and brought back that new metal, ArmAlColite?" Bud nodded. It was a metal named for the three Apollo 11 astronauts who first brought it back. "The large plate will be mostly a skin of carbon fiber and tomasite fibers with a thin ring of ArmAlColite. There is absolutely no chance of any aircraft having it so there is no chance of attracting parts of the jet."

"And, you could make that outer shell look like a giant bug!"

Tom groaned, but went on to tell Bud that the wing unit—which would also be used on the tail section—was to be mounted on an arm that could be attached to a standard forklift. When the flyer asked how many Tom believed they might sell, the inventor paused before answering.

"Dad and I are thinking about three dozen. One each for the nine major aircraft manufacturers around the worlds and the rest for various accident investigating agencies in major countries."

"Well, I know we don't need one given our manufacturing and materials, but I sure hope all the other guys sign on. Imagine if all fatigue accidents had never happened. That accounts for about thirty percent of industry's deaths. Now, if only you could build an infallible pilot!"

Over the next week Tom kept a close eye on the building of the automobile factory. Damon had been called to a series of meetings in Japan regarding their space program in which Swift Enterprises was currently helping.

It was the day before Mr. Swift was due to return when there came a knock on the office door. Munford Trent, the secretary and administrator they shared along with the office, poked his head in.

"Tom. I've got a small delegation from the Materials department out here. They have a meeting with your father that either I forgot to reschedule—" he shook his head and mouthed the word 'No,' "—or word didn't get to them that he would have to reschedule." Now he nodded and rolled his eyes.

Tom laughed. "Send them in. Hopefully, I won't disappoint."

Once the seven men and women were in and seated around the conference table Tom took the final seat and smiled at them all. "Well, thank you for coming. As you now know, dad isn't here. I hope I can help, so if someone will tell me what this is about—" he looked around hopefully.

Finally, they all swiveled their heads to face a young woman Tom wasn't certain he recognized. She cleared her throat.

"Well, I guess it's my hot potato," she said.

"I'm very sorry that I can't place your face," Tom admitted. "You are—?"

"Huh? Oh. I'm Chasey Marlow. We're all sort of new, at least to this team. You see we're the people working on the materials for the new cars."

"Oh. Okay. Well, for those of you I know or recognize, hello, and for anyone relatively new here, welcome. So, what is it you've come to tell me?"

There were smiles, nods and murmurs from them all before they again turned their heads to face Chasey. She turned beet red.

"I—uh—I'm not very good at speaking so I apologize if I mess things up. But you see, we've come up against a terrible problem."

"Oh. *Terrible* terrible or just *inconvenient* terrible?"

"Really terrible. You see, between your father and Mr. Sterling over in Patterns, we were given a new formula for the materials that will form the outer shell and body parts of the cars. Over the past couple of weeks we've been testing it for tensile strength, resiliency to impact, recovery to denting—and by the way it takes *a lot* to dent that stuff—and a host of other tests. Acid, alkali, salt, small rocks and sand. A bunch."

"I think I get that. You've done a lot of testing. Right?"

She smiled and nodded vigorously, not catching the small hint of irony in Tom's voice.

"Yes. But we've run into a big problem."

"So, go ahead. Tell me what that is," he prompted her, patiently.

Chasey took a deep breath. "You can't paint it. It just sort of slides down and then flakes right off once it dries. All you are left with is the material underneath."

Tom considered this for a moment before asking, "Where does that leave us?"

"It means that we can deliver cars that are almost indestructible. The finish will stay bright and shiny, pretty much no matter what. The problem is, unless we can find a way around the paint thing, the only color you'll be able to purchase, is blue. Light blue!"

CHAPTER 2 /

SO, NOW WHAT DO YOU WANT TO DO?

TOM LAUGHED for a full minute. He only straightened his face and wiped away he tears when he saw that the others in the room were aghast at his reaction.

"I am so very sorry, folks. It's just that this isn't anything desperate or deal breaking. Blue is a nice color and if that is what we are stuck with, then we will just have to live with it. As far as I know very few people actually purchase a car based solely on its color. And besides, there might be something I can do about that. I'll give the formula for the material a good look over and perhaps I can come up with some additives to give it different colors. How will that be?"

Seven pensive faces all turned into smiles. They left a few minutes later chattering to each other in happy tones.

After they departed he went to his computer and searched for the formula for the forthcoming car body parts. He finally found it listed as one of Hank Sterling's semi-private files. Without the pattern maker's access codes he could not download or even look at it.

Tom picked up the phone and dialed Hank's number.

"Why sure you can have access, skipper," the big engineer told him. "In fact let me transfer the file into your file pool. Give me a couple minutes. But hey, while I have you one the line, can I ask you about this new car?"

"Sure. What do you want to know?"

"Well, why did your dad only specify a single color additive?"

Tom almost choked stifling his laugh. "Oh, Hank. Let me tell you what I just went up against," and he related the meeting with the materials team. He ended with, "So you can give them multiple colors?"

"It isn't easy to color the stuff without changing some of the strength properties, but I have at least six other colors I can give you with no major material concessions. How about if I send you over a color chart with the exact ones. By the way, they include black, two different reds, a deeper blue, gray and a sort of bronze. Sorry, but no white. It looks terrible and you really need a small amount of color to hide the fibers under the surface. Do you still want that file?"

"Might as well see if there is anything else I can come up with, but I think you've just made the day for seven very nervous scientists."

Once Tom had the chance to look at the formula, and see what the additives were that would color the materials without changing it, he understood why his father had concentrated on the light blue. It came from the addition of ultra fine aluminum and copper powders, perhaps as little as a quarter teaspoon each per car body. Pennies to use.

On the other hand, the deepest red came from the addition of five additives, one a deadly poison until mixed in, and costing on average of three hundred dollars extra per body.

Most people were not accustomed to paying hundreds of dollars just for a different car color unless it was a specialty color. Even then, Tom knew it would be a hard sell. But, perhaps, by averaging it out among all of the cars produced the cost could be kept down.

He did a little research and happened to find a tiny article by a never-before-published professor at a small college in Tennessee who had evidently found a way to introduce dyes into long chain polymers. Such polymers were exactly what was used as the bonding agent for the fibers in the body. It took several hours to get a phone number for the man but he was able to place a call just before five that afternoon. He identified himself to the man.

"Of course I know who you are, Mr. Swift. Gosh. Everybody knows who Tom Swift is. Wow, and you're calling me? Whatever for?"

Tom explained his locating the article and how his expertise might come in handy for a forthcoming project. "Of course, I can't tell you much about it, only to say that we would love to host you for a few days or a week early this coming month to see if you and your process can help us. You will be well-paid for your time, success or failure, and if the process does what we need, we will license it from you."

The man, Barnaby Somers, was delighted and promised to see what time he might be able to get off. He agreed to call Tom in the next few days with his schedule.

Before leaving for the day Tom shipped off the color chart to the materials team with a note saying:

Possibly more to come! TS

At home he was able to tell Bashalli, his wife of—as she was able to relate it—one year, five months, two weeks, three days and about three hours, that he had a great day. So, how was hers?

She coyly looked at him before sliding over and into his lap. "You," she told him wrapping her arms around his head and giving him a hug, "are being cuddled by the new Head of Media Services at my advertising agency!" She gave a little squeal of delight as he hugged her back.

Moving her a little away from his face, he asked, "So, what does it mean and how did it happen?"

As it turned out, the former head of that department had been hired away by a large agency down in Manhattan leaving the spot empty. And, though she had only been at the Shopton agency about three years full time, plus two others while in school, her artistic skills were much better than the others at the company, and she had already shown an aptitude for managing a team of artists. Now she would be managing them plus the two copywriters, the small video team and the in-house voiceover people. Eleven altogether. And, in a seventeen person company, that was a serious position to find herself in.

To celebrate Tom had her take the pot of stew she had simmering on the stove off the heat, get dressed up, and they went out to the nicest restaurant in Shopton where he insisted she not look at prices but concentrate on what sounded delicious.

She ordered lobster with a prawn salad and asparagus. And ate every bit of it.

When they got home, she was on top of the world. Her husband's approval and support meant just about everything to her. Coming from an oppressive—to women—country like Pakistan, and even leaving when she was barely more than ten years old, had always left her with just a little doubt as to her abilities. Now she finally was realizing how good she was and it felt extra good!

She was still floating on air the next morning when she served him breakfast in bed. It was Saturday and she insisted that he stay home. With little to do at Enterprises he gladly agreed and they spent most of the day in their pajamas, reading and talking. But, at about six she had a sudden thought.

"Tom. You know that Sandra has been teaching me how to fly?"

He nodded and mumbled "Umm-hummm."

"Could you take me up in one of the airplanes and let me show you what I have learned? And to give me some pointers on how I can become better?"

He glanced at the clock. It would be dark in about ninety minutes so he suggested the following morning. "In fact, rather than take up one of the propeller jobs, how about if we go up in the

Toad so you can have a taste of multi-engine jet flight?" Seeing her bite her lower lip a little he kissed her and said, "It is actually easier than any of the *Pigeons* we build. Better avionics that can be relied on to help you fly. Plus, I'll be right next to you."

The Toad was Tom's personal version of the SE-11 Commuter jet he had designed for small airline use. Seating nine in his prototype version, it featured twin jet turbines mounted high on the top of the wing with the fuselage slung underneath, giving the jet a bit of the appearance of an amphibian when viewed from the front.

Bashalli barely slept that night and was awake, showered and dressed by the time Tom came down at eight. She placed a piece of toast into his hand and turned him around shoving him back up the stairs, down the hall and into their bathroom.

While the water heated up, he munched on the toast and then took a hot and fast shower.

"Do not bother shaving. I love you scruffy today," she called through the door.

He laughed at her eagerness. It carried through on the drive to Enterprises and the short walk to the Barn—the open-sided hangar standing close to the underground hangar of the *Sky Queen*—where the Toad was normally kept. She settled down into the left seat and performed the pre-flight checks like a pro, took the microphone and called both the Enterprises tower as well as up the nearby hill to what everyone called the Super Tower, a combination extended range Swift control center and regional flight center operated by the FAA.

Both gave her permission to taxi and for immediate takeoff.

She reached over and took Tom's hand. He could feel her trembling a little, but decided it was more from excitement than nerves.

"Swift Two rolling on taxiway one," she radioed.

"Roger. Clear air with zero traffic for thirty miles. Light breeze will be over your nose at two-six-zero relative. Barometer steady at two-nine-nine-eight and temperature is fifty-seven. Climb to five hundred and turn left to zero-eight-five for flight level two thousand... contact Super Tower on secondary frequency."

"Wilco," she replied as they approached the turning point that would place them on one of the main East-West runways.

"You are doing great, Bash," Tom complimented her.

Sandy had already told him that his wife was a good, careful and steady flyer. "All she needs are some solo takeoff and landing experience and I think you can get her certified!"

"Do I need to bring the throttle for the left engine up to make this turn?" she asked Tom.

"No, just throttle both engines back a little and take the turn nice and slow. The yoke controls the nose wheel. If you want, I will do throttles and flaps and gear for you... or you can do them. It all happens in standard order and nothing has to be done too quickly."

She nodded several times as she turned them onto the runway and applied both pedals to bring them to a halt. On the radio she called out, "Ready to go."

"Permission granted. Happy flying, Mrs. Swift."

She placed her right hand on the twin throttle levers and then asked if Tom could put his on top of hers, "Just to be certain I do not go too far or too fast," she told him. It was a very smooth takeoff with Tom giving her the "Rotate" mark, and she soon reached over and pushed up the lever to raise the landing gear. As she hit her first altitude mark she turned them in a slow curve to the new heading and continued to climb. As they approached the radio turnover point she called Enterprises' tower and notified them she was switching over.

They flew for more than three hours with Bashalli at the controls the entire time. She even, after asking Tom if he thought she was ready for it, landed them with only a slight bump and hop.

The smile she had on her face early that morning hadn't left. It remained on her face as they drove up to Tom's parents' house where they had been invited to a late lunch.

Bud and Sandy were already there when they walked inside.

After greetings, Bashalli told them all about her flight and how good it felt and how excited she was. It was only twenty minutes later that Tom prompted her to tell them about her new job.

"Oh. Right. That." And that led to another fifteen minutes of her joyously telling the group all about the increased responsibility.

Once she wound down again, Anne asked about Bud and Sandy's trip to California.

"We didn't do anything special," Sandy insisted, giving Bud a sideways look.

"Didn't do anything *special*?" Bud asked incredulously, ignoring her. "How much time do we have?"

He began telling about the flight out and how Sandy had, at first, been seated next to a young woman who obviously had had a few drinks before boarding. She barely had looked old enough and it had made her very chatty. So much so that Sandy finally reached up and pressed the attendant call button.

" 'Can I get you something?' the nice redheaded attendant—from a bottle, Mother, if you can believe that!— asked once she came up the aisle."

"I'll have a drinky-poo, if you please," the young woman had slurred. "Crum and rola-coka."

"And I'll have a different seat mate than little miss drinky poo if you can manage it, please." Sandy had told the attendant in a firm voice.

Sandy got what she wanted and the other young woman did not. She was moved to the back of the plane and put on a half-minute tantrum before passing out.

Bud's next story was all about Sandy trying her hand at surfing.

"Now, you have to understand that the surf out by Los Angeles is pretty tame. Maybe four footers. There are an incredible number of water sissies who wear full wetsuits even when the water is as warm as it gets in the summer." Bud shook his head. Sandy pretended to not be listening and her mother could tell that she must have done something funny or embarrassing and didn't really want everyone to know about it. But, Bud was in his element and moved on with the story.

"My folks still have my old short board from when I was a teenager, so I pulled it out, cleaned a half-dozen years of dust off it, waxed it and we hit the beach the second morning. Sandy insisted on watching me do it a few times. I'm afraid I wasn't a very good example because I fell two of the three times.

"She took the board, paddled out a ways and turned in just in time to catch the only five foot wave of the day. She pushed herself up, planted her feet, and went flying backwards, you-know-what over teakettle. She shoved down so hard that the board took to the air, passed over the heads of three other surfers and buried itself nose first in the sand right at the water's edge."

"At least I got a round of applause from the crowd," Sandy said with disdain.

Bud chuckled. "You did at that. Unfortunately the lifeguard came over and asked her to not go back out since she might be a hazard to others."

"Did anything else interesting happen?" Bashalli asked, seeing Sandy's discomfort and hoping to change the subject.

Bud looked at Sandy who vigorously shook her head. "No, Bud. Don't you dare!"

"What?" all the others at the table asked in unison.

Sandy turned beet red, so much so that you could see the color in the part in her hair. It had obviously been quite embarrassing to her, but had it been so bad she could not, or would not, share the story with her family?

Bud looked around the table. "I can't tell you about it. I have to respect Sandy's wishes. Just suffice it to say that nobody got hurt, no animals were harmed in the making of, et cetera."

Now, Sandy was feeling the pressure of five pairs of eyes on her. Even Bud had turned to see what she was going to do. She looked around and sniffled, a bit dramatically noted her mother who had lived with this for more than twenty-one years. She drummed her fingers on the table and took another look around at the people sitting there.

"Okay. But this goes no further that these chairs. I never want to hear another word about it, here or anywhere. Got it?"

They all promised complete secrecy.

"Fine. Then here's what happened. We all, that's Bud, me and his folks and even his grandmother, went to the country club near Rolling Hills Estates where Grandma Barclay lives. Beautiful grounds and a wonderful new swimming pool." She trailed off and turned red again, but soon took a deep breath and began talking again.

"Anyway, Bud and his dad went out to the putting green for a while and we ladies stayed around the pool. It was about—" She stopped again blushing furiously. "Go ahead, Bud. You tell them."

Bud gave her a look and she nodded putting her face in her hands.

"Well, okay. As Sandy said dad and I went to shoot some balls around the putting practice green while gran, mom and Sandy took in some sun. And, from what I found out later, a few rum drinks with little umbrellas and chunks of fruit. Dad and I got back just as the police arrived—"

"Police?" Anne and Bashalli chorused. Sandy still had her face hidden but she nodded.

Bud picked back up. "So, we run over to see what's happening. I was afraid that gran might have died or something, but there are three officers surrounding Sandy and she is sitting there with handcuffs on—"

"Handcuffs?" came the female chorus. Another look at Sandy and another resigned nod.

"Why?" Damon asked, more levelly than his wife or daughter-in-law would have been able to.

Now, Sandy looked up and spoke. "They were thinking of arresting me for indecent exposure," she admitted with narrowed eyes that just dared any of them to say anything. "See, after a couple of the drinks they called Scorpions, I decided to take a little dip in the pool. What I didn't realize is that the back strap of my bikini top had loosened, so when I dove in it popped off on the one side of the pool while I swam underwater to the other."

"Sandy evidently climbed out and was about do dive back in again when an old biddy saw her and screamed to high heaven," Bud added.

"I didn't know I was showing anything so I stretched and dove back in and came up with my bikini bra draped over the top of my head. *Then* I figured it out. I was back to being decent before I got out again, but the old woman had screamed for the manager and he came on the run and the old woman is some big donor to the club and rich as can be and he bowed and scraped and cow-tow'd to her and called the police."

"They let her off with a warning once my mother told them off. She didn't put up with a bit of guff from them, and then she marched right over and told the old woman just what she thought of her. Needless to say, we were informed that we were not to return, even though gran and gramps were charter members of the club. Sheesh!"

"Bud's grandmother called me a blonde bimbo. Can you imagine?"

They all had a good laugh and agreed that the entire affair was more of a tempest in a teacup than anything to be ashamed of.

"Besides," Damon told his daughter, "if you never go back all they will have is a memory. Pleasant for most, I presume."

"Daddy!" Sandy said as she playfully punched him in the arm. "So, story time is over except to tell you that as Bud and his father were leaving the putting green, an older man hit a ball a little too hard and it rolled off the surface and onto the pathway and right under Bud's foot. *He* went you-know-what over teakettle. Has a nasty set of scrapes on his left shoulder to show for it and everything." She playfully stuck her tongue out at her husband.

It was agreed that a change of subject was in order.

"So, Bashi," Anne Swift asked they were finishing the last of the meal. "Now that you've conquered the skies, what do you want to do next?"

"Mother," Sandy said in mock exasperation. "Bashi wants what every woman wants. Now that she has a great husband and a fulfilling job, she wants *a baby*!"

The last gulp of milk Tom had in his mouth came shooting out through his nose!

CHAPTER 3 /
HITCHED 'N STUFF LIKE THAT

TOM WAS speechless. Bud was speechless, as was Damon. Anne got a tiny knowing smile on her face and Sandy looked like the cat who had swallowed the canary.

Only Bashalli wasn't silent. Or particularly pleased. "Sandra Swift. You take that back!" she practically shouted. "I most certainly do *not* want a baby. Not right now at least. *Why* would you say something like that?"

Now it was Sandy's turn to look shocked. She had only said it as a tease but it certainly had been taken wrong. As she sought for words to say tears came streaming down her face.

"Oh, Bashi, I am so sorry. I was kidding. I just wanted to see how Tom might react. I never thought…"

Now Bashalli was in tears and Anne was getting misty.

Tom was grabbing for all of their napkins trying to wipe up his errant milk from the table and his face.

Damon shook his head and said to his son, "You let your sister clean that mess up. She's the one who brought it on."

Tom looked at his wife and sister as they hugged each other and cried on each other's shoulders. It was, to his knowledge, the very first time there had been any angry words between them.

He and his father got up and began picking up the dishes, carrying them in silence to the kitchen. Once there, Damon closed the door to the living room and looked at his son. Tom looked back and they both broke down in laughter.

"I hate to say this about my own offspring, but it serves your sister right for spouting off like that. I only wish you had had the foresight to turn your face to spray that milk all over her." That brought on renewed laughter from them both.

"But I guess, on a more serious note, that it does bring up the subject of grandchildren. Your mother will kill me if you tell her I said this, but she has been wondering out loud about when she will be 'grandma' to one or more mini-Swifts. She has promised to not nag either you or Sandy about it, but it is a fire burning inside her that will not go out. Not even if you doused her with your AntiInferno flying fire truck." He referred to Tom's latest major invention, a repurposed seacopter capable of concentrating nitrogen and carbon dioxide out of the air, liquefying them, and then directing them onto large fires from high overhead.

Tom assured his father that his lips were sealed.

"Bash and I have discussed it a little and we both agree that we do want to have kids. But not for at least ten years. I've got too many things to do that would keep me from being home enough right now, and she is so proud of her job at the ad agency that she wouldn't want to even take a few months off. So, it will have to be Sandy and Bud, or nothing, I'm afraid."

Tom sliced a large cherry pie his mother made earlier that day and dished it up onto plates while Damon went back out and picked up the last of the lunch dishes.

No further mention of unintended exposure episode or babies was made.

What was talked about was Tom's next great idea. Or more properly, his total lack of a next great idea.

"I thought I might take over the management of the new car factory build from dad, with his permission of course. You seem to have more than enough on your plate right now so I thought you could use the break."

Mr. Swift looked thoughtful and then nodded. "It would be a great help if you could take some of the responsibility off my shoulders. But I think I'll keep final say control for now. What I could use is your expertise in getting that first inflatable building up and solidly installed. I have a feeling that your knowledge in creating the strong foam to fill all those brace tubes might be necessary."

"Why is that, dear," Anne inquired. "I thought Tom perfected that for the Mars colony."

"We did the necessary environmental study including a year-long project to measure all the hydrology, weather and other things that effect any patch of land that large. We discovered a few things. First, that area, just a few thousand yards away from Enterprises' back wall, gets an almost continuous ground-level breeze of three to five miles per hour. Now, by itself, that isn't much, but where Enterprises sees top wind speeds of about thirty, the new area gets a flow coming off the nearby hills of up to fifty-two."

"Wow. I didn't realize that, Dad," Tom admitted.

"But, what does that mean?" Bashalli asked.

"Well," Tom replied, turning to face her, "my expanding foam already is going to have to hold up more than twice the weight. If Earth's gravity is measured at one unit, the gravity on Mars is about thirty-eight percent of that. My computations for the foam's strength covers that extra weight but only at winds about what we get at the tower at Enterprises. Like dad said, that's just about maxing out at thirty. This makes a big difference. Of course I'll take that on, Dad. Count on me."

Bashalli beamed at her husband. She was incredibly proud of what her Tom could do and what he was willing to take on.

Before they all left it had been decided that Tom would finish up the few small things on his agenda over the next week and then get firmly into the inflatable project.

As they were walking out the door, Bashalli gave Anne a big hug and whispered in her ear, "Do not worry, mother Swift. It may be about ten years but Thomas and I intend to give you that grandchild you truly want. I think you will be a wonderful grandmother."

Anne kissed her daughter-in-law on the cheek and in a choked voice, whispered back, "Thank you, Bashi."

Tom and his father were sitting in their office two days later when there was a small knock on the door. This was usually the point where their secretary poked his head in, but the door failed to open. They looked at each other as the knock was repeated. Tom pushed his chair back and got up from his desk, crossing the room and opening the door.

There stood Chow Winkler, their personal chef and good friend. Chow had first met up with the Swifts when Tom was just turning sixteen and Damon was building their nuclear test facility, the Citadel, out in New Mexico. When the Swifts left to go back to Shopton, the old time western prairie cook had begged to go along, and they had accepted his offer to be their cook.

"Well, hey there, pard," Tom greeted the older man with a smile. "And, since when do you just knock and not come on in?" He looked around the cook. "Uh, I see that you don't have your food cart so this must be a social call. Come on in!"

Chow shuffled into the office, taking off his ever-present ten-gallon hat and setting it on the back of one of the conference area chairs. Tom noticed that this was a new hat, and it looked to be smaller than the old one. This made sense as the cook had been on a diet and exercise program for nearly two years and had dropped almost ninety pounds. As a result, he had to replace all of his clothes and had recently complained that his hat kept falling down onto his ears.

Unlike most days when he wore some of the most outlandish and brightly colored western shirts available, today he was wearing a pale blue chambray shirt tucked into his jeans which were, in turn, tucked into his brightly polished boots.

"Kin I ask you two an important question?" he asked.

Damon got up and came over indicating that they should all take seats in the conference area. Once they sat down, he told Chow, "Of course you can ask anything you want. If we can figure out the answer we'll give it to you. Now, what can we do for you, Chow?"

Chow scratched the top of his mostly bald head. He looked from one to the other of them before replying. "Wahl, ya see, I got a pre-dic-ee-ment that I'd appreciate some o' your kind advice on."

Tom grinned. He was relieved that things had not begun with any bad news. "What can we help with?"

"Okay. Ya'all know my lady friend, Wanda, right?" The two inventors nodded. "Okay then. If'n ya recall, she an' me were gettin' real cozy afore she moved out West fer a year or so, then she up and moved right back to Shopton last year."

"And, as I recall, you rekindled your romance with her at that time," Damon commented, making the cook's head bob up and down in agreement. It had been a very happy Chow back then when Wanda had come back into his life.

"Yep! Wahl, now I've been gettin' a sort of itch in the back o' my brain that it's just about time I finally tossed off my bachelor duds and got hitched n' things like that." He looked at his bosses apprehensively.

Chow relied heavily on the approval of the two men before him. Even thought Damon was nearly six years his junior he often felt as if the inventor was more like a father and Tom was more like a son.

Tom and Damon almost collided with each other as they both jumped up and reached out to shake Chow's hand.

"Wow, Chow! That's wonderful." Tom exclaimed.

"I whole heartedly double that sentiment, Chow," Mr. Swift was quick to add.

Finally, the cook's face relaxed and he smiled at them.

"I'm mighty pleased to hear that," he told them. "Ya cain't imagine how I've been sweatin' this out fer the past coupl'a days."

Sitting back down, Tom asked, "So Wanda said yes, huh? When's the wedding?"

Now, the westerner's face went slack and his eyes opened wide.

"The truth is I've been so knotted up thinkin' 'bout this I haven't asked her yet. Golly. You do think she'll say yes, don't ya?"

Damon reached out and patted Chow on the knee. "I think she'd be foolish to say anything *but* yes, Chow. She is a wonderful woman and you are a wonderful man. And, I agree with you. It's about time you settled down and had a steady home life with someone you love."

Chow's face screwed up for a moment before he spoke again. "Kin we have the weddin' here? That is unless she's got her heart set on another church weddin'. Prob'ly not since her first marriage was some big church affair an' that didn't last but about five years or so."

"Anywhere, Chow. Just give us the date and we'll make it happen."

The cook left a minute later promising that he was going to ask Wanda to marry him that very evening and would see if she agreed to getting married on the Enterprises grounds.

When the door shut, Tom turned to his father. "Unless you have an objection, why don't we roll out one of the new inflatable buildings and set it up near the front gate. I'm sure that Sandy and Bash and mom would love to decorate, and Harlan will appreciate us not letting a lot of non-employees wandering around in an open area."

The building he mentioned was one of the inflatable structures Enterprises built for commercial use that now came in five sizes, all based on the structures Tom designed and built for the colony on Mars. The three, soon to be four, buildings up there housed almost one hundred and fifty people and would approach two hundred by year's end.

Since the first one went to Mars, Enterprises had built and sold more than a hundred smaller structures to various industries and to the power companies with stations located in areas of inhospitable weather. Before the buildings, each averaged one outage due to water damage per month. Now, inside of the protective structures, there had been zero outages due to weather.

"I have absolutely no objections, Son. Let's just hope Wanda is smart enough to say 'yes'."

That evening, Chow was pacing back and forth in the front room of his two-bedroom bungalow on the opposite edge of Shopton from Enterprises. He had already changed shirts twice as the nervous perspiration dampened the underarms of the first two. Now, with Wanda due in a couple minutes, he was nearing panic.

When she walked in the front door a moment later he nearly fainted. Seeing him red in the face and puffing short breaths, Wanda panicked thinking Chow might be having a heart attack.

She rushed over and eased him onto the sofa, cradling his head against her shoulder.

"Oh, Chow. Are you okay?" Her voice was filled with emotion. "Don't you go and die on me you old thing! I've got years and years of plans for us. You hear me?"

A sudden calm came over Chow. *Plans*? Years and *years*?

All of his fears were swept away in that single statement. He pulled his head out of her embrace and looked at her.

"Ya mean, like as in gettin' hitched an' bein' together fer ever?"

Wanda froze. Her mind needed a few seconds to switch from worry to wonder.

"Of course I mean as in 'gittin' hitched' you old misery. Why in the world do you think I moved back to Shopton?"

Now, Chow was floating on air. "So, will ya marry me?"

"Damn straight!" she said planting a big kiss on his lips. "And the sooner the better, before you have a chance to change your mind!"

When he brought up the idea of having the wedding at Enterprises, she jumped into his lap like a young girl. "Yes, yes, yes," she said. "With everybody who you know. Do they have a building big enough? I mean, other than one of those old, dirty airplane hangars?"

Chow assured her that something could be done to accommodate the wedding guests, possibly numbering more than five hundred.

"Plus, yer fam'ly, o' course," Chow told her.

"One spinster sister, one brother and two nieces. Not much to cram in," she told him with a smile.

When Chow practically waltz into the office the next morning both Tom and Damon knew that the answer had been "yes." Tom told him about the potential for using one of the inflatables.

"Ya mean, one o' them marshmeller puffy buildin's?"

"Yep! What do you think?"

"I think you are two o' the most wonderful people in th' whole dang world, an' I think Wanda might just be askin' fer Mr. Swift ta give her away. Would ya do that?"

Damon laughed heartily. "You won't be able to keep me away!"

Both Wanda and Chow wanted to get married as soon as possible, so the date was set for the following Saturday, only ten days later.

As he suspected, Tom's wife, sister and mother went into overdrive working on the decorations and getting all the chairs, tables, linens, silverware, and food arranged.

Chow had suggested that he do the catering, but accepted the fact that he had "other duties" and so reluctantly agreed to let the man he often referred to as, "That mad Russian," his evening counterpart at Enterprises main kitchen, take care of everything.

Electronic invitations went out and nearly six hundred people responded.

The local newspaper, The *Shopton Bulletin*, somehow got wind of it and their editor, Dan Perkins, made a personal call to Tom to see it they might cover the event.

"I know you don't like the way I have handled some things, Tom," he said, "but I swear on a stack of back issues that I will only send a photographer and one reporter and that it will be in Sunday's paper only in the Life Around Shopton section and not a word about anything other than the wedding. Promise."

Tom relented after asking Chow what he felt.

"Wahl, I say let 'em come, but mebbe have one o' Harlan Ames' men standin' right close so they *really* know they got to behave."

On the day, Damon walked Wanda down the aisle dressed in his tuxedo with her in a beautiful cream-colored ankle-length dress. The ceremony had been just about twenty minutes and as the reverend declared them to be "husband and wife," a round of applause and cheering broke out that lasted more than two full minutes.

It rose in volume as Chow leaned over and gave his new bride a long kiss before they turned and walked back down the aisle.

Later, Chow, reluctantly but with sincerity, thanked the Russian chef for his contribution to making the reception a rousing success. "Mighty good!"

Sandy and Bashalli had sat together in the front row and cried throughout the ceremony, sharing a box of tissues. They hadn't stopped sniffling and wiping away the occasional tear during the reception, and both broke down again—remembering their own happy weddings—when Chow and Wanda climbed into the limousine Damon had arranged to come up from Albany that was to take them to the Shopton Regional Airport where they would be catching a flight that would eventually get them to the Bahamas for their honeymoon.

Everyone agreed it had been an incredible event, and good to his word, the full page spread Dan Perkins printed in the following day's paper was nothing but complimentary on all fronts.

When Chow showed up at work the following Monday Tom was flabbergasted.

"But... uh... shouldn't you be..." he tried to get the words out. Everyone had figured that the chef and his new bride would have winged off on their honeymoon right after the reception.

"Spit 'er out, youngin'," Chow told him. "Speak what's on yer mind."

"Okay," Tom said getting his thoughts in order. "You did get married the other day. Right?" Chow smiled and nodded. "And you and Wanda are happy and everything is okay. Right?" Chow's smile widened and his head bobbed up and down even more vigorously. "So, why haven't you headed out for a couple weeks of honeymoon? You know you have the time, don't you?"

"O' course I do, Tom. I'm a might surprised your daddy didn't tell ya. Wanda and I are headin' off ta Fearing Island tonight. By this time tomorrow we'll be flyin' high and straight fer Mars."

When the inventor looked at him in wonder, the chef continued. "Ya see, Wanda's heard me tell 'bout the couple-a weeks I spent up thar at the colony with you and she really wants ta see it. So, I cleared it with yer dad and Haz and everyone up thar, and we're doin' our hun-ee-moon on Mars. All I gots ta do is take along some special vittles and make one humdinger of a meal fer everybody in return fer their hospitality."

Now Tom understood. "So, you take this month's supply run in the *Sutter* and then come back on next month's return flight?"

"Right. Can ya spare me that long? I mean, I don't wanta leave you and yer pa in the lurch."

Tom laughed. "No, Chow. You take the time. You deserve it. And you deserve all the happiness that Wanda will bring you."

CHAPTER 4 /

SIDETRACKED

WITH THE wedding now behind them all, Tom spent all of Tuesday and Wednesday up at the Outpost in Space, the large spoked wheel sitting in geosynchronous orbit above the equator. He tried to get up there every few months but had missed his scheduled visit three weeks earlier.

Ken Horton, the station commander, met him at the airlock when he and Bud floated over from the *Challenger*, Tom's large cube-inside-circular-rails spaceship.

"Welcome, you two," he said shaking their hands, "and what brings you to our sunny shores?"

Tom and Bud grinned. "We come to freshen up our tan lines," the dark haired flyer replied.

"Actually, Ken, we have come up to see what might be done to improve the station. And, to let you know that we will no longer be able to launch anything up from Loonaui. It's the political situation you've been briefed about, and we're prepping Fearing to take over those operations. And now that we are converting the remaining cargo rockets to fly on repelatron power we no longer need the deep water slingshot effect that the Loonaui facility gave us."

The Pacific island, sitting to the Southeast of Hawaii and right on the equator, had been the first place to agree to allow the Swifts to build a rocket base capable of sending up several dozen rockets in a fairly short time. Tom had figured that a rocket capable of carrying the heavy cargoes necessary would be too large if launched from ground level. So, effectively a giant underwater slingshot was built letting the fueled and sealed rockets to be winched down to the floor of the ocean, hundreds of feet below the surface, surrounded by a large bubble of air, and then shot straight up assisted by the buoyancy.

The power imparted could launch a rocket nearly three thousand feet into the air by itself. Of course, the liquid-fueled engines ignited less than a hundred feet above the surface and used that extra momentum as if it were a very powerful first stage. Therefore, less than half the fuel was necessary to get a rocket into geosynchronous orbit 22,300 miles up. It left much more room for cargo.

"Well," Ken replied, "off the top of my head I'd say that our number one issue is space. Not that out there—" he said pointing back at the airlock, "—but lack of it in here. Let's go to my office."

He led the way. At the outer ends of the spokes—where the airlocks were located—the slow spin of the wheel gave them about 1/5 G of apparent gravity, but as they neared the central hub that dropped to practically nothing. They were able to float across the hub and into the spoke that housed Ken's small office.

Seats outfitted with hundreds of tiny vacuum tubes designed to hold a person down were pulled out from the wall to accommodate the visitors. Bud had dubbed these "Suck-Seats" years earlier and the name had stuck.

Tom got to the point. "Tell me what you need the room for. I can't promise much today, but dad agrees with me that we need to put some new funding into the Outpost."

Ken took a breath and let it slowly out his nose. "Well, for starters the long-timers are now coming back from their one month rotation ground-side constantly mentioning how much they had missed flowers and trees and such. Anything, really, that is growing and not metal or plastic. And the smells of fresh air and flowers, grass, et cetera. I have to admit, I'm one of them." He grinned and shrugged.

"I see," Tom said. "You know how we've talked about adding a second set of spokes to the station?" Ken nodded as did Bud. "Good. I've been pondering bringing up a fabrication unit like the one we now use at the Construction Company. You've both seen it. The one Hank Sterling built that can vacuum-form large pieces. If we built it as a module to fit inside the *Sutter* she could manufacture the components in space and then your people would assemble them over here."

The *Sutter* was Tom's giant, golden, cone-shaped space ship that he originally built as a mining vessel to take advantage of the mineral-rich Pluto having been temporarily relocated near the asteroid belt by the Swift's Space Friends. The ship now sat in orbit, parked just a kilometer away from the Outpost.

"How would they attach to the current station, skipper?" Bud inquired.

"I'm actually thinking that we replace the hub with one that is nearly three times as tall. Perhaps a bit wider as well. That would give everyone ready access to the two levels of spokes plus it might give you enough room to add some hydroponics. We could even make the upper shell opaque to allow sunlight to get to the vegetation. What do you think, Ken?"

"I don't know what to think, Tom. I like the idea, but what about the station while we change from one hub to the other. What about the personnel? What about our day-to-day work?"

Tom had thought of that already. "To start with, everyone moves into the *Sutter*. We'll have to bring up bunks and set those up in the large common compartment, but it should handle everyone with ease. It has a kitchen and all the other facilities you would need for the five or six days I believe it would take to swap out the current hub."

"Sure, but how about our broadcasting spoke? A huge chunk of the free world relies on that staying in operation."

Tom nodded. It was another thing he had thought long and hard about. "First, we stop the wheel spinning. Slowly enough to realign all the antennas as we go. Next, we detach that spoke and very carefully move it off a few hundred feet or so keeping things aimed. It is actually easier to do that than keep up the 24/7/365 constant adjustments that the computers and servo motors need to perform today."

"Oh," Bud perked up, "so you slide the old spokes back a little, tow the old hub out, bring in the already assembled new hub, reattach the old and add the new spokes and then finally the TV and radio spoke?"

Tom nodded.

"If we are getting more spokes and more room, can I make a suggestion?" Ken asked.

"Shoot."

"Can we put all the antennas on the bottom of the new hub so they stay in one spot? It'd do the same thing as moving the stationary spoke off and sitting it there."

"Excellent idea, Ken," Tom complimented his station commander. It was one of the weaknesses that everyone only realized once the station had begun operations.

Over the rest of the day Tom and Bud interviewed each of the residents of the station asking them a set of questions to see what the overall needs and desires were. These would be tabulated back on Earth and matched against what Ken had been telling them about.

On the trip back down, Bud asked, "Can you do all that? I mean, new hub, old spokes, new spokes and get everything to match up?"

Tom thought about his answer before telling his friend, "I think so, but I'm not entirely positive. It would be much better to just build a new station but the cost of all those materials and all the rockets needed to carry it up in a timely manner is prohibitive. Dad bet the bank on this one, and it just started to operate in the black eleven months ago. Besides, if we're going to build a larger outpost, it might as well be really large. As in maybe as many as a thousand people." He looked to see what Bud might think of that suggestion.

"Jetz!" his friend muttered. He turned to face Tom. "Just how big would that station have to be anyway?"

Tom laughed. "Oh, only about a quarter mile wide—maybe up to fifteen hundred feet—and a mile or so long. It would be a cylinder, like some science fiction authors have described, with a lot of the area built around the inside walls. You could have perhaps twelve or fifteen stories all up and down the thing and rotate it at a speed to give a good, let's say two-thirds-G, apparent gravity."

"Okay. Remedial teaching time for little Bud," the flyer said. "*Apparent* gravity?"

"Sure. It isn't real gravity—it isn't a product of great mass—but it works like it. As in the current Outpost at the outer ends of the spokes where you can stand with your head facing the hub and it feels like there is some gravity holding you to the floor. Well, the wall. With me so far?"

"Uh, yeah. And I think I might actually be able to jump to the end of this already. So as the *whatever* spins it is apparent to anyone standing with their feet heading the correct direction, and I guess that is the outside of the cylinder, that they have some gravity."

Tom made a small adjustment to their course as they were now entering the outer atmosphere. Finally, he replied. "Correct. So, Doc believes and research backs him up, that as long as we can provide for at least two-thirds Earth standard gravity, but better at three-quarters-G or more, people will be able to live normal and healthy lives for years and years without the need to return to Earth periodically to rebuild muscle mass. And when they do come back down, the closer to normal one-G we can make it, the easier it will be to readapt, if necessary at all."

Now they were plunging downward and both could see the East coastline of the U.S. Soon the thin sliver of land known as Fearing Island, home of the Swift's rocket and undersea fleets off the coast of Georgia, could be made out though the wispy layer of clouds.

"What about that gravity system we use in the *Sutter* and here in the *Challenger* and even the little runabout we used to go take a look-see at that strange black hole? The combination of the special under-suit and the tiny repelatron emitters sure make it feel like we've got normal gravity."

Tom had to agree, but pulled out the neck of his shirt and looked down at the dark blue bodysuit as he cautioned, "You and I both know that a couple days inside these things and you begin to get a little claustrophobic, or at least your body does. I believe we have to let people walk around in normal clothes they can take off and not float around. But, I will say that special areas designed for exercise and running would be a perfect use for the technology." He made a mental note to add that to his growing list of considerations.

They landed without incident and soon the boys were winging their way back to Shopton in the Toad.

The entire way back Tom was pondering the possibilities of building his giant space station. The logistics alone would take a bank of super computers to keep track of. But he knew his biggest obstacle would be the cost of materials. And, locating them, and transporting them to a staging area, and launching them... and then, and only then, begin the arduous task of assembly. It was not a task he felt at all ready to tackle.

What he did feel ready for was the giant inflatable structure that would be the first building erected at the new automotive factory site. His first order of business the following morning was to go check the status of the fabrication of all the panels that would go into building it, plus two new similar structures that would eventually be taken up to the Mars colony. That meant a visit to Uniforms.

Although the department was responsible for producing all the specialty uniforms—including space suits—for all employees at all Swift facilities, over the past year plus they had been primarily turning out the giant, tube-embedded panels of multilayered material that eventually formed a complete inflatable structure.

And not just for Mars or for the forthcoming Swift auto plant. The staff had been expanded to fifty-three, and they had moved into new quarters several months back when orders had come pouring in for dozens and dozens of the various sizes they offered. Still more requests came in for specialty sizes or configurations. They were only just getting into a position where they might satisfy some special orders.

The manager of the department, Marjorie Morning-Eagle, was a large woman. Not fat large, but imposing large. Her Native American heritage provided her with permanently bronzed skin and large muscular arms and legs.

People called her "The Major" and not just behind her back. She could be gruff when necessary and gentle when she desired.

Tom hiked the one mile out to the hangar that now was the home of Uniforms. It afforded them a work area nearly five times as large as they before plus double *that* amount of space for storage and assembly.

"Good morning, Major," Tom hailed the woman who was

standing, hands on hips, looking away from him. She was supervising a new team of workers as they were making a practice run on the connection of four large panels. She turned and the frowning, almost menacing look on her face melted into a bright smile.

"Good morning to you, young Tom Swift," she greeted him stepping away from her team and coming to see him. "What brings you to this incredibly wonderful new facility you provided for us. And, I am sincere when I tell you that if I ever have a child I want you in the delivery room so I can name him—or her—Tom in your honor. It will be so much more meaningful than, 'She Who Holds Towel to Doctor's Sweaty Forehead,' or something equally silly."

Tom grinned at her. "I come bearing a request and a need for information. It's about the giant building that you will be putting together for the new auto plant. Got a minute or five?"

She nodded and motioned him toward her office about fifty feet away. Instead of the simple, raised platform she used to have, she now had a fully contained office with triple-pane glass and insulated walls, ceiling and floor. With the door finally closed it was perfectly quiet.

"So, speak."

Tom told her about the wind conditions at the new site and his desire to make the building as strong as possible.

"I see three ways to do that," she told him after considering the matter of a moment. "One," she touched her index finger with her thumb, "you come up with a super strong foam or some other liquid that can be forced into all the little tubes. Of course, this building is supposed to come down in a year or two so you don't want anything too permanent or you will end up having to destroy the tent."

She looked at Tom and he shook his head. "You're right. We would rather not do that, not after all the work your ladies—sorry, your *team* goes to, to build the thing. Next?"

She touched her middle finger. "Two, we build it with thicker walls and a sealed floor plus put in air locks so you can pressurize it for more strength." She and Tom both shook their heads. Now she touched her ring finger. "Three, because this doesn't have to get all rolled up and shoved into that giant gold spaceship of yours, we just make the tubes bigger. More capacity, more foam, greater strength!"

Tom looked at her as he pulled a slip of paper out of his shirt pocket. Handing it to her he told her to read it.

"Ask Major about increasing tube size for strength" Now she let out a raucous laugh and slapped her desk. "I shouldn't be at all surprised at you, Tom. For starters you came to me with the offer for this hangar one day before I was going to come begging you and your father for at least a little more space and maybe another one or two people."

They agreed that the Uniforms department would build a trio of test panels each only five feet wide but fifty feet long. Tom did a few calculations on his tablet computer and decided that the best candidate would need to carry a load of one hundred and fifty pounds in the middle of the span and not deflect by more than five inches to meet his needs. One panel would incorporate the current tubes but with half again as many as the current inflatables used, one with the current number but double the tube size, and the final one would use the standard number of tubes but these would be purpose-made in a triangular shape to hopefully offer greater all around strength.

"Have them for you a week from today if that's okay," she offered.

"Works for me, Major. And, thanks for the name-the-kid compliment." He winked and left her office.

On his way back he placed a TeleVoc call to Hank Sterling, his chief pattern maker and the engineer he turned to for special projects of all kinds. He described the triangular tubing.

"I'm seeing them as being about one inch on each outer side with one of the three planes having extending flanges that can be sewn through to attach the tubes to the outer shell of the building. My guess is that the Major would want at least one-half inch on each side for that. What can you do for me?"

Inside his head he heard Hank laugh. "Plenty. The Construction Company took delivery of a new type of extruder about a week ago. No more dies or forms. Everything is done using electromagnets, micro-fine iron beads and computers to create whatever shape you need. I'll sketch what I believe you just described and send that drawing to you in about ten minutes. Unless you need it sooner."

Now it was Hank's turn to hear Tom laughing inside his head. "No, in fact it will take me about that time to get across the tarmac. I'm hoofing it back to the big office from their new facility out in the old hangar three. Take fifteen if you need it!"

The inventor's current pace got him back to the office in a little under nine minutes but Hank was faster. His file was date/time stamped two minutes earlier. He looked at it as he dialed Hank's number on the telephone.

"Got the drawing and it looks just like what the Major ordered.

And I agree that a thin sewing flange should be sufficient. The question now is when can we get production time and—okay I see that there are three questions here—so, when can we get production time for a short prototype run, how long does it take to reset the equipment to a new form, and how accurate is it if we wanted exactly four hundred-seventy feet—nuts, there are four questions—and if it all works what lead time would we need for a run of about three hundred-and-fifty thousand feet?" Tom sighed. "Five questions... what are our choices of materials?"

Hank was laughing now. "Want to try for six?" he asked.

Tom considered it for a few seconds before replying, "No. That's it for now."

"Okay, so I can tell you that I can get production time for the short run day after tomorrow—oh wait, that's Sunday—so Monday, after lunch. It should take about three minutes for the computer to align everything. It over-produces by ten feet on any project. That's because it takes five feet to get up to speed, runs at full speed until it hits the real quantity requested and then rapidly slows down, but that leaves you with inaccurate stuff at both ends. It gets trimmed, chopped up, ground into pellets and reused, by the way. So, what else did you ask? Oh, right. I'm looking at the request log and if you can wait we could do the entire final run on the following Thursday and Friday. The extruder will not be in use for anything else those days and your final batch will run through in a little over twenty-four hours. It can do about two hundred-fifty feet a minute."

"And, materials?"

"Just about anything from PET to ABS to PVC to corn-based plastics to Tomasite. The current tubes in the Mars structures are HDPE mixed with a tiny amount of tomasite and we think it will last thirty years on Mars and twenty-five here on Earth."

"Unless you can think of a way to make it physically stronger and more resistant to UV rays, then let's go with that," Tom requested.

When he got the triangular tubing late Monday afternoon it was in a large roll and loaded onto a thin pallet in the back of a truck. Hank met him outside of the Administration building and they drove it over the Uniforms. The Major was thrilled to see it and was amused to find that Tom had thought of adding the sewing flange. As she felt the ends her face clouded.

"Good work, inventor boss of mine," she told him. "Now to see if I can find needles strong enough to pierce that hard plastic. Otherwise, I'm afraid this may have been a big waste!"

CHAPTER 5 /

UNCOMFORTABLE STIRRINGS IN D.C.

AS THE gavel swung down onto its base, Tom sat attentively next to his father. The Chairman—a senator from Alabama—called the special session to order. They received the call on Tuesday to appear on Wednesday. It gave them no time to prepare even if they had known the purpose of this "emergency committee meeting."

Both Tom and Damon would have preferred their old champion, Senator Peter Quintana of New Mexico, be at his usual position heading this committee, but the man was now simply Pete Quintana, and retired. After five terms he had reached both his sixty-first birthday and the end of his patience for the comings and goings of continuous government work. And so, he had retired two months earlier, heading back to Taos and his hobby of painting.

"Mr. Swift and... uh, Mr. Swift? You are not unfamiliar with sitting in those chairs providing testimony to this committee. Your honesty and forthrightness is well known and I expect nothing less than your full cooperation. Are we clear on that?"

Damon Swift cleared his throat as he nodded. "Of course, Senator. But it would help us greatly to have a better understanding of the nature of this session. In the past we have been given the courtesy of being told why we have been called to Washington. May we assume that this was simply an oversight on this occasion?"

"I hear implied sarcasm and a bit of a scold in there, *Mister* Swift," the senator said warningly. "You will be informed as to the nature and reason for this session in due time. For now you and your boy will sit there and listen. There will be time for your response later."

Damon glanced at his son. For his part, Tom was sitting there, eyes slitted, experiencing a sense of foreboding that he had never felt before.

"Neither a scold nor sarcasm implied or meant, Senator," Damon told him. "But, as we have always tried to be as cooperative as possible, and cannot think of anything we may have done recently that would incur either the ire or scrutiny of this or any other governmental group, I may have allowed my dismay at the change in attitude toward us seep into my voice."

He left it there carefully watching how the southern man would accept his statement.

The senator scowled but looked down at some papers on the desk in front of him. Selecting one, he spent the next full minute reading before looking back up at the Swifts.

"Right. So here is the heart of the matter." He picked the sheet of paper back up and shook it gently. "In point of fact you have not been cooperative with this committee and indeed with this government that has supported you to the tune of—" he searched through the other papers before finding the one he wanted, "—more that *fifty-three billion* taxpayer dollars! What have you got to say about that?"

Tom heard his father take a sharp breath in. "Over the last century plus that Swift Enterprises and its predecessor, the Swift Company, have designed, developed and sold our products to this government as well as to the corporate and private sectors, we have never delivered less than asked and frequently a great deal more. And, it is just over ninety-one billion, sir. Slightly less than forty percent of our sales over those years. Where is this leading?"

The senator slammed his fist down on the table causing the others around him to jump and the woman to his immediate right to put her hand on his forearm, shaking her head.

"Where this is leading is that you have kept things from us. Secrets that this government and the citizens of this nation deserve to have. You have worked with aliens from beyond our solar system, you have entertained electrical beings with powers far beyond what we possess. In short, *Swift*, you have withheld valuable resources from your country that our military should have received!"

He pounded his fist on the table again, his face growing bright red and his eyes flaring with anger. A moment later he shoved his seat back and into the knees of the Page standing behind him, jumped up and stalked from the chamber.

A stunned silence followed, only interrupted by a meek voice from the rear of the room muttering, "Oh, my. He'll burst a gasket!"

The Congresswoman who had been sitting next to the now-absent man cleared her throat and addressed the Swifts.

"I must apologize for that outburst. That took us all—" she glanced at the other seven people around her who all nodded, "—by surprise. While I cannot imagine what is going on in the senator's mind, I do have to tell you that this hearing was called because it is the opinion of some in the House and Senate that Swift Enterprises may have kept certain secret information and technologies from us that the Government and taxpayers have paid you for. Is there anything you can tell us?"

Tom and Damon shook their heads. The older man said, "As I stated before, we have delivered everything and more than we have ever been asked for or paid for. For instance, when requested to build a propeller-driven high-altitude reconnaissance plane with a twelve hour flight time, we delivered a jet aircraft, faster, higher-flying and for twenty percent longer for the same cost. And, while we hold certain technologies for only our internal use, none of them have been part of any local, state or federal contract."

Tom nudged his father's arm. Mr. Swift nodded.

"Madam Congressperson," he began. "If someone could tell us what information or technology we are being accused of—"

"You are not accused of anything, young man," the woman stated, interrupting him.

"Okay. Then anything we are being investigated for that is suggested we might be withholding. If someone can tell us that we might be able to give you a full response. And," he added after a few seconds' pause, "if this is something old it would help to understand why it has waited until now."

Damon moved his right foot over to tap his son's ankle, a signal that Tom should now stop talking.

Another senator, this one the senior senator from Alaska spoke up.

"We appreciate the position you are being asked to submit to, but this isn't about any one incident. It has to do with a systematic behavior by your company. I have a list of more than a dozen issues here," he held up a multipage document, "going back to about four years ago and your incursion into South America with that giant space yacht of yours."

"Umm, space yacht?" Tom asked. Then he brightened. "Do you mean my flying laboratory, the *Sky Queen*, sir?"

"Whatever you call it, that aircraft of yours went down there and helped find valuable uranium resources that nobody in this government were ever told about. At least, not by you."

Damon spoke before Tom could. "Sir, that uranium was the property of the country in which it was discovered. The United States could have no claim on it whatsoever. And, as to the matter of 'nobody was told,' I believe that you will find in the Congressional Record of that time that we did notify the President *and* Congress of the nature of that trip—partly a rescue mission to find me—and that Tom's device the Damonscope had indeed discovered a deep vein of ore."

"And, it was all privately funded by us," Tom added.

There was some muttering between the committee members before the first woman asked, "Are you suggesting that our current information is in error?"

Both Swifts nodded with Tom stating, "At least so far as that incident, ma'am."

"What about these mysterious submarines you built for a foreign government?"

"Do you meant the SeaSpears we build for the British Navy?" The woman checked her paper and, finding nothing, looked blankly at Tom.

"I suppose..."

"We received permission from the President, himself, to take on that project. While I can't tell you everything, they were built to British specifications to provide patrol and protection to a ring of installations around the main British isle. And, after one year we were given the go-ahead by them to offer the subs to our own Navy. They declined, at least at first."

"Hmmm? Let's set that aside for now, but what about his report of you creating a death ray gun?"

Tom couldn't help himself. He let a laugh escape. As he tried to control himself the new chairwoman scowled at him.

"I'm sorry, Ma'am. But I believe that item on your list refers to our e-guns. They are like the tasers police and military personnel use every day, just in the form of a gun that doesn't require a long coil of wire and needles to stick into the person being shocked. They may be technically capable of killing as their power settings can go high enough to stop a charging horse, but we never use them at anything other than stun strength. You see, even our own Security department people do not carry traditional guns. We do not believe in the use of deadly force."

"Oh," was all the Congresswoman could say. She looked uncomfortably to her left and right and found nobody on the panel willing to look her in the eye. "Well, let's go through this list anyway."

Over the following hour each of the other issues on the papers was brought forth and each one was answered—in most cases debunked as being entirely false—by Tom and Damon.

Only three issues were not resolved. These were: the Swift's secret communications with the beings known as their Space Friends, from first contact through their face-to-face interaction nearly two years later when Tom finally was able to crack the problem of getting them down to the surface of the Earth;

Enterprises' lack of immediate notification to the Government when it was discovered that a pair of megalomaniac siblings were building a slave-operated base on the back side of the Moon; and the Swift's Martian colony.

The answer to the first one did not sit well with the committee. It had to do with the Swift's not believing that mankind was ready or mature enough to deal with a race that could hold unimaginable technologies, technologies that might be turned into weapons by unscrupulous governments or people.

"Need I tell you that it is hardly your place to decide what is good or bad for this country?" came the question from a Congressman from Florida. "If we decide that turning a new technology into a weapon is right, then by god it is what we'll do!"

"And that, sir, and with respect, is exactly why we have not believed that mankind can be allowed to access their technology. Even *we* haven't asked for anything more than their methods of almost instant communication across light years. We do not want the responsibility or the pressure from our own government or that of other nations. Besides, it was their choice to contact *us* and not any single government on Earth."

The second matter was tabled in favor of discussing the colony Tom had built on Mars after Enterprises had been refused the contract to build one on the Moon, and had even had to rescue and partially rebuild the lunar complex when it began to be destroyed by space debris.

"You have steadfastly refused to allow a contingent of our armed forces to be stationed up there. You won't even transport an observation team to inspect what you've put up there. What are you hiding?"

Tom laughed out loud. "We are hiding nothing. And since we are a private company with our own resources having gone into the construction and transport of all supplies and personnel, we get to say whom we take up. Enterprises has never provided or handled anything that might be termed a weapon in our history. We might provide aircraft but you turn them over to others to turn them into something deadly."

Damon mumbled, "That's enough, Tom," before addressing the committee himself.

"For the same reason we would not turn over any alien technology we might come into knowledge of, we cannot trust any government to go up to Mars and to militarize it. We do not lay claim to the planet, only to the area we currently colonize. And you are welcome to build the necessary spacecraft to go up yourselves, but we will not assist you in that endeavor. Mars, like the Moon, is a neutral body and we hope it will remain so."

The meeting ended just before lunch. Tom and Damon left in a taxi moments later to go back to the airport and to fly back to Shopton. It wasn't until they were in Tom's Toad commuter jet that Damon mentioned what had happened.

"I have to tell you Son, that I do not like the attitude of some members of that committee. You hit the nail on the head with the whole 'you're not ready to handle it responsibly' thing. I swear I almost could spot a bit of blood lust in that Floridian's eyes."

By the time they touched down it had been decided to let the matter rest and see if anything else came of the meeting.

Tom went down to his underground office and lab while Damon headed back to their shared office in the Administration building.

But, halfway down the second floor corridor he did an about face and headed back outside and to his car. He drove out the main gate and headed around the perimeter of Enterprises and to the site of the partially-built automobile facility.

"Hey, Damon," greeted a burly man, Steve Piper, who was the construction supervisor for the new plant. "What brings you to the various holes in the ground?"

Damon gave him a brief and highly edited version of the trip and meeting earlier, ending with, "So, I just needed to come see something different and positive. And from the look of things, you've made some amazing progress since I was here two weeks ago."

"Well, you need to come over here more often. Oh, and speaking of coming over here, is there any way to get you to authorize a back gate in the Enterprises wall? I understand the potential security issues, Harlan Ames has given me several ears full about that, but it adds twenty minutes or so, round trip, for anyone wanting or needing to drive inside the grounds."

They had reached the construction manager's trailer and stepped inside. After pouring two cups of coffee, Steve sat down facing Damon.

"Even if it is just a small gate that is only open during the workday and only wide enough to fit the smaller electric runabouts?"

Damon let out a laugh, a bit louder than he had intended. "Sorry. Anyway, I think I can do you one better."

He outlined a plan that seemed, in the broadest sense, to be overkill, but on discussing it the construction man could see the reasons.

Damon planned to take one of Tom's tunnel digging machines, the ones he built to do all the underground work when constructing the transcontinental bullet freight train system, and to create a roadway under the bulk of Enterprises coming up inside the planned security walls of the automotive plant.

"Tom was going to downsize it until I suggested that having the two bores with the raised central area was the best way to go. Separate traffic lanes along with a wide area that can be used as a walkway. Plus, it will be just short enough that there will be no need to equalize any pressure build-up in front of vehicles so we will simply add ventilation ducting inside the tunnel to give people fresh air."

"And it'll run from where to where?" Piper inquired.

"My vision is to place it on the South side of the central complex of buildings but well before you get to the nearest runway. We've got about a quarter mile buffer out there and might as well use it. We'll take a straight shot running it about one hundred feet underground until is time to slope up to come out in this facility close to the main gate."

The construction man asked what the Security Chief had to say about it.

Damon laughed again, this time more gently. "Harlan agrees with the plan to put in an automatic set of gates at each end. As long as an authorized individual is wearing their TeleVoc pin and doesn't send a silent alarm, the gate associated with the direction and mode of transportation opens just long enough for them to get through. If they are driving, only the direction they are entering or exiting opens. Same thing for foot traffic."

"I hate to play devil's advocate, Damon, but what if somebody sneaks in?"

"That's where the TeleVoc pins come in. As soon as anyone not wearing one is detected approaching, such as somebody trying to hitch a ride in or on the back of a truck, the outer door refuses to open. If by any chance someone unauthorized does manage to get inside. The doors all close and lock down until a Security detail gets inside to clear things." He added that with no interior walls or enclosed areas along the walkway, it would be impossible for anyone to hide.

Piper agreed that it would be about the most secure entry to Enterprises and to the Swift Automotive plant once everything was in place. "Speaking of which... when?"

"The *Super Queen* is out in Texas where two of the units are digging the last of the underground tunnels for the North to South spur of the Bulletrain. They pick up one of them tomorrow and it will be on site back here after it gets cleaned up, checked out and ready to go by a week from Monday. After that we believe it will take just five days to do the dig and tunnel coating. It will be about two miles inside Enterprises' walls, the distance across the fields to this location and then a hundred or so feet inside of the security fence. It will cut off about nine miles of travel from what you have to do today."

After taking a tour of the work that had been accomplished recently Damon left and finally got back to his office.

His secretary, Munford Trent stopped him as he reached for the doorknob.

"Tom's in there. I routed a phone call from a Congresswoman I hear you both met today. When he came over from his lab he had a big grin on his face, so I assume it's good news."

"Let's hope so. The meeting this morning didn't exactly go well."

Tom jumped up from his desk as his father entered the large office. "I could kind of hear Trent telling you about the call. Want to hear what it was about?"

Before answering, Mr. Swift crossed to the side table next to the large conference area of the room and poured himself a tall mug of hot coffee. As he sat down in one of the overstuffed leather chairs, he nodded and said, "Tell me all."

Tom took another seat and grinned at his father. "It was that woman Congressman from Connecticut who took over the meeting when the chairman left suddenly. Get this—she apologized to us. She had to do it off the record, but she says she was horrified at his outburst and anger toward us. Told me that the chairman was served divorce papers the day before and took his frustrations out on us. All that the meeting was supposed to do was to have us assure them that we have delivered faithfully on our contracts and that we aren't withholding anything that might be 'vital to the United States and our security.' That last bit were her exact words."

Damon let out a breath he realized he was holding. "Well, that's a load off my mind. Did she say anything else?"

Tom nodded. "Yes. She told me that we might be getting called into a meeting with the United Nations and that they will probably try to insist that anything we know about alien technology be turned over to them. It was a warning that today's meeting might be one of several where we get raked over the coals." His grin had disappeared. "On the positive side she told us to invoke national security as a reason for not answering any of their questions, and that if we are pressed or threatened that we are give them a letter she is sending us. It will be here tomorrow."

Mr. Swift's left eyebrow arched. "That almost makes it sound like a get out of jail free card. Hmmmm. I think we need to talk to our legal department about this. Did she end with that?"

"Yes, other than to say that with one exception—probably the actual chairman who left abruptly—the committee voted to tender an official apology to us. That will also arrive tomorrow."

It was a very curious turn of events. And while it helped with the sting of the morning's events, it now brought up the spectre of future times where they would have to defend their business decisions. And, their moral ones as well.

CHAPTER 6 /

LEGAL ADVICE

AS HE entered the shared office the next day, Tom could see his father was scanning more than a dozen sheets of paper spread across the top of his desk. The older inventor looked up briefly, gave a small nod, and muttered, "M'rning."

Tom sat down at his own desk and began going through the daily emails. Fortunately for both men, Munford Trent screened out nearly 95% of the mails that arrived, sending auto-replies to "begging letters," a standardized, "We are sorry, but we can't buy/sell/produce your invention for you because..." or to forward threatening letters to the Enterprises' Security and Legal departments. He did let personal emails and those he felt either or both of the Swifts would want to answer personally and that meant between eight and twenty per man per day.

Today, Tom found only nine. The first made him smile. It was from his old Junior High teacher, Mrs. Trunbridge. In return for her helping him to see a solution for a tricky water shortage problem in Africa he had returned the favor by developing several unique music instruments for her to enter in a national grant contest for her school. And though they were disqualified on a technicality, two of them were now being produced under license and those payments went directly to her school to fund their music program.

Today's note was a thank you for the third annual payment that had been large enough to not just fund the music program, but she told him that there was now enough to restart the Home Economics classes that had been shelved five years earlier.

She wrote:

You cannot imagine the joy running through many of the girls and boys here at the school. Everyone seems to want to know how to cook and do basic sewing. It appears that some of our young boys have figured out that girls actually like them better when they can do more than just sit and play video games! Next thing you know, we'll be teaching oil changes to girls.

He was left with a big smile.

The next three were personal appearance requests with one of them coming from a college in Florida that began with:

Dear Favored Alumni...

Not only had Tom never heard of the school, he obviously had never attended it nor had he ever visited it. He made a few notes for Trent to type into an answer—including "I have no idea who you folks are, but there has obviously been a mistake—" in a return note.

After checking his calendar he had to decline the other two invitations.

Only one of the final emails intrigued him. It was from an old acquaintance and former Enterprises employee, Linda Ming. Linda had worked directly for Arv Hansen in the Modeling department. A specialist in electronic miniaturization, she had been instrumental in creating the sub-sized circuits and controls for about thirty of the scale test models of his and Damon Swift's inventions.

Linda had departed Enterprises two years earlier to marry an old High School flame who had come back into her life in her late 20s. He re-read the final two paragraphs paying attention to two sentences specifically.

> As everyone around me warned, Todd turned out to be a bit of a cad, and I don't mean in the computer design way; he still had at least two other women in his life and after a year made no excuses for dallying around. Financially I have been left holding the bag and it has precious little inside for me, so I was wondering if I might crawl back to Shopton for at least an interview?

Tom called up the original email on his computer and wrote her a personal note. *Of course she can come back*, he thought as he typed. *For crying out loud, she was a great asset here and I'm sure Arv would love to have her back—* he stopped typing. Perhaps he ought to check with Arv before sending the email.

So that he wouldn't bother his father, Tom tapped the TeleVoc pin on his collar and made a silent call to the model maker.

After explaining the email and Linda's predicament Arv's voice came into his head with a loud and clear "Yipee! Gosh, I'd give the old eye teeth, if I knew what those actually were, to get Linda back here. So, heck yes. Tell her to come as soon as possible and to plan to move back to Shopton the following day. I've got it in my budget to hire her and pay for her move. Wow! Imagine that. Linda wanting to come back."

Tom completed his email and sent it off suggesting that tickets, paid for by Enterprises, could be arranged for any day after the following one. Trent would take care of everything for her. He hit the send button and sat back and pondered what to think about the events in Washington the day before.

He made a decision that required a bit more direct communication than a TeleVoc call, so he pushed his chair back and left the office. As he passed the outer office he told Trent about Linda Ming. "If dad asks where I've gone, tell him I went to the Legal department to check on our rehire policy. I should be back in a half hour or so."

On entering the offices of the team of law professionals that Enterprises kept on the floor above the shared office, he greeted the receptionist and asked if Jackson Rimmer, the Chief Counsel, was available.

"Sure is, Tom," she replied with a bright smile. The woman was a year younger than him and had the brightest whitest teeth he had ever seen. Bud once commented on them telling the inventor, "I'll bet she uses those to see in the dark!"

"Thanks, Marlee. If you'll buzz him I can see my way back to his office."

A minute later, handshakes out of the way, Tom sat in a comfortable leather chair opposite the lawyer. He got right to the point.

Rimmer sat patiently as Tom detailed most of what had occurred in the Congressional hearing including the not-so-veiled threats.

"What do you think we ought to do about it?"

Jackson nodded and leaned forward, placing his elbows and forearms on his desk. "For starters, I'm happy to hear your impressions. Your father called me at home at seven this morning and we met here a half hour after that. He told me much of what you just said, but with a different, and perhaps a bit too philosophical tone. You let the full emotion of everything come through and I thank you for that." He sighed and sat back again. Steepling his fingers and placing them in front of his mouth, he sighed again. "Okay. For starters I believe that Enterprises needs to start hunkering down and getting ready for some legal attacks. Well, not attacks but challenges over how we do business.

"As a major contractor to the U.S. Government we derived about forty-six percent of our gross income from taxpayer money during our most recent fiscal year. At least it isn't over fifty percent. If it were, or if it gets to be that then we have to live under a law signed off by the President last year that states, in part, that any company so funded in excess of half their gross income must fully open their books to any requested audit by Congress or the Government Accounting Office."

"But, does that include just financial stuff, or project and product files, specifications and company secrets?"

"It hasn't been used to quite that extent nor has it been challenged, but it is something that might have to be decided at the Supreme Court level, and that could tie up some or all company business for a year or more. But it gets worse."

Tom made a wry face. "Do I want to know this?"

Jackson nodded. "Yes. The law goes on to state that if profits come from products and subassemblies purchased from U.S. companies, particularly if they, too, are contractors to Uncle Sam, and the target company refuses to follow the law, then those supplies can be halted by a simple majority vote in the House and Senate. If Enterprises can't get the raw materials domestically, then our costs of making goods will go up considerably. I shudder to contemplate what might happen if the international G-20 put their weight behind a U.S. decision along those lines."

"Oh, surely they can't think it would be of any help or good to take those drastic measures," Tom stated. "We did a study a year ago that showed that purchasing goods through Enterprises saves the taxpayers in the neighborhood of a billion and a half dollars a year over other companies." He looked plaintively at the lawyer.

When Jackson Rimmer said nothing, Tom asked, "So, worst case scenario. Where would that leave us?"

"Either purchasing from smaller countries and dealing with possibly inferior quality goods, or with unfriendly nations like Kranjovia or even North Korea. At least until sanctions would get put into place. And that leaves you with having to dig what we need out of the ground or extracting it from air somehow and making everything right here."

"Or?"

"Find some way to do it all up on Mars at the colony. Or, the Moon. That's about all I can think of," the attorney told him.

"Hmmm. Now *that* brings up an interesting idea," Tom responded. "Tell me, what can any governmental or legal body do if we don't obtain the things we need from any *Earth* source?"

Jackson Rimmer's eyes went wide and he once again leaned forward, this time moving his head even closer to Tom. "Way back in 1967 the United Nations voted unanimously to keep all of space and all the planets and moons in our solar system as free trade zones. Period. Never to be changed. They did it that way to ensure that no one country could control anything out there. Even the Soviets voted in favor."

"Right, and I guess that's because they knew they wouldn't get to the Moon first."

"Possibly. Possibly not. Nobody understands the whys from back then. But the upshot of this is that if you bring things down from up there—" he pointed to the ceiling, "—it can't be taxed or controlled in its use except where it presents an undeniable, and provable danger."

Tom left a few minutes later, very pleased, after asking about the rehiring of Linda Ming. Jackson Rimmer told him that as long as she departed under positive circumstances—and there was a position for her—that there was no reason not to bring her back.

When Tom breezed back into the office his father was waiting for him. Unlike earlier, he now had a sly grin on his face. "Welcome back. I should have suggested that you tell Jackson about our little visit to D.C. while you were there talking about old employees. So, I hear that Linda Ming might be coming back? Good. I liked her a lot. A very talented woman. I imagine Jackson told you to go ahead."

Tom nodded. "Yes, and we also talked about Washington. I don't want to sound like a tattle tale, but he seemed to think that you soft-soaped your version." He now raised one eyebrow.

After sucking in a short breath through his teeth, Damon Swift reluctantly agreed that he had been less than fully honest in his appraisal of the situation. "I hope you got him straightened out on that."

Nodding again, Tom now asked, "So, what had you all smiles when I came back? Surely it isn't because of Linda."

Damon walked over to his son and gave the younger man a little turn. "Come on. We have an appointment," he said a little mysteriously. Nothing more was said, even when Tom asked directly where they were going. Pretty soon he didn't have to say or ask anything; he realized where they were heading. As the former hangar and current home of the Uniforms department loomed ahead of them, Tom turned to his father, saying, "Ah, I suppose this means that the Major has called to say the test panels are ready."

"She did and they are. I needed to get out of the office for a bit so I thought I'd join you. Both she and I are curious how you intend to test these panels without taking them into the wind tunnel. So...?"

Now it was Tom's turn to grin but say nothing.

They arrived a minute later and climbed out quickly and easily from the tiny runabout. Tom started to marvel at how "spry" his father was even at the age of forty-eight, but stopped himself when the thought hit him. *Gee, I sure hope nobody is surprised at me when I get to the young age of forty-eight!*

The three panels sat on the ground, their tube systems fully inflated with the self-hardening foam. Next to them sat a pair of metal sawhorses. Tom explained the test process.

With his father's help, they soon had the sawhorses placed about forty-five feet apart and the first of the panels set on them. He climbed up onto his end and began to walk to the other while Damon moved to the middle and held a yardstick next to the center point. As Tom neared the middle of the panel, the older inventor called out the number of inches the panel was drooping under Tom's one hundred-sixty-two pound weight.

"That was a disappointment," Tom said when the panel with the smaller tubes, but an increased number of them, sagged more than three inches beyond the point Tom wanted. Panel two, with larger tubes was slightly better but still "failed" the test by three-quarters of an inch.

"Fingers crossed, Son," Damon told him as they hoisted panel three up.

By the time Tom reached the center point he was suggesting that his father come up as well. Marjorie Morning-Eagle brought over a step ladder and helped Damon up. There, he and Tom bounced on their toes a little while the Major called out the numbers.

"You've got a winner there," she said when it was found that even with the two of them, the flex was five-sixteenths of an inch under the maximum.

"Get me all of those crazy tubes I need and I can start the big top in three weeks," she promised.

Tom and Damon hopped into the little runabout and returned to their office. On the way back Damon informed Tom that Harlan had received a letter threatening Tom's life. No reason was given, but the Security man wanted everyone to be vigilant. His father had mentioned it is such an off-hand way that anyone else might have thought nothing of it. Tom knew better and promised to be extra cautious. It wasn't something new to him, but it wasn't something to ignore.

"So, skipper," Bud said as he breezed into the underground lab two hours later, "what say you and I get out of here for the afternoon?"

Tom eyed his friend. Generally, an offer such as this led to the reveal of a soon-to-be date with their wives that Tom would have forgotten all about. But this time he was certain there was nothing overlooked in the "time with the ladies" arena.

"Well... can you tell me what this is about?"

Bud grinned. "This time I promise there is no motive other than I feel the need to stretch and exercise these under-used lower limbs of mine and I was thinking how long it's been since you and I took a good, old-fashioned hike in the hills West of here. Do you remember all the trails we used to hike on the weekends and during the summers?"

Nodding, Tom now grinned back at Bud. "Yep. I sure do." He paused, looking down at his desk as if searching for something.

After a few minutes Bud coughed and asked, "Is there anything on that desk that you absolutely can't carry around as a memory in that head of yours? I mean, I don't expect scintillating conversation out there, so if you've got a project or two you need to think about..."

"No," Tom said a little ruefully. "The truth is that right now I've got a desk full of nothings. Nothing that works, nothing that needs fixing and nothing that is jump-starting my brain. So, let me make a quick call and I'll join you upstairs in about five minutes."

As the dark haired flyer was crossing the hangar floor heading for the elevator to ground level, Tom made his call. A minute later he nodded to himself, grabbed a couple things out of his desk drawer, shoving them in various pants' pockets, and left to join his friend.

Two hours later they were three miles into their hike when Tom heard a rustle in the bushes behind them. They stopped with Tom placing his index finger up against his lips to tell Bud to not say anything. Two minutes later there had been no additional sounds so they resumed their walk.

"You recall what's up that little ridge?" Tom asked when they stopped to take drinks from their canteens.

"You bet I do. Wanta go up and see them?"

"You lead the way, flyboy, and I'll follow."

In little more than five minutes they stood before the opening to a cave. The entry was about three feet wide and just over five feet high.

"The old Mantego Mine, isn't that what it used to be called?" Bud asked.

"Sure. Otowan Mantego, the only person from Haiti to ever come up here to mine for gold dug this by hand way back in about nineteen-twenty-two. Well, probably for a lot longer than that but he struck a small vein in twenty-two and died from hypothermia that same winter when he tried to ride out the coldest January and

February on record. Townspeople who remembered him for being a colorful character brought his body back down and buried him in the Shopton cemetery."

They stood in silence for a moment out of respect. "So, do we go in?"

Tom looked at Bud who was practically hopping from one foot to the other. "Okay. We explored everything and it was incredibly safe back five or six years ago, so why not!"

With Tom in the lead—he had thought to bring a bright LED flashlight with him that he now used to light the way—the two young men entered the cave. Mantego had been an engineer by profession before the gold bug got him, so the walls of the cave had been meticulously carved from solid rocks and heavily-compacted clay soil. Any spot that might have appeared weak to the man had been shored up using heavy timbers that had then been coated with creosote to ward off insects and rot.

Back they went, down the entire one hundred-fifty-seven feet of the horizontal shaft until they arrived in what they used to call the "Grotto." It was an area about thirty feet across that had been dug down an additional fifty or so feet. Stairs had been carved out of the rock circling the lower area.

It had been in that lowest area that Mantego found the vein of gold. Neither Tom nor Bud could recall how much he had managed to get out but it had probably been in the range of a few thousand dollars worth back in the day, and perhaps a million dollars by modern values.

After taking a ten-minute rest, Tom and Bud retraced their steps back along the cave. As they got to the three-quarter point Tom turned his flashlight off. Their eyes had grown accustomed to the dim conditions and now light coming from outside seemed quite bright to them.

Tom, in the lead again, was startled when a shadow flitted across the opening ahead. He stopped and motioned for Bud to do the same. This was fortunate as the explosion that came a second later dropped ton after ton of rocks and dirt down into the entry of the cave, stopping just a few feet in front of them.

Carefully, hoping that there would be no further cave-in, the boys backtracked a few yards and then stopped. A strange scratching sound came from above their heads and suddenly a voice could be heard from what was a hidden speaker.

"Swift? If you are alive down there with your buddy then you won't be for very long. That explosion collapsed at least twenty feet of the entry and that means you'll run out of oxygen long before you can dig your way out!" Harsh laughter from at least two men could be heard.

"So, before you die have a good think about how this all could have been avoided if you just hadn't messed with people's families. So long!" The speaker went silent.

Tom and Bud were completely cut off from the outside world.

CHAPTER 7 /

A PLAN IS HATCHED

TOM TURNED his light back on and shown it in Bud's direction. The flyer, contrary to what might be expected from their situation, was smiling.

"How long do we give them?" he asked.

Tom reached into his front right pocket, took out a small circular object and gave it a squeeze. "Might as well go now," he replied.

Bud took the flashlight, turned and headed back to the Grotto. Once there the two skirted around the perimeter of the dug out area until they reached the opposite side.

"My guess is that those men out there never actually came all the way in or they might have seen the three other shafts heading out of here," Bud offered.

"I think you're right, but—" Tom stopped talking and walking. "Bud?"

"Yes, Tom."

"How do you suppose that they knew we were coming here and had planted the explosives and that speaker?"

In the light Tom could see his friend scratching his right ear. "I have no—" Even in the light of the LEDs Tom watched the color drain from Bud's face. "Oh, no. Oh, golly. Oh, Tom, I think it's *all my fault.*"

Tom took the light from Bud's now trembling hand and pushed down on his shoulder. They sat. "Tell me why you believe it could be your fault."-

"Well, yesterday I got home and there was an offer for a new magazine called '*Hiker and Spelunker*' in the mail. Now that I think about it, it didn't have any postage on it. Anyway, it was all color and glossy and talked about how the magazine would highlight stories about average Joes about their experiences in hiking and cave exploring. It said it was a great friendship-building thing to do. That put the idea in my head to come out here on a hike. I'm so sorry, skipper. The bad guys must have planted that knowing this is the only real cave in the county."

"I probably should have mentioned that I received a death threat." He told Bud what he knew about the note.

"I'm sorry, skipper."

Standing up Tom told him, "Not a big problem. Harlan, Phil and their team ought to have the bad guys in hand by now. I called them before I left the office and told them where we were going. Because of that letter Harlan said he and a few of his men would be tailing us." Now the inventor headed into the closest shaft, this one angling up at about ten degrees.

It was a little longer than the first shaft but they soon rounded a corner and spotted sunshine. Stepping outside, they both took deep breaths of the fresh air. Tom pulled out a miniature radio and called, "Tom to Harlan. We're out on the opposite side of the hill. Do you want to have us hike around or wait for you?"

"Nice to hear your voice, Tom," the chief of Security replied. "I've called for a helicopter to pick us all up. You, Bud, my team and a couple of bundles of trash we discovered up here. See you in ten."

The large double-rotor Swift DB-1 helicopter came up and over the crest of the hill seven minutes later. It hovered above the two and lowered a wire cage with a padded seat inside. As it reached them Tom opened the door and swung it to the side motioning for Bud to get in.

"No doing," Bud shouted over the noise made by the downdraft of the intermeshing rotors just ninety feet above them. "I got you into this so I'll be the last one out! Not arguments." Tom looked at him and Bud glared right back. "Get in, Tom."

With a shrug, Tom got in, sat down and put on the five-point harness while Bud swung the door closed and latched it. The flyer gave a thumbs-up signal to the operator and the basket quickly rose. It was back inside of seventy seconds and Bud repeated Tom's actions. He was soon on board where he was greeted by Harlan Ames, Phil Radnor, Gary Bradley and two other Swift Security men.

Not particularly joining in were a pair of rough-looking men who sat at the back of the compartment, their hands shackled to the arms of their seats and their legs all connected by chains.

With the side door now closed and Zimby Cox and Red Jones piloting them back toward Enterprises, it was quiet enough to converse in normal tones.

"Any idea who our friends are?" Bud asked as Tom took a drink from a water bottle.

"Funny you should ask that," replied Phil. "It seems as if our *guests* never considered that they might be caught so they came complete with wallets and drivers' licenses and all sorts of cash. Big bills, too. Along the lines of twenty thousand between them. Anyway, they are Sam Babisco—" and he pointed at the left one, taller than his companion by several inches, "—and Neville McGahan. That's with a G-a-h-a-n, by the way. Neville here also came with an 'in case of an emergency' card of sorts. Take a look." He handed a card to Tom who took it and let out a whistle. He passed it to Bud who responded, "Jetz! Double whistle from me!" He gave it back to Phil.

Tom and Bud had recognized the name on the card. It was the man for whom Tom's mother, Anne, had once worked as a secret microbial biologist: Quimby Narz. The FBI man was well known by Harlan Ames and had been involved in several FBI-led or -assisted investigations of intruders or spies at Enterprises.

Harlan cleared his throat and spoke. "I'll be having a little chat with our friend Quimby as soon as we get back," he promised. He did not look happy.

"Speaking of getting back," Tom said. "What about my car?"

"Being driven to Enterprises as we speak," Gary Bradley, the number three man in Security told him. "Once we hit the ground we left a man with the car to keep an eye out for any tinkering or bomb planting."

"Yeah, but they brought the bomb with them," Bud said with a lop-sided grin. "Hope they enjoyed the hike."

"Hey, better to close up that old cave than to scratch the skipper's car," Phil noted. "Besides, I hear that the city council voted last month to close up the whole thing. They finally had one too many kids being reported as missing only to find them hiding out or camping inside."

They touched down lightly a half-minute later and everyone but the two pilots got out. With the rotors feathered to provide no lift, the QuieTurbine engines made almost no sound. It wasn't until they had all stepped away by fifty feet or so that the rotors were again tilted and the large helo lifted off, heading back to the hangar complex at the North-East corner of Enterprises.

The next morning Bud visited him in the big office where they talked about the good parts of the hike. As they exhausted that line of conversation the phone rang. It was Harlan. He asked the inventor to come to his office. Bud tagged along with him.

"Got some good news and bad news, skipper. First, Agent Narz was dumbstruck on hearing that the would-be assassins had anything with his name on it. I emailed a scan to him as we talked and he pointed out how the card differs from official FBI cards. I think we have to believe him on this."

Okay," Tom said slowly, "and the bad news?"

"The driver's licenses were also fakes. Once we looked at them under a fluorescent light we could see that the holographic image wasn't consistent and didn't flow over the top of the pictures. So now, I've called the Shopton P.D. and they will take these two off my hands and keep them until Narz comes to get them."

Tom let out a *harrumph* sound and thanked his Security chief.

They left a few minutes later no more knowledgeable than when they entered the Security building. Tom headed out to the Uniforms hangar while Bud wandered over to Communications to see if Sandy had the time for a cup of coffee.

They were both feeling a bit discouraged and in need of something happy.

Bud got his happiness in the form of a huge hug and kiss from his wife. Tom got his when the Major greeted him with a huge smile.

"We've begun building the first panels for the monster," she told him. When Tom's forehead crinkled in curiosity, she explained. "That's what we've started to call this giant building. We've got 'Baby Puffs,' 'Middies,' 'Moonies,' 'Martians,' and now 'Monsters.' What do you think?"

Tom laughed in spite of how he had been feeling after talking to Harlan. "Are those internal terms of endearment, or will we be marketing them that way?"

She laughed. "Strictly internal for now. We all feel a little jealous that Barclay gets to tag things with silly names. We thought we'd get in on the action. Putting that aside, I have good news. Those triangular tubes Hank gave us turned out to be a little hard to sew through so he changed the formulation of just the flanges to a slightly softer plastic and bang! We have a winner. It'll mean we can assemble the panels about twenty percent faster."

"That is good news. So, when should I plan of telling the crew over there to expect the inflatable?"

"Well, since I don't intend on levitating things with the sheer power of my mind, I believe we need to assemble perhaps sets of six or eight panels at a time here, roll 'em up and truck them to the site, and do the final assembly and inflation there. That doesn't answer your question, but it needed to be said. So, as of this morning we requested the final tubing along with interconnect pieces. He tells me we can expect to start getting gigantic reels of the stuff in three days. It's kinda hard to get it to roll because of that shape."

Tom gave her a sheepish grin. "When I suggested the triangular shape I didn't think about the consequences for handling it before construction. Sorry."

She patted him on the shoulder. "Not to worry. In the end this building is going to be one tough mother of a structure." She now looked like she was pondering something. Tom gave her a moment to find the words to express it.

"So, what will happen to this once the permanent structure get built?" she asked.

Tom shrugged. "We currently have no plans for it except to liquefy the foam, suck that out and then disassemble the thing. Why?"

Marjorie Morning-Eagle shrugged her muscular shoulders. "I don't know. Just seems a shame to build this and then take it apart a year later only to toss it into storage. Besides, we've figured out the cost thing and now can build this for about ten percent less than the cost of the first Mars inflatable, even though it is fifty-five percent larger. That still puts it at nearly a million bucks. That's all I've got."

Tom looked at her. "Do you think that it will hold up for a couple decades? Also, can you rig the floor to allow us to erect a skeleton of arching steel and Durastress beams so that equipment we eventually want to mount up off the floor can be accommodated?"

"Uh, for starters your father didn't specify a floor of any sort. Since this doesn't have to hold atmosphere he suggested a good double ring of tubing around the perimeter with lots of places to insert the same kind of ground anchors you used on Mars. Down here the original plan was to anchor down then bulldoze a dirt berm of about five feet in height all around the outside to keep wind from getting under things. Give it a concrete floor and sure, any amount of internal stuff can be put up. Why?"

Now Tom smiled at her. "Because, my dear Major, that means we might be able to make this the permanent building and save millions on a solid-sided replacement plus the down time it would entail transferring things from one to the other. And that," he tried to do a quick calculation in his head, "ought to mean we can get the whole factory going at full speed in about four months less time than dad or I thought. This is great news! Thanks!" With that he turned and raced from the hangar leaving behind a slightly bewildered but pleased woman.

When he got the opportunity to discuss the new inflatable with his father that afternoon the older inventor was very pleased.

"That is incredible news. I've secretly hoped we might stretch out the use of that inflatable to three or four years. Both to save some money and to let the factory get its feet under itself, so to speak."

"I'm going over there to talk about this, ummm, opportunity with the construction manager and to see how the tunnel digging is going."

"I'd like to know that as well," Mr. Swift commented. "Mind if I tag along as a silent witness?"

Tom nodded and smiled. "You don't even have to be silent. Talk all you want. I value your input on this. Besides, it really is still your project. I'm just assisting!"

They began by driving around the perimeter of the buildings at Enterprises to inspect the opening to the tunnel. Tom's incredible boring and coating equipment had entered the ground four days earlier. As it had disappeared, a team of specialists swarmed down the ramps and erected the pre-built arch that would seal this end and keep any dirt or debris from sliding down onto the roadway. They had also installed the set of stairs that foot traffic would walk up and down.

Next, the two inventors headed back around and out the main gate. Twelve minutes later they were entering the grounds of the new assembly plant. The immediate change Tom noted from his visit a week earlier was the first of the tip-up walls for the Assembly building was being raised. That meant that this part of the construction was a few weeks ahead of schedule.

Steve Piper came striding across the compacted dirt to meet them.

"Hey, you two. How do you like the progress?"

They admitted to being happily surprised. Then, Tom said he might do a return favor and told Piper about the inflatable and probable use over a period of years.

"Wow, that *is* great news!" Piper told them. "I'm far enough ahead of things that I'll get the equipment and manpower over to finish the pad the whole thing will sit on right away. All we need to do is build the forms and pour the perimeter concrete ring and get things drilled for all the anchors. Just as long as they can give me about ten days I'll be ready for the tent."

Tom explained that it would take longer than that due to the need to transport things in manageable packages and to do the assembly on site. "They won't be ready to erect the thing for a full month or more," he told the other two men. "So, don't bust a hump quite yet. And, as to the holes for the anchors those might as well wait until the assembly is here and in place. That way you won't need to adjust any of the spacing."

"Good plan, Tom," Steve Piper admitted.

After a tour of the grounds and an inspection of the newly-installed ramp and arch for this end of the tunnels—breakthrough was scheduled for the following day—Tom and Damon headed back to Enterprises.

Tom had been back in the office a few minutes when the phone buzzed. It was a direct call from an Enterprises department head—only department heads had Tom and Damon's direct phone lines; everything else had to go through Munford Trent or via TeleVoc. He picked up the receiver.

"This is Tom," he told his caller.

"Tom? It's George Dilling in Communications. It just got the strangest thing popping up on my screen over here. Listen to this: 'Mr. Dilling, will you please get our fair haired boy to take a look at his computer? We've been trying to get his attention most of the day. What does a Collections boy have to do to get noticed?' That's it. It isn't an email and I can't trace the darned thing backward. But, I'm guessing you have an idea. Right?"

Tom chuckled. "Yes, as a matter of fact, I do. Thank you, George. I appreciate you not just forgetting about it as being some sort of crank thing. Bye."

He walked over to the desk and sat down. A few clicks and he dismissed the screensaver program. A swirling and almost psychedelic pattern was covering the screen, but before he could touch anything it cleared and a picture of a smiling pair of lips appeared for a second to be replaced with:

> Glad we finally seem to have your attention,
> Space Boy. Your back is about to require some
> watching. Fear and loathing will descend on
> anyone attempting what you seem to be about
> to try.

Tom typed back:

> Does this have to do with the D.C. bashing
> we received?

The answer came back almost immediately.

> Partly. But bigger things are afoot and we don't
> mean Sasquatch. Your tax dollars may not be
> enough to help this time. We are not sure what
> to tell you right now. We are very embarrassed.
> It appears that people and governments alike
> do not want a big brother overhead. They see
> it like that, and not benign.

Right now Tom wasn't certain whom to trust fully outside of the Enterprises group, so he cautiously answered:

> All I want to do is build a larger space station.
> The current one is too cramped. What do they
> think they have to worry about? I don't
> want to sound like a doubting Thomas, but
> with possibly many against us, how can I be
> sure you are with us?

Again, the answer came back almost immediately.

> Quandary time. I can't give away the farm, but
> know that old Sneaky Pete is on the lookout.
> Deepest respect both ways and it might sound
> hollow and unprovable but we need/want/expect
> you to persevere.

> We are on up and up as they say. Make this work.
> Your tax dollars depend on it!

Tom was about to respond but something told him it would be futile. In all of their brief communications, the people who referred to themselves as "Collections" initiated every communication. When he tried he might as well have been sitting in front of a fire with a wet blanket sending up smoke signals.

But, to date they had been instrumental in several successes either by running political interference or by supplying vital information.

Sometimes Tom thought they were a bit too flippant in their cryptic wording, yet he would never deny that they never communicated down to him.

One thing he did note was the use of "I" rather than "We" in the message. He wasn't sure how to interpret that. He always felt that Collections was more than a single individual and whoever was communicating with him used the plural to show that. A little shudder went through his upper body as a fleeting thought of *what if just one of the Collections people wanted to warn him and the others were not "on board" with it?*

He put that thought out of his mind and tried to do the same with the entire interchange.

Of course, this latest interchange raised one question and that was who "Sneaky Pete" might be.

CHAPTER 8 /

THE SURVEY SAYS...

JACKSON RIMMER called Tom before five that same afternoon.

"I have a little message to read to you. It comes courtesy of an unknown source in Washington, but it goes a little something like this." He cleared his throat. " 'Dear Swifts. If you thing you had it bad in the Congressional hearing then just wait until you try to buy what you need for that giant space wheel you plan to overhauled. People will make it impossible for you to buy a single lock-nut much less everything you need for that boondoggle. Be warned that the days of Swift Enterprises running roughshod over the U.S. Government is about to come to a screeching halt.' And, Tom, it is signed, 'A Friend,' if you can believe it."

Tom was puzzled. "Uh, Jackson? Did you say 'if you *thing*?' Shouldn't that be *think*?"

Rimmer laughed. "I knew you'd catch that. Yes, it says 'thing.' Plus, the word 'overhaul' is spelled o-v-e-r-h-a-l-l-apostrophe-d. It shouldn't even have an e-d, just plain overhaul."

"Some crank?"

"I believe so," was the answer. "That's not sound, solid legal advice, by the way. It is just my opinion. I've forwarded it to Harlan to see what he thinks. It does bring up the subject, again, of what you plan to do if the notion of cutting off our supply chain to force us to divulge company secrets comes to a head."

Although the lawyer couldn't see it, Tom was nodding, sadly. "The good news is that I believe I might have an answer, and it goes to a question I think you asked about, or a statement, talking about building or mining what we need on the Moon or Mars."

"Ah, yes. I recall that. Uhhh, can you do that? I mean, technically?"

"Yes, but I plan to do it even farther away from interference. I have been looking into setting up a mining operation out in the asteroid belt. Of possibly using our Attractatron mules to haul one or more good candidates into orbit perhaps only a million miles out from our orbit."

The Attractatron mules had been developed to capture and "fling" away any incoming space debris that might hit the Earth's surface. In their year plus of service they had managed to quietly grab nearly fifty space objects while remaining mostly out of the news. One of those objects had been large enough that later calculations showed it would have been at least a mile across when it would have plunged into the Atlantic Ocean just off the western coast of Portugal. The resulting tsunami would have inundated most of Western Europe. But, it was a moot point as the large rock had been easily deflected and had plunged harmlessly into the sun three months later.

"Now, I may not be a scientist like you and your father," Rimmer said, "but if I may make a P. R. suggestion? Haul them into orbit between us and the sun. That way nobody can raise a stink about the possibility of them coming in to hit us."

Tom agreed that it was probably a good idea and would not mean much difference in the mining activities. Before hanging up he requested that the attorney and his people make doubly... triply certain that nobody could claim they were doing anything illegal or that any government could lay claim to what they mined, refined and brought back to Earth.

"Will do," Rimmer promised him.

Damon Swift paged his son over the TeleVoc system. "Tom? Can you meet me over to the auto factory site tomorrow morning?"

"Sure. Can I ask why?"

His father laughter came over the system "Yes, you may. Two reasons. First, the tunnel equipment is going to pop out at around eight-fifty tomorrow morning, and I also want to have a discussion with your about your plans for the new space station. Is eight too early?"

Tom promised to be there at the suggested time.

When he arrived there was already a gathering around the ramp where the tunnel exited. Everyone seemed to be carrying around a steaming cup of coffee or tea and Tom started to wonder about it until he spotted Chow's food truck parked a few yards behind the crowd. The chef, just back from his honeymoon, had arrived at seven-thirty with the fixings for hot beverages as well as breakfast burritos and biscuit and egg sandwiches.

"Ever'body was well please ta see me swing through the gates, I gotta tell ya," he greeted his young boss. "Git ya a cup o' coffee or a san'wich?"

Tom agreed to the drink but begged off any food. "Bashalli made me some strawberry waffles this morning, old timer, and I'm stuffed!" As the cook was handing him the hot drink, Tom asked, "How's married life?"

Chow both beamed and blushed. "It's th' greatest thing ta ever hit my life, Tom. Wanda's the greatest an' she' 'bout the softest thing I ever did hold." He blushed again. "Well, 'nough o' *that* sort o' talk. When will that mee-can-ical mole o' yours be comin' up?"

Tom looked at his watch. "About forty-one minutes from now. I suggest you close up shop and join the crowd in about a half hour. I'll be sure to get you a ringside seat with dad and me."

Locating his father, the young inventor asked if he wanted to talk about the space station project now or wait. "It can wait and I think we need privacy anyway."

Now Tom was curious, but he knew that if something dire was to be discussed that his father would not have hesitated to suggest the discussion take place the previous day.

With three minutes to go anyone looking into the hole saw the end of a probe poke out through the dirt. This was something Tom had added after the bullet train project and was used to measure the final ten yards of an exiting hole. Seeing it meant that the tunneling equipment had paused when its instruments indicated this position.

Three technicians walked down the steps and soon had spanned from one side of the exit archway to the other and were measuring the probe's location relative to those points.

"It's within a half-inch of dead center," the man in the middle called up to the Swifts.

Tom called back down, "Hook up to the probe and give them the adjustment angle, then everybody back up here for breakthrough!"

Two minutes after the men had climbed back to ground level the dirt showing inside the archway suddenly gave way and disappeared. The earth blasters used to carve out the tunnel had broken nearly all of it down into gases that were being drawn along a long tube and out into a filtering equipment truck at the other end.

"Wonderful process," his father complimented him. "With everything practically done with the one machine it's easy to see how you got those tunnels dug in so little time. But, now we should drive back and discuss. Come on. I'll send Trent back here with someone from Facilities to retrieve your car."

Once they closed his father's sedan's doors, Tom asked, "Is this something I'm not going to like?"

Damon chuckled. "Well, it isn't particularly good or bad. I just need to make certain you aren't trying to pull off something we— and by that I mean Enterprises—can't justify. You see, I have been getting phone calls from people we both know in Washington. There are more and more rumblings about this one project. On the good side, any discussions about the larger picture that we got hit with in the committee meeting have gone away."

Tom looked over at his father as they pulled out of the gate at the auto plant. "What sort of calls?"

"Well, for starters some people who haven't particularly been our best friends are saying that this is a plot to put 'something' in orbit that could allow us to try some power ploy."

Tom snorted and laughed. "Power ploy? That's rich coming from people who want our Space Friends' secrets so they can turn them into weapons!"

Damon nodded. "Yes. But setting that aside, people are asking me for both assurances about the new station along with what, precisely, we intend to do with the larger facility. Oh, and there seem to be a few new people down there who don't realize that Enterprises footed the entire bill for the current Outpost. Words like 'improper use of taxpayer money,' and 'Congressional approvals should be demanded,' and that sort of nonsense."

Tom stared straight ahead, saying nothing.

Finally, Mr. Swift continued. "The upshot of it is that I just needed some time to talk to you to see if you might run up a list of the things that this new station will do that the current one either can't or can't do as well. Will you do that for your old man?"

Tom smiled. "Sure, Dad. I've been working on something like that for a couple weeks as I try to decide how to subdivide the area inside. I'll spend the rest of the day getting that together and a copy to you."

"Wonderful. It'll be a big help."

Tom's head tilted to one side and he turned to face his father as they made the final turn down the front side of the tall wall surrounding Enterprises.

"Are you going to need a foot-by-square-foot detailing or just general uses?"

"Well, general I suppose for the things where you don't have a lot of details. Things like 'Research.' Now that could mean so many things that you might want to subdivide it into a list of items such as weather, astronomy, zero and low-G manufacturing, space agriculture, and things like that. But when it comes to items like broadcast television and radio, those brief descriptions are all you need to provide. Besides, I can sort of wing a few things if you don't have much to say."

They entered the main gate where Damon greeted the young

guard. "Hello, Davey. I hear from your mother that you have started evening classes. Mechanical engineering is it?"

"Yes, sir, Mr. Swift," the young man grinned and nodded his head. "I'm pretty good at figuring it out, too. Straight A's so far!" His pride of accomplishment came through loud and clear.

"Well, as soon as you finish, if you want to apply for any other position here at Enterprises, or one of our other facilities, you just let Tom or me know. We love to promote from within."

With a wave he drove on. Tom asked to be dropped off at the elevator to the underground hangar. Then, Damon drove off for an appointment somewhere.

The young inventor sat at his desk looking through the scribblings—electronic as well as on paper—of the things he felt were necessary to do in a larger facility. Several of the notes were placed in a separate file. They were pipe dreams or things he really wanted to do, but absolutely didn't want anyone outside of his father to know about.

The eventual list was about twenty items long with nearly half of those containing added sub-categories. He was reading it one final time when an idea hit him and he had to laugh at himself for almost forgetting it.

The current Outpost in Space had airlocks at the ends of each of the spokes, but there had never been any consideration for bringing a spaceship right up to it and docking. This was mostly due to the slow spin it was given making aligning with a moving or spinning target all but impossible.

He typed out a new category on his computer right at the top of the list.

1) Docking facility(s) set at hub position for bringing one or more supply or personnel rockets right up to the station.

    a—Facilitates safe(r) transfer of people

    b—Facilitate safe(r) and more efficient transfer of materials

    c—Make evacuation of injured personnel safer/quicker

    d—Protect integrity of atmosphere-required materials

    e—Allow for larger items to be more safely moved into station

He thought about adding other reasons, but knew that his father would understand most of the other "whys" involved. He then wrote a footnote discussing the current difficulties the Outpost underwent on an almost daily basis by lacking such a capability.

Tom looked at his screen and let his eyes un-focus. It was a trick he learned years earlier that eased strain on his eyes and let him look beyond something right in front of his face. The side benefit when up close to somebody is that he could make it so he seemed to be looking at them without crossing his eyes.

Now, it simply meant that he could be looking somewhere without having an actual image interrupting his thoughts.

There was a huge logistical hurdle to overcome if he ever wanted to build the new station.

How do I get everything up there? he wondered. *There are so many things we need to get into space that we just do not have the lifting bodies to accomplish. Now that the CosmoSoar is defunct, we're even straining the abilities of the Challenger. But, what?*

The *CosmoSoar* had been his father's first big rocket. Built using nested rings rather than stacked stages, it started out wider than it was tall. As each stage dropped away, it became narrower and more aerodynamic for the increasing speed of the rocket. After it had been retired the first time, Tom had asked permission to rebuild it —slightly different—for a couple projects. But on the last project the structural integrity gave way and it had since been deemed unsafe and un-flightworthy.

It had been all he could manage to get the current inflatable structures off the ground and into orbit where they could be loaded into the *Sutter*. She was unable to make planetfall and had even been built in space.

With a shrug, he leaned forward, focused his eyes on his screen and typed a few words into search engine. While he scanned the results he considered that science fiction writers had come up with many "impractical" and "futuristic" concepts that over the years had become realities. Now he hoped that a search string of "**Space transport large items to from ground science fiction**" might shed some ideas, however impractical.

There were any number of "To get items from the ground into space, simply teleport them..." listings and a slightly smaller number of "rail gun" suggestions. He and his people, especially Harlan Ames, had enough of rail guns during the time when Tom was creating his Attractatron system and the space mules. It wasn't entirely out, but he wanted something else.

Then, he spotted it.

Nearly a hundred listing down, the words "Space Elevator" stood out on the screen. It wasn't a new concept and not even something he had not already glossed over in his mind. But now as he read a short article, and a history of the concept, his mind began to envision just such a thing.

He sketched a globe with a pair of railings and a boxy elevator going up to a cylinder far out in orbit.

Tom sat looking at it and thinking over the many details of such a system until his father rang to ask if he was finished with the list. It was, he saw on his watch, nearly six p.m.

Survey says you are worth looking into! he thought as he bookmarked the page and told his father he was on the way over.

Five days later and with permission from both Shopton township and Essex county, a team of Enterprises experts returned to the old mining caves and carefully detonated a series of small explosive charges designed to close off the entrances to the mine but not to collapse things inside. It was suggested that some historical significance ought to be recognized and preserved.

Tom and Bud had gone along to witness things and arrived back at Enterprises in time for Tom's TeleVoc to beep him.

He tapped the collar pin and silently answered the call.

"Tom here."

"Oh! Good. This is Harlan. I tried your phone but got nothing. I have some news about your would-be cave in assassins. Do you want me to come to your office or can you come to mine?"

"Bud and I just drove in the main gate," Tom answered. "I'll just park between our buildings and be at your office in two minutes. Tom, out." He explained the nature of the call to Bud and asked if the flyer wanted to come along. Bud agreed.

"Might as well. I was part of their scheme either by accident or on purpose. Plus, I want to hear about who might be behind that brochure I received that lured me in."

Once they had seated themselves across the desk from the Security chief, Ames got to the point.

"The two we originally identified as Babisco and McGahan turned out to be a couple of soldiers of fortune who answered an internet ad for people who could work with explosives and had no qualms about using them against *government* targets." He heavily emphasized the word 'government.' "That might seem to indicate, at least on the surface, that some official body was behind this."

Bud was about to speak but Harlan held up a hand.

"That isn't to say it actually has anything to do with ours or anyone else's government. In fact, nobody knows since the posting and even the hosting of the notice is hidden behind many, many anonymous IP addresses. I put in a call to a friend I trust in the Secret Service to run a few things past him.

"Any solid results?" Tom inquired.

Ames shook his head. "Not yet, at least. He is working on getting some of his resources on the trail but it will require a few more days before he expects to find anything."

"In the mean time, whoever is behind this will have pulled down that notice and wiped all records of it clean," Bud stated sourly.

Harlan and Tom both smiled and Tom explained. "Well, yes and no. You see, the Internet is a tricky thing. There is so much equipment and so many servers and such that everything goes through to let the entire world have access, and that all gets backed up weekly, daily and in some cases hourly that there will always be some trail left behind."

Ames picked up the narrative. "Given enough time and resources it has so far proven to be impossible to completely obliterate traces of anything posted. My friend will get us the trace if he isn't stopped by people above him. And, if he is, then we have a good indication where this might have originated."

Tom looked sadly at Ames. "I am really, really hoping that this isn't something from our side. I'd much rather this be Kranjovian, Brungarian, North Korean or even the now deceased daughter of the Black Cobra than our own government." He shook his head and sank deeper into his seat, head now hanging down.

"Cheer up, Tom," Bud told him. "I'm certain it'll turn out to be someone else!"

Ames slightly changed the subject. "However, on the good news side we found out where that threat letter came from. It seems that one young man, a Congressional Page who was nearly bowled over in that meeting you and your dad attended decided that he'd had enough of one particular senator's shenanigans and sent that warning. His English might not be great, but he was sincerely warning you that the senator was against you."

He went on to tell the two young men that the Page had felt guilty about how he worded the note and went to the FBI to claim responsibility. He made no secret of both his admiration of Tom Swift and his disdain for the senator.

"In the end they released him so that he could submit his resignation. They believe he is of no threat to you. Of course, that doesn't get us any closer to the recent attack, but it does raise a whole array of other questions."

CHAPTER 9 /

BABY STEPS

TOM AND DAMON were having a lunch, provided by Chow, in their office when Harlan Ames walked in. He had a satisfied, nearly smug, look that immediately made both Swifts alert.

"Anything... well, interesting on your mind, Harlan?" Mr. Swift inquired.

"Oh, this and that," came the reply as Ames helped himself to a mug of coffee and took his time sitting down. "Ahhh. Feels good to not be on my feet," he told them, taking a sip of his hot beverage.

The two inventors looked at each other and shrugged. Sometimes their Security man could be evasive about... or not actually evasive, but more teasing about how he presented them with good news. Both knew that if something were wrong that Harlan would get right to the point, so they waited him out.

Finally Harlan leaned forward and told them, "We have good news about that pair of clowns who tried to seal you and Bud in the old caves. I had truly feared that it might have something to do with our own Government and the raking you two got in Washington. One of those, 'If you won't play it our way, you won't ever play again' sort of things."

"But it wasn't that, was it?" Damon asked, but it sounded more like a statement.

"It was not. Those two finally talked. Neither wanted attempted murder and kidnapping and other charges that would have kept them in prison the rest of their lives, and for just ten grand apiece!"

"So the money they were found with was their total payment?" Tom asked. "I find that to be a bit insulting. I'm not certain I'll tell Bud about that. He feels his life is worth at least twice that," he said with a twinkle in his eyes.

Harlan laughed. "Anyway, those two are goons for hire out of Texas. Wanted in connection with several attacks on Mexican citizens trying to cross our border. Vigilante types. They were told by the man hiring them that you two were clever illegal immigrants that needed to be given a taste of justice, their style. They claim they would have dug you out a day later and that it was all to scare you."

"Some way to scare a person," Tom said.

"Right. But intent and action are two different things. Once they realized that, and once they tried to call their boss, who had been using a disposable phone and is now invisible, they rolled on him."

"Who is he?" Damon asked, concern in his voice barely masking the anger he felt.

"Ever hear of Jeffrey Singleton?"

Both Swifts shook their heads.

"How about Innozio Brakatelli?"

Again, two shaking heads.

"Last one. Tatiana Roushcu?"

Damon shook his head but Tom suddenly stood up. "She's the Russian who killed Senator Grimsby's granddaughter, Gabrielle!"

"Right! And Innozio Brakatelli was her husband. And he is evidently out to get you."

Gabrielle Grimsby had been hired at Enterprises in spite of previous animosity between her family and the Swifts. Senator Grimsby had been forced to resign his Senate seat over her conduct and death. But the woman actually died much earlier than anyone believed, and her place had been taken for the former KGB agent. In a last ditch attempt to ruin Tom's chances of ever bringing the Swift's Space Friends to Earth, she had stolen a Swift mini-jet and rammed it into the dirigible planned to be their transportation. Whether by accident or on purpose, the jet had crashed after passing through the air vehicle and she had died instantly.

"You believe this Brakatelli guy is out for revenge?" Tom asked.

"We do, but the FBI and Interpol both have a good idea of his whereabouts and believe he will be in custody today. And, for the rest of his life as well. So, I am fairly certain you won't have another attack coming courtesy of him."

They all agreed that this was good news.

"The best part is now I don't have to worry about this being a home-grown attempt or punishment from some angry agency."

After Ames left, Tom and his father sat in silent contemplation for almost eight minutes.

Damon let out a deep breath through his nose before asking, "Now that that seems to be behind you, what are your next steps?"

"As much as I'd like to say, 'full steam ahead with the new space station,' I still have a number of problems to overcome."

"Let me guess," his father said. "Transportation?"

"Number one on the list. The remaining supply rockets are just able to keep the current Outpost supplied. I really don't want to build more of them because, quite frankly, they don't have the capacity."

"Quite frankly I don't want you building more of them either," his father said. "If they won't be used as part of the new station then I hope you find an alternative."

"Dad? What if I said the words, 'Space Elevator?'"

Damon's eyes went wide in wonder. Then, they narrowed as he considered such a monumental project. " 'Very big stuff,' I'd say. 'Impossible' would be next and perhaps, 'Impractical as all get out!' would come right after that. Do you really think it's possible?"

Tom shook his head. "I don't know. About the design and build part, that is. As for the need, absolutely. The new station is not just going to be big, it needs to get built in record time. As in a couple of years. If it takes longer than that I might as well just add on to the current Outpost."

They talked about the cramped conditions and how some experiments they might like to undertake were not possible and some paying customers had to be turned away when space and other needs outpaced the available room and lifting capabilities.

A big contract had been turned down that would have seen the Outpost become a "tune-up" facility for long-term satellites. It had been suggested that a ship like the *Challenger* might pick up ailing or older units, take them to the Outpost for an overhaul/refueling/cleaning and then return them to service.

Tom was unwilling to put his favorite space ship into that sort of use at the time. Once the Attractatron mules had been developed, it became something to look at. But the actual station had been the negating factor. The sorts of nuclear and burnable fuels involved could have jeopardized the Outpost, and keeping the spare parts in stock would have been a nightmare with so little storage area available.

And, it wasn't practical to just pull up a portable storage bin like you might do at a building site.

A new, large station could have both the space as well as the ability to mount an external module to do such service.

The contract would have brought billions of dollars to Swift Enterprises and there was no reason to believe that would disappear in the coming few years.

As they stood up, Damon slapped Tom on the back. "If anyone can build a space elevator it's you, Son. All I ask is that you not break the bank on this. If there is any way to bring in some money from all of this, both your old man and our accountants will be pleased."

Tom decided to go down to the relative quiet of his underground lab and office.

There, he sat at the desk tapping a pencil on the edge of his keyboard. There were so many things to think about and he began to outline a plan of action. He considered that just about anything is possible given enough time and funding, but what if the resources aren't available? If now or in the future any government attempted to shut off supply chains to Enterprises, it would leave them with an impossible-to-complete project, and could destroy the company.

He had to ensure that didn't happen, and so one of the top items on his list was: *Survey Moon, Mars and Asteroid Belt for continuous sources of materials.*

This would mean direct visits that would include getting core samples to test for what he needed. That might mean the *Sutter* with her mining module, but he wanted something fast. He decided the *Challenger* could be outfitted with everything needed. He, Bud, a couple technicians and a few others could handle the job and quite probably in under three weeks.

Tom knew that Bashalli and Sandy would put up protests and so decided to invite them along. Not wanting to have Bud broach the subject only to have Sandy's boss, George Dilling, balk at her being away he placed a quick call to the man in Communications.

"To tell the absolute truth, Tom, she's been doing more flight demos than working here in Communications the past two months. And, as much as I do not want her to hear this, we've done quite well without her. I love Sandy like a daughter, but at this point in her young life she has not gracefully settled down into a life of less-than-glamorous jobs."

"Yeah. She'd still rather spend her time with Bud or my wife. So, can you make is sound like you're stretching things but will let her go?"

"You've got it, Tom. I'll wait for her to ask, of course."

Tom next called Bud and outlined the voyage.

"I'll be ready in about two minutes!" he told Tom.

"Well, while that is fine and you will only need to sit around here for five days or so before I'm ready to leave, what will you tell my sister?"

There was a sharp intake of breath on the line. "Ohhhh. Right.

Hmmmm. That is a poser. I kinda promised that I'd be around the house nights and weekends for a few months. Gee. What *am* I going to say?"

Tom counted to five just to let Bud stew a little before he suggested, "Call Sandy and tell her she can come but only if she can get time off from her job here. If George says 'no,' then she has to abide by that and not make his or your lives miserable. Or, mine for that matter."

Sounding a little defeated, Bud told him. "I'll call you back."

The call came a little over an hour later. "You won't believe it, but George told Sandy she'd have to take some of that as vacation or as non-paid days. She had to think about it but finally agreed to forego salary for two of the three weeks. Evidently she believes that my salary will cover for her. See what sort of pickle you get me into?"

Tom knew without seeing Bud's face that the flyer was grinning. "Gosh, Bud. Sorry," he said not sounding at all sorry about it. "Too bad you didn't know all about Sandy before you married her. Ah, well. At least Bash will be more likely to take the time off and come."

When he called her, Bashalli was thrilled at the prospect. "But three weeks is a long time, Tom. Is there any way you might bring me back early?"

He explained that the longest time would be the Mars and Asteroid transit times and that coming home after even Mars was a little out of the question.

"But, I'll tell you what I can do. I can have one of the computers hooked up to your desktop at work and you can do remote work as well as videoconference. If you like I can have a camera set up in your space that you can manipulate to watch everybody."

"Oh, no. That would most definitely not go well with anyone. I will ask for the time off but will promise them my attention eight hours each work day."

While preparations were being made and the *Challenger* outfitted with an array of digging, coring, and analyzing equipment, Tom went to visit Arv Hanson.

After he explained what sounded like a far-fetched project, the model maker nodded and asked, "When do you want a scale model to test?"

"I ought to not be amazed at you anymore, Arv," Tom told his. "but I am constantly. I haven't even tried to draw what I might want and you're ready to give me a test version."

"It's what I do," Arv told him. "Besides, what it looks like and what it does are two different things as I see it. I also think that testing the whole idea of an incredibly long cable system might help you come up with a design that makes the thing practical."

Tom admitted that it made sense. "Tell me more of what you might do at this stage," he requested.

"First, start by telling me if this is to be a counterweighted, pulley approach, a cog and ratchet approach or a friction engine."

Tom stared at Arv, but the model maker wouldn't say anything more. After a minute Tom broke the silence.

"I haven't even gotten that far. But I can see massive issues with using a pulley. That's just too much movement of the rope, so to speak. Any number of ways it can foul up or strain or stretch. Or worse." Tom made a breaking motion with his hands. Arv rolled his eyes and nodded.

"If it were me, I would still suggest a counterweight and pulley. It might be a little trickier, but trying to create something that will creep up and down, probably using some sort of wheels and pressure to grip the cable, is a crap shoot. Wet cables could get slippery and that means loss of traction and *that* means a potential crash landing. Plus, it takes a lot less to move a load when you have that matching weight on the other end of the line."

"What about the cog and ratchet system you mentioned?"

Arv rubbed his nose. "It's something I've seen before but don't like the idea for this run of thousands of miles. It works in office buildings, but..." He shook his head.

"So, I might be stuck with the pulley after all," Tom stated.

"But it isn't as bad as you might think. One way to find out is for me to make you a couple test versions. I guess we can suspend them a mile of so up using a balloon or even a remote-controlled drone to give the cable even more lift."

Tom agreed to the plan.

Arv told him that the first one, the counterweighted pulley system, would be built so that the weight moved up and down well to one side of the elevator compartment. The second version using a friction grip and mechanical drive would use a single cable and technically be easier to build both in scale as well as full-size forms.

"We'll take baby steps for now with the small ones," Tom decided. "When can you have one or both?"

"The mechanical straight-cable version can be knocked up in a couple days. It will take a bit longer for the counterweight and pulley version as I need to find some cabling flexible enough to not require a pulley about a scale mile wide!"

Two days later and with things at Fearing progressing nicely, Arv invited Tom and Bud out to the North end of Enterprises to an area that would not interfere with any flight operations. Waiting for them was a large spool of thin cable and a four-rotor drone. Arv explained that the drone was autonomous and would take off at Tom's command, lift to a height of one mile trailing the cable underneath.

"That's about the limits of its lifting ability and the point where it can still provide a taut cable for the test," Arv told them as he attached the free end to a ground anchor.

The drone's small gasoline engine was started and the four rotors began to spin. Soon they were whirling at high speed. Tom nodded, Arv pressed a button on a small remote he had in his pocket, and the rotor hubs tilted the blades catching the air and sending the craft aloft.

It took ten minutes to reach top altitude during which Arv readied the boxy elevator. He showed the other two the "guts" consisting of a powerful Swift Solar Battery and a trio of rubber wheels attached to electric motors that touched the cable at 120-degree angle from each other. It would, Arv explained, provide the best balance between power and pressure to move the box.

As the box began its ascent Tom watched it through powerful binoculars. "Wish I'd brought a pair of BigEyes," he muttered. Arv, smiling, walked to the small car he had driven over and pulled out three pairs of the hand-held devices. Soon the box disappeared to normal view but the BigEyes, with their tremendous amplification abilities, let them see it as if it were just a dozen yards away.

After another minute Bud asked, "Is it me or is that box going slower?"

Tom, looking more closely, answered, "It *is* slowing down. Any ideas, Arv?"

He was about to speak when Bud cried out. "It's coming down!"

Sure enough the box and the cable were falling back to the ground. Tom, Arv and Bud ran for their two cars and climbed in just in time to not be struck by the falling mess of cable or the box.

The cable writhed on the ground like a nervous snake, but the box shattered into nearly a hundred pieces.

Arv yanked out the remote and pressed the DESCEND button. Much faster than it went up the helicopter drone came back down and landed.

It was obvious to see what had happened. The connector for the cable, even made from strong metal, had snapped apart sending everything down.

Eyeing the mess, Arv offered, "If you can forget you ever saw this, I will have the other version ready to try tomorrow."

Tom nodded and he and Bud helped collect the cable and elevator box before heading back to work.

The following afternoon at three they came back out.

Arv was waiting with the same drone and a spool of cabling, similar to the spool the day before, and another, larger spool. Attached to the drone was a one-foot-wide pulley made from Durastress. Over the top ran a cable from the larger spool, and on the end just below the pulley was attached a tube of about two inches in diameter.

"That's the counterweight," Arv explained. "It weighs about the same as the box, and the box has a scaled down version of the wheels to move things along. They barely have to lift any weight at all this way."

The smaller spool contained the "anchor" cable that would remain attached to the ground and the drone. The elevator wheels would use it to grip onto for movement.

Because of the extra weight, this attempt would only go up about three-quarters of a mile, Arv explained.

Up the drone went carrying its cargo of the counterweight, the moving cable and the anchor cable. Once it neared the top Tom gave the signal and the drone went into a hover keeping the anchor line tight and straight.

"Here's hoping..." Arv said as he pulled out a new remote control and pressed two buttons. They all watched as the box began to rise. Slowly at first and then with increasing speed. BigEyes were again used to keep an eye on things and gave them a good view of the counterweight as it barely missed colliding with the side of the box. But, shortly after that the weight began to slow its descent and the box its rise until the weight came to within a yard of the ground and stopped.

Arv gave a little bow as Tom and Bud applauded him.

"Can I bring it down while I'm still ahead?" he asked.

Tom gave the go-ahead and the process reversed. In exactly the same time it took to come down, the weight went up, this time bumping slightly into the box but doing no damage, and the box arrived back at the starting point in front of them.

"Other than the little collision I'd say this is the functional model of what we need to build. As soon as we get back from our prospecting flight you and I will sit down and try to come up with a modified version and a solution to the bumping."

Arv told them to head back; he had an assistant who was coming out to help gather things up.

The rest of the day and the next were spent in final preparations for the trip.

CHAPTER 10 /

WHY NOT NESTRIA?

WHEN THE time to depart came, Bashalli arrived at Enterprises with a large portfolio of papers and what looked like a fishing tackle box of pencils, pens and other tools of her trade. "These are the preliminary designs I must finish by the end of next week," she explained.

"Why not just bring computer files?" Bud asked.

"Because *you* might use computers and *Tom* might use computers and even Sandra, but I use paper, pencils, pens and paints to do my designs," she told everyone. "I like it the old fashioned way!"

When they arrived at Fearing Island the *Challenger* was ready for them. Red Jones and Zimby Cox would accompany them as additional pilots, two specialist technicians that would operate all the sampling and analysis equipment as well as Chow and Wanda Winkler who had declared that their recent honeymoon on Mars had left both of them with many friends they hoped to visit at the colony.

" 'Sides," Chow had exclaimed, "ya gots ta have lots o' good vittles on a trip like this'n." He had looked hopefully at Tom knowing that the inventor might veto their participation. Chow had, months earlier, declared that he was going to step away from going on most of Tom's adventures.

One look at the earnest face of the old ranch chef and the inventor's heart melted. The chef had a new vigor for life now that he was married. There would be plenty of room and both Bashalli and Sandy liked Wanda, so they would be able to keep themselves busy.

"Absolutely, oldtimer," Tom told him. "I wouldn't have it any other way."

The short hop to the Moon was soon behind them and a criss-cross pattern of orbits, just about one mile above the lunar surface, was begun. This phase would last nearly two days most of which would be spent not looking out of the large view panes that filled the front wall of the second and third floors of the ship.

When Bashalli had inquired why Tom had blanked out the panes he briefly unmasked them allowing her to watch the surface zooming under and past them. Ten seconds later she had turned a little green from the sense of vertigo it gave everybody, and Tom had again made the windows opaque.

He, Bud and the other two pilots spelled each other at two-hour intervals so that by the time their scanner survey was complete each had spent only a dozen hours at the controls.

Next came a series of more than fifty corings taken at sites that showed the most potential.

However, potential and reality didn't match and Tom called a halt to the attempts after thirty drillings. Other than ArmAlColite, bauxite, a variation of iron only found where the solar winds had bombarded it with free hydrogen atoms, several types of glass and a trace of water, there was little of importance to Tom. He did register one area with a high percentage of an exotic glassy mineral he hoped to mine in the future, but three days after arriving they headed outward to Mars.

The three ladies and Chow elected to stay at the colony while Tom and the others performed the same multiple orbit survey, this time at a height of fifteen miles. Only a dozen or so sites showed anything interesting and so Tom chose to keep the ship working for two more days rather than go back to the colony.

Chow and the ladies had a wonderful time. It was the second visit for each of the women and third for the cowboy. The colony leader, Haz Samson, showed Bashalli and Sandy all the changes that had taken place since their visit just after the colony had opened. For starters, there were several inflatable habitats now and not just the one.

One of them was totally devoted to aquaculture while another now had minimal growing facilities and maximum living and recreational areas. In fact, it featured the first basketball court on Mars as well as a velodrome—a sharply-angled bicycle racing track —that was a favorite of the colonists for exercise.

Tom and the others returned on the fourth evening in time for dinner. Chow had brought along an incredible array of foods packed in the hangar of the ship. Everyone agreed that they needed to get the cook to come up several times a year. If nothing else his meals were huge morale boosters.

The longest part of the trip started the following morning. The asteroid belt ringed around the entire orbit of the sun, but there were some areas where a greater number of larger chunks tended to congregate. It was one of these the *Challenger* aimed for.

On the trip out, Sandy and Bashalli were given lessons in the operation of the ship. Wanda had begged off telling everyone that she was more into steering horses than even automobiles and *certainly* not spaceships!

When they arrived within about one hundred thousand miles of the main part of the belt, Red, who was piloting, had to be extra cautious as millions of small pieces needed to be dodged around or carefully pushed out of the way using minimal forward repelatron power. From that distance Tom used the ship's SuperSight equipment. The precursor to Tom's BigEyes, the system used both an exceptionally powerful lens system along with computer enhancement to bring distant object into close view.

In this case, pieces of asteroid a mile or so across seemed to be no farther than a dozen miles away.

Tom used the SuperSight for his first survey of nearby objects, selecting more than one hundred to be looked at using his Megascope Space Prober for a much closer and more detailed examination.

It took four "days"—a 24-hour clock set to Shopton time was standard on all Swift craft—to complete the visual survey after which Tom knew of nineteen objects he wanted to get samples from.

Only once did they have any trouble when a small piece of debris, probably not part of the belt but coming inbound from farther out, caromed off of a larger asteroid and careened directly toward the *Challenger*. Red Jones was back on duty and he had no time to call out a warning to "Hold on" to anyone as he yanked the ship to the right.

A crash was heard in the galley and Wanda's voice called out for help. Bud got to the small kitchen first and could see that Chow had been injured in a fall. His right arm was at a bad angle and his face was pale and sweaty with pain.

Nobody on board had much medical experience but Tom was able to contact Enterprises and get Doc Simpson some video of the chef's injury.

"It's a simple fracture, skipper. No bone poking out and the potential for bleeding in there is only moderate. If you haven't already, grab the med kit and pull out one of the hypo-sprays marked with the number seven. Push that against his upper arm until you hear it hiss out. Wait five minutes and give him another one but closer to the break, maybe as close as two inches. The hypo has five doses in it. Wait five minutes more and then gently but firmly pull at the wrist, straight out, until the bone sort of clicks into place. Give him one more shot right over the break and then get him in one of your self-adjusting splints. Keep him quiet for a day or so. After that, unless there is other damage in there, his body will sort of forget it's broken and he can get up."

While Chow didn't want to be any bother, Wanda asked if they could go back to Earth, and Tom had to make a decision.

With the bone set and splinted, Chow was immediately ready to get up and "Git about fixin' ya some san'wiches." Tom told him that Doc ordered twenty-four hours of rest.

"Then we'll see. Okay?"

Chow nodded. He told his new wife that she didn't have to worry and the mission could continue. As he spoke, she had begun to cry a little.

Sandy and Bashalli had a talk with Wanda. They understood the emotions; they had both been there with Bud and Tom. Many times. She could see their reasoning and thanked everyone for taking care of Chow. She took over galley duties.

The asteroid survey started in earnest an hour later.

Each large chunk, most at least a mile in diameter and some as large as ten miles wide, was orbited for the sensor survey and then several core samples were taken at various points. Everything was broken down and fed through a continuous-stream spectrographic analyzer. The results were better than Tom hoped.

Rich deposits of both standard metals and elements were mixed with veins of rare earths and specialty elements such as titanium and magnesium. One of Tom's favorite metal alloys, magnetanium, was a mixture of these and had both incredible lightness as well as durability. He had been prepared to build his new space station out of alumi-steel coated with Durastress and tomasite, but this find would allow for faster manufacturing of all the outer skin of the station as well as interior walls and structures.

But it was a discovery on one of the last asteroids to be checked that made his heart beat faster.

It had a core made of several of the heaviest elements known on Earth. These might be easily converted into capital by selling them for many purposes that currently had to make due with minuscule amounts of these elements.

All too soon it was time to return to Earth.

Each of the target asteroids was tagged with a short-range beacon operating in a frequency range that Tom's ships would be able to track from within two hundred thousand miles or so. Tom decided to not extend that range. And, although considered exceptionally unlikely that anyone would be able to come try to lay claim to them, each position was both catalogued and registration made identifying them as mining claims by Swift Enterprises.

By the time they reached Earth six days later Chow was feeling nearly back to normal, but he did have to get a permanent cast on his arm.

Doc congratulated Tom and Bud for setting the arm as straight as they had been able to.

"He'll have one hundred percent recovery!"

For a couple days Tom rested at home. Bashalli had to return to work the day after getting back, but she also had been able to stay ahead of any due dates on all of her projects while away. Even her department had barely felt her absence as she was in near-constant video communications with them.

When he did get back to Enterprises, Tom sat down with his father to discuss both the practical and legal angles of their rich findings.

Mr. Swift looked at Tom. "I think that we need to speak to a friendly face about this. And I know of just the man. Unfortunately he isn't in a position to help us any more, but at least if he thinks we have a case, then I'll feel a lot better about giving permission for some of these tremendous costs of yours."

Tom grimaced. He knew full well that there was no way in the world for Enterprises to pay for everything he needed or wanted to do, at least not over any period of less than about thirty years. It would be vital to be able to mine raw materials, purify them and then sell any excess down on Earth to other manufacturers to offset much of the expenses.

"I promise to start small," he said with a hopeful look.

Damon shook his head but couldn't help but grin. "Right. Tom Swift and small. 'Dad? Can I build a smallish jet aircraft? It won't cost a lot and it will be easy to store.' Remember that one before you built the *Sky Queen*?"

Tom laughed. It was true as were about fifty other instances his father might mention. Damon buzzed Trent and asked him to get in contact with Peter Quintana in New Mexico. When his father spoke the name of the former senator, it flashed into Tom's mind that his recent communication with "Collections," just who their mention of a "Sneaky Pete" most probably meant.

"I have the senator on line five," the secretary announced a minute later.

"Pete," Damon said picking up his receiver. "It's Damon Swift. Can I get you to sit in front of your computer and accept a VideoChat?"

"Important enough that you want to see my sorry self, Damon? Of course. Give me five minutes to wash the dirt from my face and hands and get into my office. Usual sign in stuff?"

"Yes. See and talk to you in five. Oh, and Tom will be in on this as well."

"Great! Bye."

Four and a quarter minutes later a red square began blinking on the screen of Damon's computer. He pressed a button and his display was now coming up on the large flat screen over in the conference area of the office. He and Tom moved over and sat down where he picked up a remote control and pressed another button. The face of former Senator Peter Quintana was looking at them expectantly.

"Well, hello you two," he greeted them. "What's up? And make it really interesting because I am bored to tears out here."

Over the following eleven minutes Damon and Tom explained both the blow-up in Washington and the project Tom wanted to undertake, including his intent to bring one or more asteroids closer to Earth so that the *Sutter*—built originally to mine in space —would be able to break down the materials into various metals and elements and ready them for shipment down to Fearing Island.

"It's a big project, Pete, huge, and we absolutely must be certain that Uncle Sam or the U.N. or G-20 or whatever can't and won't want to invade Enterprises and pull some tricks to gain control."

Letting out a big gush of air, Pete Quintana asked, "And did you say you have an anchor point? Where is it? I ask because if it is on U.S. or our territorial soil you might be in trouble."

Tom replied rather sheepishly, "We don't have an actual point nailed down yet. But I have several options and only need to start with the real negotiations once you tell us we will be safe. It's important to build our space elevator because we need a much larger platform than our current Outpost can provide. Something in the order of twenty times the size."

"Wow! Okay, so why not just move your base of operations up to your moon, Nestria?"

Damon looked at his son before answering. "It's a fair question, Pete," he told the former politician, "but I think you know as well as we do the kind of brouhaha that would cause in certain international circles. We were forced to give up ownership claims even though it was moved into Earth orbit by our Space Friends for *our* use. Otherwise we might have continued having the same sort of issues up there as we did in the first place."

He referred to a series of attacks and attempts to wrest control of the little satellite, Earth's second official moon, by foreign agents from the unfriendly nation of Brungaria. They had eventually been repelled and the leader believed, for nearly a year, to be dead, but he eventually turned back up to torment the Swifts. In the end Damon and Tom had signed away ownership rights and the object nicknamed Little Luna had become a free scientific colony under no one nation's or governmental body's rule.

Nodding as he recalled the problems and the protracted negotiations that finally led to peace on Nestria, Pete Quintana now had to ponder the whole issue of a space elevator that would be under total control of the Swifts.

"Okay. I accept that and believe that your space elevator is something we, and I mean the U.S. Government, can't question or hinder you on, especially if you have obtained solid permission for an anchor point that is not under any control other than a foreign nation itself. I pride myself on being a bit of an international law expert and so I think I can say that if you meet those conditions, you have an air-tight case for going ahead."

Damon and Tom both wanted to smile but kept serious faces as they thanked the man who had been instrumental in helping get their nuclear research and power facility, the Citadel, okayed and built in the senator's home state.

"Thank you, Pete. So, how is retirement going for you?"

Pete Quintana made a face and blew a raspberry. "It, to quote the vernacular, bites. Bites big time, Damon and thanks for asking. Remind me to get some salt and a lemon the next time you get a cut. My daughter, who decided to move in with me to take care of this frail old thing, had me build a shed—a *shed*, can you image it out here in all the heat!—in the back yard where she expects me to spend at least six hours a day not bothering her. Phooey! Just between the three of us—" and for no good reason he looked from side to side as if somebody might be close to him, "—I've spoken to our Governor about taking over the remaining term of my replacement in the Senate. He was diagnosed with throat cancer last month and will announce that he is stepping down later this week. Prognosis is good by the way because they caught it early on, but he's going to lose most of his vocal cords. Can't have a blowhard who can't talk. So, it looks like I'll be back in the saddle inside of two weeks." He let out a joyful giggle.

"Do you get to regain your positions within committees?" Tom asked.

Pete nodded. "Most of them. Well, at least three of the five I was on. And those positions will let me smooth things out for you. Of the other two there was one I was desperate to get off of, so that's a little blessing, and the other was the special committee for wasting money okaying the purchase of lavish gifts for our ambassador's around the globe to give to undeserving pseudo-dignitaries. Hah!"

Now, all three men smiled and even chuckled a little at the notion.

"So, Tom? You go ahead with your plans for mining the raw materials. I'll see that permits to bring what you need down to Enterprises are not 'mysteriously held up' somewhere along the line, *if* they are needed at all. I'm almost certain I have the exact text of the law that allows for import without taxation of materials from space. That's how you were able to mine and bring down that ArmAlColite from the Moon a few years back without it costing you anything. I'll do another of these video-visit things again in a few days. Adios, amigos!" and with that, the connection was broken.

Mr. Swift turned to Tom. "You can't imagine how relieved I will be with Pete Quintana back in Washington. I can't count the number of times he's been our guardian angel down there."

Tom smiled and replied, "Plus, he's an incredibly knowledgeable man. I miss not having to explain even tiny, unimportant concepts to politicians. Let's hope his regaining the reigns of those committees does the trick."

"In the meantime, you need to get working on finding that anchorage point. Having it only on the equator, or at least within a hundred miles at most, is limiting. Loonaui was a great find a few years back, but now that it is off limits to us that leaves a considerably smaller list of options. If you need my help, let me know. Otherwise don't hesitate to work with the Legal department until we have Pete back at the helm in D.C."

CHAPTER 11 /

REFITTING A GIANT

THE *Sutter* would naturally be the go-to vehicle for any asteroidal mining operations. After all, Tom had built her specifically for mining in outer space in the first place. It was only because of great foresight that he had built the huge, funnel-shaped craft so that both the drive section at the wider, rear end as well as the forward eighty percent of the internal working could be disconnected, removed and replaced so the ship might complete other kinds of missions.

She was a beautiful ship with a large "sail" near the upper, back end to house a crew and all the controls and systems, as well as a wide and long common room perched at the top of the main body that served such purposes as crew lounge, exercise facility, entertainment center and mess deck.

The ship also contained an artificial gravity system. Those working inside wore, under their regular clothing, a skin-tight body suit interwoven with special metallic fibers. An array of small and low-power repelatrons covered every ceiling in any space where gravity was desired. These were tuned to only repel the metallic fibers, so the end result was that people were pressed down making it feel as if they were held down by about half gravity.

Because the effect was spread out all over the body, only a few people had complained that they felt like something was pressing down on them. For most others it took only about an hour to get used to.

When Bud caught up with his friend, the inventor was standing in a partially darkened room on the main floor of the Engineering building walking all around a 3D projection of the ship. His telejector system provided the nearly photo-quality model that currently ran eighteen feet in length and about ten at its widest point.

Closing the door, Bud waited and watched while Tom walked completely around the floating ship again, this time pausing at several points to take a few notes on his tablet computer. When the inventor looked over at him, Bud smiled.

"Trying to figure out what to do so the *Sutter* is ready for your first mining expedition?" he asked. "And, before you answer, is my name on the crew list?"

"Well, yes and yes, but tentatively on the second one."

Bud looked disappointed and was about to protest when Tom stopped him. "By that I mean you might not be crew... with so many things to accomplish back here I may need to take a pass at this one and that means you will be captain!" He smiled at the flyer.

Bud's face split into a huge smile, so wide he couldn't get out his tradition exclamation of "Jetz!"

Finally he settled down and asked about the entire project.

"Well," Tom began, "it all starts with you and me taking the *Challenger* back out, perhaps along with a couple of the Attractatron space mules. We'll be visiting the asteroid belt and picking up at least three chunks to bring back. Once we do, they will be parked in a solar orbit about one million miles closer to the sun than we travel. From that point—"

Bud interrupted him with a question. "Uhh, I'm still not in sync why aren't we putting them into orbit around the Earth? After all, a closer sun orbit means they travel faster than we do and that means they get ahead of us pretty quickly and that means more hassle getting things back in position. Or, am I not understanding something about astrophysics?"

Tom shook his head, stating, "You're not missing something. That will be the case, except we have the advantage of the mules and their ability to drag the asteroids back into proper position. In fact, if they run just five minutes a day to shove things backward, we can keep the rocks within a half degree or so of the same relative position to Earth for as long as we wish. Same thing with the *Sutter*."

"And once you get through mining them you just nudge the remains into the sun?"

"No. I considered that, but in order to keep the balance of things, we will mine them, never taking greater than thirty percent of their mass out, and then return them to their old positions in the belt."

Bud admitted that he saw some logic in that approach.

"What sort of stuff do you want to mine from them?"

Tom rattled off a long list of minerals and metals he believed would be found in one or more of the asteroids. "It's a matter of how much and in which chunks," he told his friend. "That's where our initial survey comes in. Our recent visit identified at least thirty or more pieces of Maldek that are candidates for our initial selection. As you recall we tagged the best ones."

"Yeah. But, Maldek?"

Chuckling, Tom told Bud about the supposed one-time planet. "Bodes Law calculates that to be balanced as it was being built, our solar system should have once had a planet between Mars and Jupiter. As in right about the orbit of the asteroids belt. Some catastrophe broke it apart, possibly before it was fully formed, and allowed it to scatter pieces around the orbital path. I actually don't know how the name Maldek became associated with it, but it is one of the names given this potential planet. Oh, and Bode also postulated that some of Jupiter might have been the cause of the breakup, and that also left some asteroids right along Jupiter's path. They're called the Trojan Asteroids. A few get drawn in every year and crash onto Jupiter's surface."

"Wow. Glad we don't have any of those around Earth," Bud exclaimed. As he looked at Tom he noted the inventor wasn't agreeing with him. "Uh, we *do* have Earth Trojans?"

Tom nodded.

"Okaaaaayyy, why not mine those?"

"It's a good question and comes mostly down to scale. Earth Trojans are relatively small. Many too tiny and far away to detect from the ground. We've never made a study of them, but dad and I feel they are not good candidates for the metals and minerals we want. However, the asteroid belt has mega-tons of iron, titanium, nickel, tungsten, copper, aluminum, and some of the rare-Earth metals. We can use all the non-ferrous ones we can get, and by selling off much of the rare metals we will bring in huge amounts of capital."

"Enough to pay for everything?" Bud asked hopefully. He was pleased when Tom confirmed exactly that.

They spoke about the forthcoming mission for another hour before heading to the cafeteria for lunch. There, Bud asked Tom about this proposed new space station.

"I'm fairly certain that it won't be a station like the current Outpost. For starters, practically none of it will be built here on the ground. And, I've gone off repeating the wheel approach as it makes for confining spaces. We need big, open spaces and that means my long space cylinder approach. Once the *Sutter* has mined and refined what we will require for the first year or so of construction, she will be refitted with an entire production facility. Every panel, beam, brace or other component of the inner and outer hull will be manufactured up there."

"But, where *is* up there going to be?"

"At first I was aiming for one of the LaGrange points. But even the closest one is way out near the Moon's orbit so that is out unless we want to build and launch a lot of stuff inside rockets again. I do want to be much higher than the current Outpost and far away from any possible interference with space debris."

"What does that leave you?"

Tom looked over the rim of his glass of iced tea. "A tethered station, probably about thirty thousand miles out."

Bud nodded as he thought this over. When he looked up it was to ask, "So, this *tether* thing? Is it like the Gravitex we used for that space kite and your cyclone eradicator machine? Do you build the new station in low orbit and then sort of let the line out... like a kite?"

"No. This needs to be a real, solid attachment from the ground. We start by building this incredibly long and durable cable with a big enough and massive enough weight at the end to keep it taut using just the Earth's rotation. Then, we build something that people have been talking about since the late eighteen hundreds—a space elevator!"

Bud let out a low whistle. "Right. Like the ones Arv tested. And those weren't rousing successes, were they? Tell me you've solved those problems," he requested.

"Not a lot to tell... right now. I'm still trying to finalize a design. Once we have the cable and the elevator we can move things up or down at will. We go up at a reasonable speed, faster if the elevator is unmanned, and can come back into the atmosphere without the need for heat shielding since we can come in as slow as we like."

He described more about how the station would be completely built from the materials mined in space and processed by the *Sutter*, and extra materials or unneeded metals could be ferried back down to the anchor point, transported to Enterprises and then sold on the open market.

When he finished Bud had just one more question. "What will the elevator look like? A box like Arv built?"

Tom's head tilted to one side. He actually had not thought that far into it. "I would suppose that it will just be one or more platforms connected around the central point where the cable passes through. Well, the cable and the counter weight. There will be some sort of drive mechanism to propel and retard speeds, but it won't need to be big and boxy or anything like that."

He thought a moment before adding, "In fact, the more open it is the lighter it will be and the easier it becomes to move it. So, unless I run into problems just think of it as several mesh-like platforms surrounding a central core. Strap things down and *voilá!"*

Bud didn't ask what the central cable might be made from and Tom was glad of it; he had no idea at the moment. But he knew that whatever it was would need to be made very visible to aircraft traversing close to it, and would need to be either thin enough, or designed in such a way to avoid much of the drag prevailing winds might place on it. After all, stability was required, but not so much that he believed a solid rail or pole would be appropriate.

It would mean making the incorporation of lights or possibly some other detection method mandatory, or finding an anchor location that had no air traffic. There were very few locations like that, but you couldn't be certain that an emergency might not force flights through any restricted zone.

There were so many design considerations that Tom began to second guess himself on the viability of a space elevator up to his new space platform. If he could build it, that would make transportation a breeze and save multiple billions of dollars over using rockets, even those featuring repelatron power. Without the elevator, the space station would have to be compromised to be smaller and less usable than he wished.

If there were no elevator for what he wanted and needed to do, a new fleet of perhaps one hundred ships, fifty-percent larger than the ones used for the first Outpost, would need to be built and kept in almost constant use. Even at the cut-rate price tag of about twenty million dollars apiece, he knew that for the cost of three ships he could build his space elevator.

Everything expense-wise above that would go toward the construction of the new outpost. Tom wanted to have as much funding available as possible for the station itself. And, what a space station it would be.

As he had described to Bud, it would be built like a giant cylinder, or, be a series of squat cylinders—discs?—that could be added to one another as time went on. His initial vision of a completed half-mile-wide, two-mile long space station probably needed to be pared down to a thousand feet across, and the length would be... well, he didn't actually know what the eventual length might be. The design was something that could be added to over many decades.

He told Bud that the first idea he had of ten- or more story buildings ringing the inside of the entire hull would be reduced to just four or five stories.

But, that had the advantage of allowing an increase in the spin giving the inhabitants something more like eighty-percent normal gravity.

With concessions came benefits. Bud could tell that his friend was happy to discover the added benefits as they talked about the station. When Tom was happy, so was Bud.

The two young men parted ways for the day as they left the cafeteria.

As he wandered around the Enterprises grounds, along the winding path between the main buildings, Tom's mind began envisioning the construction process. The *Sutter* would begin to churn out hundreds and even thousands of curved panels starting with the outer skin and any connecting pieces. If he could mine enough titanium—along with either aluminum of magnesium—he could combine those into a thin, relatively light alloy could be easily seamed together and then coated inside and out with Tomacoat. The resulting hull would take small meteorite strikes and the harshest solar radiation and be none the worse for it. People inside would be safe. A mule, to be stationed nearby, would handle anything of a dangerous size.

When enough plates had been connected into a ring of perhaps one hundred-feet, the first end would be sealed with new plates tailored in the *Sutter* to provide a flat, pressure-resistant closure. And, a docking system that would be set in the dead center of the end and would not rotate with the rest of the station. Docking would be a relative breeze. Then, the next ring—open at both ends —would be constructed. A final ring, closed at the outer end would be added and the entire station sealed. This would be the outer hull of the first disc in a series of...?

From that point construction would begin inside where either individual buildings, or more likely multiple floors or levels all around the inside of the hull, would be built. Following that, separate compartments, workspaces, apartments and other facilities would subdivide the space. The "roofs" of the interior structures could be planted with gardens for both the enjoyment of the inhabitants as well as augmenting the hydroponics facility Tom could see being an integral part of the station.

And *that* would be modeled on the facilities at the Mars colony and the knowledge they had gained in operating them to peak efficiency. If at all possible Tom wanted the station to be self-sustaining.

His vision included precisely-spaced avenues running the length of the tube that would be at hull, or ground level letting people walk "outside" of the enclosed spaces thus making it even more Earth-like.

A space solartron would float outside soaking up solar energy and churning out everything from oxygen to food-making materials such as proteins and carbohydrates.

He had to smile to himself as he had the thought that it wouldn't be like having Chow's incredible cooking, but it would beat the reconstituted foods the current Outpost was saddled with.

As he entered the Administration building, he thought, *Heck. The station could eventually be made of three or four or even five of these long tubes where not just a few hundred or so people might live, but perhaps five hundred or a thousand, working, playing and living in space.*

He took the ride-walk belt down the center of the second floor. Tom put such grand thoughts away when he greeted Trent as he walked past the outer office and opened the large door.

His father and Jackson Rimmer were waiting for him.

"Ah, Tom. There you are. I was about to TeleVoc you. Jackson has some good new for us."

Tom shook the attorney's hand and they all sat down in the conference area.

Rimmer got right to the point.

"I've had a long conversation with the newly-reinstalled Senator Peter Quintana and his Chief of Staff this morning. Now, he isn't making outright promises, but he did give me every indication—both in his specific words as well as subtle subtexts—that the necessary committees, groups and even full Senate and House of Representatives will back Enterprises up on your space station project."

Tom was about to express his joy, but Rimmer forged ahead. "Not without a price, however."

Now, Tom's mind shifted gears. "Is it compromises that are going to force us to do things someone else's way?"

"I don't believe so. What the senator hinted at is more along the lines of guaranteed working and living space for a rotating team of scientists. Some of them you already know as they routinely visit the current Outpost. What Mr. Quintana told me is that he will most likely need to be in a position to promise that ten to twenty accommodations be always available along with an array of permanent and interchangeable equipment and supplies."

"Okay, but I'd like us to retain final okay like we have at the Outpost. Harlan has been able to clear all but two individuals and those later turned out to be not very nice people!" Tom said looking at the lawyer to see if there was anything else.

There was.

"On the plus side, as I reminded him, we would not cover transportation costs so long as we might be forced to use conventional rockets. We would, however, provide free transportation at practically any time if we had access—and I stressed that it must be exclusive access—to build and operate—*freely!*—a space elevator system devoted only to the new station. I could practically hear the smile he got on that one."

"So, I take it he agreed," Damon inquired.

Jackson Rimmer smiled and nodded. "One hundred percent. He gets it and the people he is and will be dealing with get it for the most part. Anyone who has issues or troubles understanding it will be handled on an individual basis."

"That means we're free to go ahead, right?" Tom asked.

"That means we are full speed ahead, to use a nautical phrase," Rimmer told them.

It lifted a huge load off Tom's shoulders. He got another big grin on his face as he thanked their legal genius.

"Oh, just one other small thing," Rimmer told them as he was standing to leave. "I did make it abundantly clear that it is only the transportation that is gratis, not the time they stay or resources they use while up there." He winked at them and departed the office.

When the door closed, Damon cleared his throat causing Tom to turn to face him.

"You aren't home free, yet," he cautioned his son. "There have been some pretty ugly stirrings from the United Nations. A lot of talk about 'stopping the Swifts' is being bandied around, so I hear. This domestic win is one hurdle in a field of many. Just remember that. Of course," he said, softening his tone, "this is probably one of the two biggest, so I suggest you go home, grab a nice shower, take your lovely wife in your arms and ask her if you might have the honor of wining and dining her this evening. Of course, I realize she doesn't drink, but you get the picture."

"Yep! And, Dad? Thanks for everything you've done. I know that you've been on the phone a lot, pulling strings, or at least substantial threads, and calling in a few favors. I promise that I won't let you down on this."

Damon shook Tom's hand before grabbing him and giving him a long, warm hug.

As Tom reached the main gate and was waiving goodbye to the guard he happened to glance across the road and up the hill where the new private neighborhood and control tower built for both Enterprises and the FAA were located.

Originally, the neighborhood overlooking Swift Enterprises, despite Federal mandates to the contrary, had been financed by a foreign agent intent on spying on the complex below. When his involvement had been discovered, a mysterious fire had destroyed most of the closest street of partially built homes. He disappeared, so the Swifts requested to be given stewardship of the land.

It now had more than two-dozen homes that were used by Enterprises to house important visitors and people doing temporary work at Enterprises.

Tom's eyes went wide and his heart began to beat when he saw the large delivery truck coming down the last straight stretch of the road. It was out of control.

Before he had the chance to take a second look his mind registered the terrorized face of an older man who appeared to be practically standing on his brakes, but to no avail.

"Run!" Tom yelled to the guard.

Davey was one of nature's reactors. Meaning that he didn't stop of ask what might be happening or taking time to look around. He heard "run" and that is what he did.

Tom also was a reactor. He knew instinctively that he would not make it out of the gate and around the corner before the truck hit so he jammed the transmission into reverse and floored it. Everything went into slow motion as his adrenaline levels soared, and he suddenly knew he had run out of time. The truck was just yards away and his car *wasn't accelerating fast enough*.

CHAPTER 12 /

LONG AND STRONG IS AN UNDERSTATEMENT

TOM SPUN the wheel and was barely out of the way as the giant truck plowed into the archway over the gate and into the grounds of Enterprises. The doubly reinforced archway sheered the top of the truck's cab right off and tore through nearly the entire fifty-four-foot trailer behind. But, it had been specifically engineered to keep large vehicles from crashing through and it did what it was designed for.

Tom jumped from his car screaming for Davey. He hadn't had time to ensure the guard's safety. He needn't have worried. Davey was not only safe, having run about fifty feet away in record time, but the young man was already on his radio calling for an emergency vehicle from the runway support team and for Doc Simpson plus an ambulance.

The driver, a man looking to be in his sixties, was hanging in his shoulder harness. His eyes were closed and Tom could see a rib that had broken through his chest.

Doc arrived a minutes later with three of his medical technicians. He nodded to Tom after checking the man's pulse.

"He's alive. Banged up really bad, but short of massive internal injuries I think he'll live!"

The rescue and fire trucks arrived but with no fire to fight only the "jaws of life" needed to be employed to tear off one side of the cab. The man, finally loaded in the ambulance with Doc and a technician, shot down inside of the wall to the private "Executive" gate and headed for the big hospital in Shopton.

Tom was a little shaken and decided to go back to his office.

By the following morning word came that the driver was doing well. An investigation by Harlan and his people showed that the brake lines had failed taking with them any ability for the driver to slow down. It appeared to be material fatigue, not sabotage or anything suspicious.

Being Friday and with not much to do, Tom volunteered to supervise the clearing and temporary rebuilding of the main gate area.

Davey had been given the day off. Even though he was a "reactor" his body had pumped out so much adrenaline that Doc declared him unfit for work until after the weekend.

By the time he arrived back at work on Monday Tom had several mental notes that he knew he needed to work on for the space elevator and the station. And as he sat in the shared office his father came in, saw the look of concentration on his son's face and did a quick turn around leaving the office as quietly as possible.

The young man was in such concentration he didn't notice a thing.

He did notice when Bud came in just before lunchtime. And even though he saw how much Tom was concentrating, the flyer couldn't help himself.

"Ground Control to Major Tom," he softly sang. It required several more lines of the song, along with him picking up a small loving cup Tom had been awarded years ago and using it like a microphone as he raised his voice and swung into the chorus.

"Huh?" Tom sat back and looked up a little startled.

Bud stopped singing and put the small trophy back. "I came over to do three things. First to see if you wanted to grab some lunch if you haven't already arranged to have Chow bring it in. Two, to see if there is anything I can help with. I've got nothing, nada, zip, zilch, on my calendar for the next eight days. And, three, to tell you that I have come up with a good name for this space *elevatorial* thing of yours."

Tom groaned in anticipation of one of Bud's rightfully famous pun names. "Okay, Bud. Hit me with it, but gently. My head hurts from all the thinking I've been doing."

Bud smiled and moved his hands outward as if presenting something sitting right in front of him. "High Space L-Evator." He wiggled his eyebrows. "Well?"

The inventor closed his tired eyes a moment and spoke with them remaining shut. "Sure, Bud. It goes to higher space around the planet and not really what I like to think of as outer space. The first part is fine. But elevator? Isn't that a cop out?" He now opened his eyes.

Bud was shaking his head. "You've got no imagination for these things," he teasingly chided his best friend. "L as in the twelfth letter of our English alphabet, then a little hyphen just to be tricky, and then the 'evator' bit but with a capital E. L-Evator!"

Tom had trouble getting his mind around it. "Not 'upsy-downsy space yo-yo?'" he asked.

Bud shook his head again. "Not even 'Long Distance Otis-mobile,'" he told the inventor. "I figure that this one is so sensitive that even I can't justify making light of it. I just thought that the play on elevator made it sound a bit more modern. Makes it sound like a big thing and not some ride to the fifth floor box affair. What do you think?"

In spite of his hurting eyes and head, Tom had to smile. "I think that you've come up with a good name and done the right thing. Not that your other puns haven't been, well, let's say somewhat accurate, but you're right about the seriousness of this. So, short of adding 'The Memorial Budworth Barclay...' to the beginning of that, I'll put the change in on all documentation and files."

Bud was very pleased. It had taken him the entire previous evening to come up with it, much to the displeasure of his wife. She finally had headed up to bed with a favorite old mystery from her early teen years and refused to put it down when he finally came to bed. But it had been worth it to see how Tom adopted it right away.

"And the other things?" he now asked.

"Lunch, yes. Not here because I need the walk. And something for you to do? Can you go up to the *Sutter* and supervise the final installation of the refining machinery in a few days? Take Sandy if she can get George Dilling to give her more time off."

Bud agreed to ask.

While they ate Bud asked several questions, the most important had to do with the cable that would suspend the, now named, L-Evator.

"First, how massive is this going to be and then how the heck are you going to get it all up there?"

"The first one is easy. It will be just four and three-eights inches across." When Bud looked like he had a follow-up question, Tom second guessed him and added, "It will be made from a twisted bundle of five different things. Durastress for the great tensile strength that will give it, copper to provide some data link capability, titanium for lightness, a nearly unbreakable form of nylon and finally Kevlar. Like the cables used on suspension bridges there will be about eleven smaller bundles of small cables all spun around and around for added strength. It is going to weigh in at just under a pound per foot, so about five thousand pounds per mile."

"Jetz! I was figuring on it weighing five or six times that," Bud said. "But that still leaves tons and tons to haul up into space."

"Yes, and that is why we won't be doing that. Instead, and this is also part of what you will eventually supervise up there, we make the cable in space and lower just what we need down to the anchorage. Of course it is going to take all the power the *Sutter* has to maintain a stationary spot above the anchorage and to have enough to keep all of your tons and tons under control. But, she has the power and Enterprises has the space pilots who can jockey her around while you and I connect things down here."

Bud looked disappointed. Tom knew that he wanted to be part of the "upstairs" action, but he told his friend, "I'll need you down here. We might need to find and retrieve the cable end using the *Sky Queen*. If I'm stuck at the anchorage point I need you to go get that cable for me."

"You can count on me, skipper!" Bud declared. "Tell me more about what I am supposed to do at the *Sutter* this trip."

Tom took the next half hour and described the process of making the giant ship ready for her next task.

"In all it ought to take four days before mining begins."

"I'm already looking forward to it," Bud announced as they left the cafeteria.

A week later they had another lunch in the shared office. Afterward the inventor suggested they go to the underground lab. Quite a few things had happened and Tom wanted to let his friend know about them.

When they neared the entrance and elevator building to the underground hangar, Bud asked, "Have you come up with the final design for the L-Evator? I recall a failure and a partial success with what Arv built."

"No. We've come up with the near final design. At least for the cable and counterweight system." As they headed downward, taking the stairs, Tom explained.

"After we attach the main, stationary cable from the ground up to the point where the station is to be built, we will be mounting what amounts to a giant pulley. It will be about three hundred feet across and lets the movable cable go up and over and back down again."

Bud stopped as they reached the main floor of the hangar. "Hang on a sec. You've got a big cable that just runs straight up and down *and* another cable? Why?"

"Come on into the office. I'll show you the diagrams."

When they were seated Tom called up a large image on his monitor.

"Oh, now I see," Bud said. He was looking at how what Tom had called the "moveable" cable attached at one end to the set of cargo platforms—currently shown on the ground—and then running up to the pulley and around to the counterweight. This cable would allow travel in both directions while the straight—anchor—cable gave everything something to move along.

"But, that means twice the cable, huh?"

Tom agreed.

"And everything just sort of slides past all the other bits?"

"Well, that is where a bit of engineering comes in. Let's start with the platform end. The moveable cable attaches to the top of the platform core, but to one side of the central shaft where the counterweight will travel as they pass each other. That counterweight will wrap around the anchor cable and use its drive mechanisms to grab hold of and push either up or down on that main cable. As it moves, the cargo platforms at the other end go in the opposite direction.

"Once in space where there are no outside forces like winds, everything will move smoothly. But in the atmosphere I need to build some arms at the top and bottom of the cargo core."

"Okay," Bud said not quite understanding. "Now tell me why?"

"In a word... stability. Remember videos of old rocket launches? You've seen those arms that attach the rocket to the gantry. Well, picture them swinging to one side as the rocket takes off."

Bud smiled seeing that image in his mind. "Right"

"The arms for the platform will let the core keep a steady distance, centered if you will, from the main cable up until it is time for the counterweight to pass through."

"I get it! They swing aside for the passing maneuver and then swing back to continue doing their job!"

"Another gold star for Bud," Tom declared.

"Let me see if I really get this. The stationary cable sort of acts like an elevator shaft keeping everything going just up and down and not side to side." Tom nodded. "The other cable stays taut and just lets the weight and platforms move up and down the main cable." Another nod. "And the pulley at the top keeps the moving cable from getting bent."

"And there you have the L-Evator primer," Tom told his friend.

Bud's face changed from a smile to a concerned look. "It's a lot of cable, though, isn't it?"

"Yes, it is. But by using two cables to support and control the weight of the counterweight, that lessens the strain on the main cable for the cargo platforms and means I can engineer it to be long, strong, and relatively thin."

"Jetz! I'd say long and strong is an understatement!" Bud told him. "What's the pulley thing going to be made from?"

Tom called up a different diagram. Pointing at it, he explained how the pulley system would consist of another cable to be firmly anchored to a two-mile-wide asteroid that would act as a stand-in for the eventual space station.

"We need that to hold up the end of the main cable. Centrifugal force like a ball on a string that you spin around. The string remains straight. In our case it is the Earth spinning and the weight out there keeping the cable straight."

From the asteroid the cable would run down—about one thousand feet—to the wide pulley. That would be mounted inside a cage-like arrangement to ensure no slippage over the sides of the wheel.

Everything would be constructed from a magnetanium and Durastress sandwiched material.

"As we complete small portions of the new station's outer hull, we'll attach that to the outer side of asteroid via a cable that will be drilled completely through the asteroid and remove a corresponding mass from the asteroid itself."

"So, if I'm still with this program, by the time the station is complete, no more asteroid?"

"Another gold star!"

"Just one more thing before I go," Bud requested. "If the movable cable needs to go around that pulley, just how strong and flexible will it really be?"

Tom put a hand on Bud's shoulder. "That pulley is just wide enough so that no additional stress or strain gets put on the cable. There will be more non-metallic components to that cable as opposed to the other. Things like alumisteel won't be in it. That is too stiff. Instead, more Durastress and other engineered materials. Any metals will be made from finely-braided wires for both strength and flexibility. It has to be strong enough to hoist a fully-loaded jumbo jet into space and still be flexible."

"And you think you've got it handled?"

"I hope I do, Bud."

"Me, too, because I won't be able to help you on that front. Unless it is shaped like a football or has a joystick, I'm sorta out of my league!"

The rest of Tom's day was spent in working with Hank Sterling. It would be the Chief pattern maker's job to coordinate getting all the large components built. It was quickly decided that the pulley wheel obviously could not be lifted into space as a complete piece. Likewise, the manufacturing capabilities that the *Sutter* would soon feature would not be able to turn out the heavy-duty device. That equipment was going to be devoted to making the thousands of slightly curved and interconnecting outer hull sheets.

"I think we need to build this pulley like a pizza," Hank told the inventor. "A big, single-topping pizza cut into perhaps twenty-four slices."

"Ah, I see. So we make the mold or jig for one and then just pump them out until we have enough. I guess the *Challenger* is going to need to have her top rack put back on so we can carry them up. How much will each, uh, slice, weigh do you think?"

"Under a ton I would believe."

"Good. We can maybe nestle a pair of them running in opposite directions, tie them down and get those up. Only a dozen trips that way. How long to make the entire set?"

Hank did a few calculations before answering. "A week to build the jig and then two days or so for each section."

Tom told him to go ahead and get started in about a week. "I still have to finalize a few items before I give the go-ahead."

Hank nodded and agreed to be ready when the time came.

They turned their attention to some of the other things the engineer would be managing. There were many of these so it wasn't until nearly six that Tom left to go home.

"Another interesting day?" Bashalli asked after she had given him a big kiss.

"They all seem to be interesting, Bash. Some good interesting and some not-so-good interesting. There are just so many things to keep track of. It's kind of like if I were building ten different and very large jet aircraft at one time, then adding an ocean liner, a new type of submarine, and learning how to do micro-surgery all at once."

She stayed in his arms for a full minute before kissing his neck and letting go.

"Then, the least I can do is to keep you fed well," she told him. "I was going to give us the leftover lasagna from the other evening, but I think that I will cook up the rib eye steaks that your mother gave me for tomorrow. Baked potato?"

Tom grinned, took his wife back into his arms and whispered in her ear, "With all the fixings, please!"

Over their dinner he described what he and Bud had talked

about. As an artist, she could readily picture in her mind how everything would look.

"That sounds like pure genius at work," she complimented him. "Just as long as you are certain that this giant wheel pulley is the correct size." She now frowned a little. "What if it is not?"

"Well," Tom chuckled, "it can't be too large, but I suppose it could be too small. Hmmm? I'm not sure."

"Can you have Mister Sterling build it so it might be expandable?"

After thinking about this a moment he asked her to explain what she meant.

"Well, if we take the pizza idea, can it be built so that the slices may be moved farther away from the center to make the outer dimension larger?"

It made sense. Such a concept might take a little redesign so that as the ends of the slices moved out, something could swing up to fill the new gaps. When he discussed with Hank the next morning, it was decided that it was very much doable.

"I called you here to discuss legal and eventually, I hope, contractual matters," Jackson Rimmer informed Tom as he sat down that same morning. The call had come in five minutes earlier and the inventor wasted no time getting upstairs to talk to the attorney.

Tom leaned forward. "Is this about the new station?" he eagerly asked.

"Yes, it is. But it is more than that. Now that I have it through my head that we need to lock down an anchorage point for a period of at least thirty years—"

"Or up to one hundred," Tom added.

"Or that, I am going to need a list of all the applicable spots on the planet. I will research all the legal angles. *Does* the U.S. have a good relationship with that nation? *Is* there any treaty precluding a private concern from doing what you want? *Could* any government, ours or neighboring to the anchor country, have legal recourse or treaties or whatever precluding it? And about five additional items I won't bore you with right now. The question is, where do you want to build this?"

Tom grinned ruefully. "Loonaui would have been great except for the new government. We had the base and it was built on solid rock going down a couple thousand feet at least. But, that's a no go today."

Rimmer nodded.

"Fine. So we have the South American countries of Ecuador, Columbia, and Brazil. Then across the Atlantic in Africa there are —"

"Sorry, Tom but I have to stop you on African countries. There is so very little stability in the region and also problems with airspace rights to get supplies to any place other than coastal nations, and on the east that's not possible because it's Somalia!"

"Right. Okay. Then if we continue around the world we have Singapore, Malaysia, Indonesia and islands below the Philippines and above New Guinea, then some islands and atolls across the Pacific and finally back to South America."

"Well, let's see what the others have to say."

"I'll keep my fingers crossed," Tom said.

"Now that I give it a little more thought I'll see what the folks in Gabon have to say. There are friendly and have a few islands off their coast that they protect. Like Sao Tome and Principe. It's a few miles off the actual equator but from what I hear that is within your limits."

Tom thanked the lawyer. Before he left he mentioned, "We need to ensure that we can have a minimum area of about one thousand feet by one thousand feet and it needs to be fairly flat. I'll have to take a look at a map to see if that Sao Tome Island can provide that."

"I can save you a little time, Tom. I've actually been there, years ago. Over half the island is hilly to mountainous, but there is a very large forested area on the eastern side. It had a few two-lane dirt access roads into several potential anchor areas. They might like to get those paved as part of the deal." He looked at the inventor, who nodded.

"Doable," Tom declared and got up feeling very optimistic.

CHAPTER 13 /

X MARKS THE SPOT

WITHIN THREE days of investigating his top five choices, Tom had received four disappointing responses. Ecuador, and Brazil had said no, and the State Department had nixed Columbia as the intended area was close to one of the most dangerous drug regions. Not even in the waters just outside Ecuadorian or Brazilian official territory. Gabon in Africa had politely declined the island stating that they did not wish to seem rude but that their people, known to be quite superstitious, would rebel against the government for allowing such a thing they called, "A rope to the gods!"

As mentioned, on the other side of that continent, Somalia was not even considered. Most of the others possibilities could not offer the sort of terrain needed.

The final refusal came from Indonesia. Their political situation was "tense and uncertain," at the moment.

This left New Guinea, but Tom was having major reservations about that area as it frequently saw typhoons and other storms.

He needn't have worried. The next day *they* sent their regrets saying that, "Information has come to our attention from an international source that indicates you may have less than honorable intentions for this ladder to the sky project! We can not be part of this."

Tom shook his head as he read this last message while standing in front of his father. "Well, that tears it," he said with more than a hint of disappointment. "It looks like the UN has poisoned the waters for us. We can't use Loonaui any more because the new government has impounded our base. At least they let us take all of our installations out. The nearby islands are too nervous about the new government there, and most other spots are too prone to storms or political unrest." He looked at his father. "Any suggestions?"

Damon shook his head. He could see the anguish in his son's face and felt his pain. But, the truth was that their refusal to built a space elevator and then turn it over to the whims of an international body that couldn't agree on practically anything had set that body against them.

Tom went home that evening feeling defeated. Bashalli met him at the front door and was about to launch herself into his arms when she saw his face. She held back, asking, "What is wrong, Tom? Please tell me that it is not news of someone losing their life!"

He shook his head as they entered the house and closed the door. After crossing the living room and patting the sofa next to him to indicate that she should join him, Tom poured out the disappointing details of what appeared to be a failing project.

After telling her about the rejections, he allowed his emotions to come out and shared his frustrations and anger. She sat next to him, simply holding his hand during all of this. At the end, when he appeared to have run out of anger, she leaned over and gave him a gentle kiss on his right temple.

"You do know, Tom, that I love you very much and it hurts me to see you in such agony. But I have to ask, and this might only be my ignorance, but why do you need to put your installation in a foreign country?"

Tom leaned back and looked into her eyes. "Well, Bash, this needs to be on or exceptionally near the equator—"

"Yes, I realize that, but why so close to a physical piece of land? Why not out in waters far enough away from any country that they cannot possibly take exception?"

He stopped and thought it over.

"From a purely technical point of view, we have to anchor the thing to solid bedrock perhaps a thousand feet deep. If we are out in the ocean too far away from land it becomes a nightmare just getting down to the sea floor, much less digging into the planet that deep."

"Ah, now I understand. But, at what depth can you do this?"

"Ummmm, perhaps as deep as seven hundred meters or about two thousand feet. Less would be better. In fact, if this didn't have to be on the equator for stability reasons, I'd just put it out on Fearing Island and be done with it!"

"See if I understand the problem, please," she asked of him. "If it is not at the equator, what is at the far end does not travel in a straight line. Does that make it wobble about, and does an anchor point on the equator remove unwanted wobble?"

Tom nodded and kissed her nose. "Got it," he told her. "I knew I married a smart woman." Now, he sobered and sighed. "Perhaps in the future I can come up with some way of overcoming those stresses, Heck. I might even make future ones portable. How about that? Want a space elevator? Just call Enterprises and we'll have the base of one delivered to your door—" He stopped. "Well, enough speculating on a future that might never happen. I just wish there was a place to put this first one."

They ate dinner in silence. Tom wanted to help with the dishes but Bashalli shooed him out of the kitchen. "Go watch something mindless on the television," she told him.

Tom wandered out to the living room and plopped down on the sofa. He picked up the remote control and flicked the TV on. *One hundred and fifty channels,* he thought as he scanned up and down the program guide, *and so little to watch!*

He was about to abandon the idea and switch off when his brain raced back to consider something he had seen about fifty channels higher up on the list. His finger pressed the UP key enough times to get him back.

A smile crossed his face and Tom felt that hope was coming back to him.

It was a documentary on the Galapagos Islands! Ecuador had relinquished ownership of them several years earlier because of the expense, and the fifteen-plus island group had declared their status as an independent nation shortly after that. Tourism accounted for most of their income with an enhanced breeding program for their special turtles accounting for the rest. Zoos the world over paid top dollar for Galapagos turtles. They still were not a rich nation, and were always looking for ways to increase their national product that were in keeping with their conservancy requirements.

Tom picked up the phone and dialed his parents' number. His mother answered.

"Swift residence and I see by the caller I.D. that this is either my doesn't-call-his-mother often enough son, or his wonderful and polite and loving wife. Well?"

"Hey, Momsie. I take the jab as you intend it. With love. I'll try to be better. Promise. In the meantime, can I speak with dad?"

Anne Swift sighed. "It wasn't so bad after you left and I still had your sister to pester me, and even after she and Bud got married, those first three months were great. She was out of my hair but on the phone daily asking how to cook this or that, or how to sew on a button. That sort of thing. But, she's gone all self-sufficient lately." Another, very dramatic sigh. "Yes, your father is home and yes, I will put him on." A third sigh, this one accompanied by a small sniffle and the sound of the receiver being set on the table. In the background, Tom could hear his mother calling out, "Damon. It is your son who would rather speak with you even though he sees you at work practically every day!"

Tom grinned.

"Hello, Son," his father greeted him. "I'm suspecting that your mother would like a bit more frequent communication with her first born. At least, she is lightly hinting at that. So, what can I do for you?"

Tom said just two words. "Galapagos Islands."

There was a moment of silence before Damon answered. "Ahhhhh. Yes. And, we did them a huge favor several months ago. You may not know it but I sent the repaver equipment down to refurbish their single airport runway in the town of Puerto Ayora on Santa Cruz island. It had only been good for their small inter-island planes. The other three islands they fly to had dirt runways. If you are thinking of asking them, I believe we might sweeten the pot, as it were, by offering additional use of the equipment. Is that what you called about?"

Tom was stunned. He had half expected to have some sort of resistance put up by his father. But, this was phenomenal. The young inventor felt a sense of relief.

They spoke about some of the logistics for about five minutes before Bashalli gently but firmly took the receiver out of Tom's hand. She spoke into it:

"Father Swift? It is Bashalli. Will you please tell Mother Swift that Thomas and I would like to have the two of you over for dinner tomorrow? From what I have overheard it seems that you and your marvelous son have come up with a new idea for this project of his, and while I am certain that you could talk about it for hours, it would probably be best for you two to get together tomorrow morning to do that. I will call Mother Swift before lunch tomorrow to discuss the dinner. Good night."

She handed the phone back to Tom.

"I think Bash believes we need to table this for the evening, Dad. What do you think?"

"I think I am getting the 'eye' from your mother and should be hanging up any second now. Goodnight, Son."

"Night, Dad." Tom hung up.

The next morning both of the Swift men headed to work before eight even though they had not discussed it. Damon arrived first followed into the office by Tom ten minutes later. During that time, Trent had left his desk and retrieved a selection of pastries and some steaming hot coffee for them.

They sat down in the conference area and started to talk about how to approach the island nation's government.

"Unless we are advised otherwise by our Legal folks," Damon said, "I believe a direct approach is called for. It might be best," he said looking at Tom to judge how the younger man might take the coming suggestion, "if I did the talking with the Galapagosian representative."

Tom took another bite of his cherry Danish and nodded his agreement. "Fine with me!" He looked at his watch. It was just 8:03 and he did a little mental arithmetic. "We'll have to wait a bit. It should be about seven down there right now. Or six. Let's figure out what you are going to tell them and then call in about two hours."

They pulled up a map of the island group on the large monitor on the wall.

"The equator runs across the top of Isabella, that longest island that looks a little like a seahorse," Damon pointed out. "I would not want to suggest taking over any part of their territory for this, but this other map," he tapped a few keys and brought up one showing both the land and ocean topography, "shows a good working depth of five to six hundred feet about a mile off the coast. That is acceptable for your anchor mount, isn't it?"

Tom agreed. "Yes. I'd like at least three hundred feet of water weight pressing down but I believe we can successfully drill the necessary holes at five times that depth."

"Let's get Jackson Rimmer down here to see how he suggest we approach this."

After he sat down and the inventors had filled him in, he smiled at them.

"For starters, Damon I believe you need to let me handle this."

"Why"

"Because, believe it or not, my first language is Ecuadorian Spanish. My father was stationed down there when I was born and it is the language I learned before we moved back up to Nebraska when I was seven. And, just as Brazilian is an offshoot of Portuguese, the Ecuadorians—and by default the people on the Galapagos Islands—speak a special Spanish dialect. With me talking I can assure you that there will be no mistakes"

It was agreed, and when the time came, Damon called the Communications department and asked the on-duty switchboard man how best to complete a call.

"Well, Mr. Swift. As far as I know they had a trans-Pacific line laid down on the ocean, but Ecuador cut that for lack of payment about a year ago. When you spoke with them a few months back on that airfield project, I had to route you through shortwave operators in California, Mexico, El Salvador and Panama. If you can give me five minutes I ought to be able to get you connected.

Who do you want to speak with?"

"Well, probably their new highest ranking government official. President, mayor, commander or whatever he is called. They changed about a month ago."

"It's a she," Jackson whispered.

"Oh. Make that whatever *she* is called."

The connections were made in record time and they soon had El Primier Minstro Señora Evelyn Estes on the speakerphone.

Jackson Rimmer made the introductions in Spanish. In perfect English she replied, "Ah yes. How are you this fine day Mr. Swift, Tom Swift and Mr. Rimmer?"

Damon now spoke for the group. "We are all fine and wish to give you our congratulations on your new position."

"Thank you for your kind words. My predecessor had many good things to say about your company and how you respected our lands when you worked to make our islands less remote from each other. How might I repay that gesture? I assume that this is not a 'Are the runways still working,' call."

"No. Uhh, how do we properly address you? We do not want to cause any confusion or insult."

"Well, if this is a pleasure call, you may address me as Evelyn. If this is a private and *very* pleasurable call, then I am Eva, but if this is an official call then Madam Minister is fine." She favored them with a little laugh.

"Madam Minister it is, then," Damon said. He began to explain the basics of Tom's project, but she interrupted him after a minute.

"Is this the space project we have been hearing about? The one the United Nations has sent warnings to all member nations to avoid?"

"I'm afraid that it is," he replied.

"Then, it is a very good thing that we are not part of the United Nations, that we have been steadfastly refused even the courtesy of discussion of the possibility, and that we had the recent foresight to demand that they at least guarantee us, in perpetuity by the way, a one hundred mile circle of sovereign water territory. So, tell me more about this. I am intrigued."

They did, both from the technical as well as the practical points of view. During the discussion they lost contact two times, which led to a definite request from the Minister.

"Is there some way in which we might obtain satellite links that cannot be cut or interrupted? We only would need a few lines, if that is what you call them, for government and emergency purposes. Is this even possible?"

Damon laughed. "It is not only possible but it is practically doable within a week at most. If we might be granted permission to fly down with the necessary equipment I believe that everything could be set up inside of two days. We could offer you as many lines as you wish."

It was decided to give each town on the populated islands three lines: one for government use and two to be shared by the general population, and to give the seat of government five lines.

"We also would like to offer to build you more airfields if you wish them," Tom put in.

"Ah, I think that might be nice, but it brings up a very delicate question, and one that may be the hinge on whether we can grant you permission to build your station down here. It is the matter of protecting the lands of our islands. We could not grant permission for you to build a large facility on Isabella or any other of our islands. I am afraid that might also impact the ability for you to fly down here with larger aircraft." She paused, and added, "but you probably will be wanting to bring down all supplies in ships?"

"Actually, no," Damon stated. He glanced at Tom.

"It's Tom, Madam Minister. What I envisioned is bringing down only a single ship. We have a large flat-topped vessel, the *Sea Charger*, that we have been using as a research ship. It has a deck like an aircraft carrier, but four times as wide, so we can make our landings on that. She was damaged a couple years ago in an attack and although she is completely seaworthy, I believe we would like permission to permanently anchor her off your coast and use her as our supply and construction facility. She is completely self-contained and recycles all waste, makes her own fresh water, and is non-polluting."

It was decided that Tom should fly down to Santa Cruz the following day—and be there the day after—to discuss things face-to-face. The call was finished a minute later.

After a little discussion with his father, Tom decided to fly his Toad down. Bud would accompany him as would their wives.

They departed the next morning at five a.m. Both Sandy and Bashalli curled up on the back seats under blankets and slept all the way down to San Antonio, Texas and their first fuel stop.

"Mmm we there?" came Sandy's voice as the jet lightly touched down.

"No. You go back to sleep, honey," Bud called back.

They flew on toward Panama City where they would stay the night and make their second fuel stop—they would have ample for the trip out and back again. The ladies dug out the picnic lunch as they flew over central Mexico.

The next morning was uneventful as they headed back into the sky and out across the Pacific Ocean. As they climbed, Sandy used a pair of Tom's BigEyes electronic binoculars to look down. After gasping a few times she handed them to Bashalli who leaned across Sandy's lap and also let out a little gasp of delight.

A very large pod of whales could be seen twenty miles off the coast cavorting in the water. But, all to soon they flew past them.

Tom set a course that would eventually take them across the top of the island of Isabella where he hoped to make a moderately low run to scope out the area. They would then make a sweeping left turn and head for the Santa Cruz airfield.

As they approached he let Bud take over the controls.

"Take us down to about one thousand feet, flyboy," he commanded. "Sandy? Hand me the BigEyes, please." She did and he began to scan the water below them. As they traversed the area between the smaller island of Marchena and Isabella, it was easy to spot how the water swiftly became more and more shallow. By the time they were a quarter mile off the shore of Isabella he could even see turtles, sharks and other aquatic creatures scooting along in the shallower waters.

Bud announced they were crossing over dry land and Tom was about to put the BigEyes down when something pinged off of the canopy to his left. That was followed by another one.

"Bullets!" Bashalli shouted. "Somebody is shooting at us!"

Indeed, one of the bullets had deflected and smeared up and across the clear tomasite canopy. While they would never be able to penetrate into the cockpit, it was an uncomfortable feeling to be shot at.

Tom quickly copied down the GPS coordinates of where they were when first hit, and the approximate angle of the shot. Grabbing a map he did a little mental math and stabbed his finger down on the probable location of the fired shots. He pulled out his pen and made a big X on the place.

"Uh, skipper? We might have a little problem. One of those bullets may have gotten into our port engine. It is starting to go out of balance." This was something they all began to feel. "I've got to shut it down before it tears itself off the jet!"

CHAPTER 14 /

THE REVEALING SWIM

THE REST of the flight was uneventful. When Bud shut down the port engine it left them with sufficient power to safely finish their flight and to land on the small and relatively short runway in the new capital town.

Leaving the ladies inside the jet, just in case, Tom strode across the tarmac and into the small building that served as the airfield owner's home and the official terminal. Bud climbed up onto the wing above the canopy and inspected the turbine.

Everything inside was made from tomasite and Durastress, both resistant to damage from something as small as a bullet. He pulled a flashlight out from his pants pocket and shone it inside. There, as he suspected, was the remains of the bullet that had hit and wrapped around one of the front turbine blades. He carefully reached in and gave it a little pull. It was wedged tightly onto the blade but he managed to loosen it and take it off.

A further inspection found no other signs of damage or bullet fragments, so he climbed down and was carefully revving that engine when Tom returned.

"I guess we have to wait. Evidently Madam Minister Primo ate something last night that didn't agree with her. She is *enfermo* and *el médico* has declared that she must remain *quieto* until *mañana.*" He grinned at the other three. "We will be sent a car in about an hour to take us to the guest residence. It's a good thing we are married. The manager looked out through his window, saw you two beauties, and told me that if you were not our *esposas*, that you would have to sleep in the jet."

They didn't have that long to wait. Five minutes later a small car pulled up beside the Toad. A young woman probably about twenty-six or twenty-seven sat inside. She waved at them and gave them a smile, and pointed at her side window, miming that it would not roll down.

Tom walked over and opened the driver's door. "Hello. Are you here to drive us to the residence?" He repeated the question in his junior high Spanish. "*Está que nos lleves a la residencia?*"

Her smile became even brighter, although to Tom she looked a little weak.

"*Usted es lindo, pero usted habla divertido.* And that means, very roughly, that I appreciate the attempt, but you do not have the local dialect correct." She held a hand out to Tom. He helped her out of the car. "I am Evelyn Estes. It is a pleasure to meet you, and I apologize for not being here sooner. My mother, I believe the airport manager spoke with her, served suspicious chicken last night for dinner and I have been a bit sick to my stomach since midnight. I think she told him that I couldn't come today. Sorry."

Bud, Sandy and Bashalli had by now climbed out of the Toad and were standing behind Tom. He introduced them all. She shook their hands and gave the two girls little kisses on their cheeks.

Her face went a little pale and she excused herself, running to the side of the paved area and throwing up.

When she came back she apologized. "I guess I am not ready to be out quite yet."

Tom excused himself and returned to the Toad, removing the first aid kit. He rummaged around in it and came out with two bottles. One was a well-known pink liquid and the other was the bottle of strong antibiotics that all Swift aircraft and ocean-going vessels carried. He gave both to her, and she gratefully washed down a pill with the antacid.

With Tom at the wheel they left the airfield and headed the five blocks to the official residence. Like most homes it was a single story. Unlike most in the surrounding neighborhood, it must have been nearly two thousand square feet, twice that of the surrounding homes.

An older woman, perhaps fifty, bustled out the front door exclaiming, "*Eva. Usted es una chica traviesa. ¡Vuelve a tu cama.*"

"*No, madre. Debo atender a mis deberes. Tráenos café. Café dulce.*" She looked at her new friends. "Come inside and let's sit in my office. It is not air conditioned but it does have a very efficient fan."

Once they were sitting and sipping the cold, sweet and slightly citrus-tinged coffee Tom brought up the subject of the shots that hit the Toad.

Eva almost dropped her drink in shock. She muttered a few phrases under her breath that Tom was certain were less than lady-like before looking at him.

"I cannot express my anger and sadness for that. Had I not been taken ill I might have remembered to contact the small village in the hills at the North of Isabella and told them of your arrival. You see, the last planes to fly over were from Ecuador and they dropped leaflets telling the people that they would all die if our islands became independent." She snorted. "That is rich, isn't it? They basically told us to go to hell and cut our telephone cable and left us to perish, and yet they have the nerve to tell my people that it is *our* fault?"

Sensing that it might be time to change the subject, Bashalli inquired about the coffee.

"Ah. A farmer in the hills of this island imported one hundred coffee bushes nearly ten years ago. Each year he carefully took cuttings and put them into something that made them sprout roots and then planted those. Now, his plantation has nearly five times as many. To make his crop go farther he began to grind up some wild sugar cane along with the roasted beans. It gives sweetness as well as the taste some have suggested is like lemon. I am afraid it is a weakness of mine and has been since I was introduced to it three years ago."

They all agreed that it was delicious.

Tom could see that their host was tiring and suggested that they might all like to see the sleeping quarters.

Evelyn stood up and took them out the door and down the hall to a single door.

"I am afraid that we have but one guest room. I will go sleep with my mother and give you my room."

The four Americans refused to entertain that idea. "No," Sandy told her. "Tom is my brother, Bud is my husband and Bashi and I have nothing to hide. If there are two beds..."

"Yes. Of course," she replied opening the door to expose a room of nearly twenty feet square. "Two beds I believe you call queen sized?" When they all nodded, she smiled. "I will have our gardener go back to your plane and get your luggage if that is fine with you. And now, I believe I need a nap."

Ten minutes later a knock came on the door and a small man stood there with all four suitcases held under his arms.

"I is bring to you señor and señora's clothing?"

Tom nodded, thanked him and reached into his pocket.

"Oh, no, señor. *Sin denaro. Despedida!*"

It wasn't until dinnertime that Evelyn reappeared. She looked much better. "The miracle of modern medicines," she declared before translating it for her mother, who gave her a look of disbelief.

Over a meal of wild pig, a vegetable that looked a little like a stringy potato, and some fresh berries that none of them could identify, Tom and Evelyn discussed his space elevator project. By the time it came for everyone to go to bed she was completely in agreement with him on all but one small issue.

"When you are digging these eight long holes to anchor the bottom of the device to, you will need to find a way to keep the debris from fouling the waters around you. On these islands we have several varieties of turtle and one of them calls the beaches and waters off the Isabella shore their home. It would be most tragic if their habitat were to become inhospitable to them."

It gave Tom a lot to think about. It had been agreed that the digging needed to be at least two thousand feet off the shoreline, which would put it in water just three hundred feet deep. Each of the eight holes would be about three feet across and a thousand feet deep, meaning that more than half a million pounds of materials had to be removed. Per hole. Where Tom had once thought to use traditional digging and boring techniques, he now realized that there was no place to deposit it all.

So, that meant devising an atomic earth blaster than could not just work under water, but one that could eject the gaseous debris and small bits of material up by as much as a third of a mile!

The girls undressed in the bathroom and slipped into bed before Tom and Bud did the same.

Tom wanted to discuss things but before he could say anything he began hearing the rhythmic snoring and breathing of his three companions. Giving up for the night, he soon drifted into sleep.

At breakfast the next morning Evelyn's mother approached Tom and in broken English told him, "I like no medicine my daughter is give from you. Is not Galapagos medicine. No give no again, *por favor!*"

Her daughter hissed something to her and the older woman walked away shaking her head. "My mother has never traveled off of this island all her life. Not even to one of our other islands. Her mother made medicines and her mother's mother made medicines. She wanted to teach me how, but I went away to school when I was fifteen. A small school in Oregon. If you can believe it I studied political science! When I came back I was just twenty-one and had experienced the outside world. Hamburgers. Soap operas. Ice cream. Doughnuts with bacon on top! I tried to follow my mother but my mind was always elsewhere. Then when our islands and Ecuador split, my uncle was asked to become our first minister. He lasted almost two years but cancer was taking him and so he told the population that he wanted to turn the governing of them over to someone else. There would be an election to decide. And, we had one. To please him I put forth my name. To both my surprise and my delight at knowing how people felt about my uncle, I won with nearly all of the votes."

"That is pretty impressive," Bud said around a mouthful of some type of vegetable mush.

She nodded. "Yes, but then my closest rival seems to have been a goat from the island of Santiago." Her eyes twinkled.

Everyone laughed and the conversation turned away from politics and to the beauties of the islands. Evelyn, now feeling completely better, offered to take them all to see the famous turtle beaches.

She made one phone call before they left. After driving along an almost invisible track in the dirt around the western side of the island, they arrived at a tiny fishing village with just four boats sitting in their slips on the single dock. One boat, not looking like much for fishing, sat apart from the others. It was to this one she led the group.

"Climb in," she told them. "This is the *official* boat. If you look out there," and she pointed almost due West, "you will see some land. That is the island of Pinzon, just about nine kilometers away. That is where we will go to see turtles, eat some food that my mother has made for us—no chicken—and perhaps swim in the warm waters."

Sandy looked pensively at Bashalli. Neither had thought to bring a bathing suit. The dark-skinned Bashalli shrugged and whispered, "I guess we cross that bridge when we come to it."

The trip took just twenty minutes and they anchored about twenty feet off the beach. Evelyn explained that while it was permissible to get this close, that nobody was allowed to set foot on the actual island.

They didn't have to. All up and down the beach were the shells of turtles sunning themselves. Every few minutes one would rise ponderously and drag itself to the water where it immediately turned into a graceful thing of beauty.

"If you men will please turn around for a minute," their host requested.

Tom and Bud turned away, heard the slight rustling sounds of clothing being removed and then heard the splash as she jumped into the water.

"It is fine. Now you can only see a hint of me. Come on in. It is deliciously warm and soothing."

First Bud, always the most adventurous of the four, and then Tom stripped down and jumped in. They turned away as Bashalli did the same until only Sandy was left in the boat.

"Oh, hecko!" she exclaimed, "here's to California all over again!" and was in the water with them a moment later. Nobody gave a thought to their lack of bathing suits as they swam around the small lagoon in which they had anchored.

Evelyn's tanned skin reminded Tom of Bashalli, and he spotted her watching him a few times, but with an amused smile playing around her lips.

Both of the girls tried to cling onto a turtle that swam past, but it must have known something was up because it sped away just out of reach.

One pleasurable hour later it was time to get back in and get dressed. They took turns with the girls going first followed by Tom and Bud and their host coming up last.

With a little laugh and knowing that it had been impossible for Tom and Bud to not see quite a bit of her, she told them, "And this means that you may all call me Eva!"

The fivesome had their picnic lunch of roasted pork and root vegetable sandwiches on a thick, rustic bream Tom had to ask about.

"Our chef back home is always on the lookout for interesting things to cook or back."

"That is a bread made from both a local hybrid grain we've had for nearly thirty years along with a plant starch from a potato we grow here, but I never ran into it when I was in the United States."

On the way back she explained her reason for taking them to the small island. "I wanted you to see just how pristine everything is and hope that you will be impressed enough to do everything possible to leave things that way."

Tom promised her that he would.

When they pulled up at the residence a man was waiting for them. In his right hand he held a rifle and in his other, his hat. He was looking at the ground.

"Pepe!" Evelyn called out to him. "*Veo que ha llegado.*"

"*Si.*"

"*¿Qué tienes que decir?*" She translated her question as 'what do you have to say?'

It turned out this was the man who shot at them as they

approached Isabella the previous day. He did it because of his anger at the Ecuadorians and because he only knew of them having aircraft that made a whining sound as it moved across the sky.

He was very apologetic and offered to pay whatever he could toward fixing any damage he had done. He was a poor man but offered two of his best goats.

Tom told him that was not necessary, and that no real damage happened. Only that it had frightened the girls. Pepe, wide eyed, apologized over and over again to the *hermosas damas*—the beautiful ladies.

Tom thanked the man for coming to apologize and then asked Evelyn to congratulate him on his marksmanship.

"It isn't everybody who can hit a moving jet at a thousand feet!"

Pepe smiled at the translation of this and soon left.

"That is another thing I hope you can bring to us. Dentistry." The man's teeth had been in terrible condition.

They left very early the next morning, opting to carry their luggage and walk the few blocks to the airfield. By six, they were airborne. They made the same two fuel stops but chose to take turns flying—including Sandy, an excellent pilot—each taking a five-hour shift, and arrived in Shopton at midnight.

The next day Tom and Damon discussed the trip and came to the same conclusion about the safety of the habitat. "We have to set up a hydrodome down there where we can process the gasses and the debris before using a repelatron elevator to bring it to the surface," Tom decided.

"Why don't you concentrate on that," Damon suggested, "and I will spend some time working on the logistics of taking the *Sea Charger* out of commission. I know she is committed to the government of Iceland for their study of that offshore volcano, so I have to check where we stand legally and morally on that."

It took them both five days before they had some answers. For his part, Damon was able to tell Tom that the *Sea Charger* would be completing her assignment in about two weeks and would head first to Fearing Island to be stripped of unnecessary equipment, fitted with an entirely new anchoring system, and prepared for the trip around the horn of South America and to the Galapagos Islands.

"Have you figured that anchor setup yet," he asked Tom. "I've got a few more days before I have to be out in California. So…"

"I'm pretty certain I have that handled. It will be a six-point system with anchors on each of the four corners and one halfway up the longer sides." He explained that each one would operate independently from the others and would use a variety of instrumentation to determine when and by how much an anchor cable needed to be let out or hauled back in to accommodate tides, storms, and other factors.

"In all I believe I can keep her level enough even in a good storm to play soccer on the deck. Well, other than having the ball get blown off that is."

He also described how each of the ship's anchors would be linked to a permanent mount that would go perhaps fifty feet into the bedrock. That was a technology already on hand. Such anchors were self-drilling and driving. Once they reached the set depth a small explosive charge rammed out horizontal wings into the surrounding rocks. Once in it would take the combined strength of three aircraft carriers to loosen one and another such ship to pull one out.

"Why not make the ship's anchors the same as the elevator anchors? Perhaps you simply allow the ship to ride up and down as the tide changes."

"I might, but I think I would need to rig some sort of brakes or controls to give the ship more stability."

"Just thought I'd suggest it. So, what about the debris processing?" his father inquired.

"Well, as I mentioned last week I think that a deep sea hydrodome is called for. We would set up in a central location between all the drilling sites. Then we move and seal down a large flexible tube between each forthcoming hole and the hydrodome. We'll probably need to incorporate a mid-point fan. All the gases enter the hydrodome where it goes through filters. The gaseous part will go straight up to the *Sea Charger* and through a processor to take out all particulate matter and to make the gases inert and ready for either release or to be captured to be stored or removed. All solids down in the hydrodome will be stored and then mixed with binders to inject back into the holes to hold down the anchors. My calculations show that this can be accomplished in a hydrodome of about three hundred feet diameter. And that's good because I want to place the holes four hundred feet apart!"

A thought hit Tom.

"I forgot about getting them a satellite link up!" he admitted.

Damon Swift laughed. "Taken care of. They go on line by Saturday. I'll have a cargo seacopter haul everything out to them including a nuclear power pod for each island getting equipment.

They asked for so few connections that we don't have anything that, well, small, so if and when they want more, each island can be switched remotely to up to five hundred lines."

Tom also admitted that he had forgotten to mention how much he would like to get the islands both modern medical facilities as well as dental.

Damon considered it for a moment. "Well, the *Sea Charger* has a full medical setup. Hospital for at least twelve if I recall. I'll have the Fearing folks leave that in as well as the small dental room. While I'd love to go to the U.N. to see about getting some of their doctors to do rotations, I suppose that is out of the question. I'll ask Doc Simpson if he knows of any people who might like a stint down there."

The next week Tom spent most of his time on the fine details of his hydrodome and the facilities it would contain. Luckily, a lot of it had been pioneered when he had discovered a long-forgotten sunken city of gold of the eastern coast of the U.S. That had required substantial cleaning and filtering when some of the ooze that needed to be removed had proven to be toxic. That meant that he already had the machinery in storage that would be needed in this new dome.

He arrived home that night feeling very good about things.

CHAPTER 15 /
DESIGN CONSIDERATIONS GALORE

THE FEELING of satisfaction lasted through the evening and most of the following morning.

There were many things he needed to give attention to today, and that began with a visit to the auto plant where Marjorie Morning-Eagle and her team were nearing the half-way point it attaching the various panels to one another. Each was larger than the panels that went into making one of the inflatables for the Mars colony by about twenty percent, and there were many more of them. As the new triangular tubing did not bend very well it had been decided to run the tubes from one side of the building up and over the top and then down to the opposite side. Only an occasional cross tube would interrupt what essentially was a hoop and cover building.

Those cross tubes would maintain proper spacing between the hoops, keeping the building in the required shape. And, because they added no real structural strength, they were to be left hollow with connectors that did not open into the longer tubes. Only at the bottoms would all tubes interconnect.

When he arrived via the new tunnel between Enterprises and the auto plant, he was very pleased to see that most of the Assembly Hall had been erected and that the Major and her team were doing their work in the next parcel of property. Heavy equipment was still grooming the area where the Administration building would be built.

As he climbed out of his car, Marjorie was tapped on the shoulder by one of her assistants and Tom was pointed out to her. She straightened up from the job of attaching an interconnect between sections of the hoops and one of the long tubes.

"Hey, Tom," she called out as she walked his direction, stretching her arms and back as she came.

"Hey, yourself, Major," Tom said as he moved forward to meet her half way. "I just came over to see what's happening. Dad tells me you won't slow down and we might have to have the erection and ribbon ceremony a week early." He smiled which told her he didn't mind this situation at all.

"What's new on this headin' to heaven contraption of yours?" she asked.

"The space elevator? Well, you know the number of tubes and

connectors and panels you have to work with?" She told him she did. "Quadruple that and you've got about a tenth of what I'm trying to keep my fingers on. My latest thing is the giant counterweight we need to use to offset the platform and cargo weight. Ideally if I want to send up, say, ten tons, having a ten-ton weight means practically no need to use any motorized drive to move things. Just a gentle push up there on the weight and it comes down hauling the cargo up. "

"And, once it gets to the top?"

"A gentle braking stops the lot. The issue is we can't be taking weight out and putting it in to suit each load, so we need to make it as heavy as possible within a small space. It's going to be a tube, pointed at each end a little to help move through the air down here. I wanted it to be about the same length as the total platform core— where we attach the different platforms— but even with the heaviest elements we've been able to mine up there so far, it would need to be five times as tall."

"I'm no space engineer, so what's the issue? Make it longer."

"Can't. Stability and rigidity are the issues. If you've ever tried to push a rope up a wall you know that it just sort of bends and eventually falls over. Our weight, if too long, would try that but instead of falling over it would just bend a little and crimp the cable."

She looked puzzled and then brightened. "Crimped means it doesn't move?"

He told her she was correct.

Before she took him on a tour of the work on the inflatable so far she told him, "I've got every confidence in you, Tom. Whatever you come up with will work. Has before and will in the future. Come on and take a look-see at our progress."

*   *   *   *   *

Tom heard unfamiliar footsteps crossing the underground hangar floor. He looked up to see Professor Somers, who had taken a leave of absence from his university to come study the polymer coloring process for the forthcoming car factory, nearing his outer door.

"Come on in, Professor Somers," he called out.

"Please. It's Barnaby, or better yet, Barney," the older man suggested.

"Well, what is the occasion that has you coming all the way down here?" Tom inquired. "Generally we don't make our guest go subterranean."

"Oh, I was just so excited by my new research into the whole color issue that I had to come tell you." He did, Tom noticed, look extremely happy about something.

"Tell me," Tom said offering the man a seat.

"Okay. Before I tell you my findings I need to admit to you that what I will propose diminishes the overall strength of the materials by a rather significant two-point-three percent. Please tell me now if that is outside of acceptability and I'll go back and try again." He looked with some expectancy at the young inventor.

With a shake of his head, Tom told him that was not going to be any issue at all.

"Wonderful! Well, I suppose that I need to tell you that I located a solvent, of sorts, that when added to a batch of the nearly ready polymer opens the chains up ever so slightly and that lets a new range of additives hook themselves into the chain, permanently, providing an array of at least fifteen colors. Three you already have within a few shades, and the rest are new. For the overlaps, this process cuts the coloring process down from many, many dollars to about ten dollars per vehicle body."

With Tom's prompting he detailed the "solvent" indicating that it was a non-polluting liquid that thermally did the trick and evaporated emitting only steam as the output.

When he finished Tom suggested he get everything together and present his report to Damon Swift the next day. "Dad will be thrilled. Now if only one of my problems could be handled so easily."

Barney asked what that might be.

"There will be, by both necessity and design, very little free space between the cable I will be constructing for my space elevator project and the inside case of the huge and heavy counterweight. Just six millimeters to be exact. I needed to do that to dampen vibrations but it brings up a rather nasty tendency for the cable to move back and forth those millimeters and rub on the inside of the weight housing. With the thing expected to last thirty or more years and with probably a trip every other day at first, I'm worried that even my super-strong materials will begin to show abrasion and stress problems."

"Have you tried GreeS?" the professor asked. "And that is not g-r-e-a-s-e or G-r-e-e-c-e." He spelled it for Tom. "I don't recall what that stands for, if anything. It is a coating developed by Randolf Standeker at a small chemical research company back about fifteen years ago. It acts like Teflon™ does in frying pans. Makes things super slick. A byproduct is that it also coats and waterproofs things. And, it is rated to last decades, even under constant abrasion. It sounds to me like something you might want."

Tom was intrigued. "How thick of a coating is it?"

"About the thickness of a human hair. A fine human hair at that."

"I have to admit I've never heard of it," Tom said. "Fifteen years ago, you said?"

Barney nodded. "Yes. Unfortunately Dr. Standeker wasn't much of a businessman and he sold the rights to a small firm that went bankrupt a year later. I'll give the doctor a call if you wish and see if he knows the legal stand."

Tom allowed him to use his desk phone and the call was placed through Enterprises' operators.

After introducing himself to Dr. Standeker, Barney described Tom's project and asked about the coating. From that point on all Tom heard was a series of, "Oh," and "Well, well," and "Yes, of course." Three minutes later he hung up.

"Bingo!" he declared. "Dr. Standeker says that the contract returned all rights back to him, that he had almost forgotten it, and would be most pleased to provide you with either the formula or with the actual coating. Here is his number is you could give him a call tomorrow. He seemed rather busy today."

When Tom did make the call the doctor was happy to speak to him. "It's so far back that I've done too many other things to worry about returning to it as a potential source of income. And so, if you and your father—how is he by the way—would like it I can either run up a small batch for you or license the formula. Perhaps a thousand dollars a year?"

Tom laughed. "Doctor, if this does what the professor says it will, then I would suggest that ten times that amount would be a fair fee. Unless you would like us to investigate the commercial possibilities, then we would pay you a percentage of all sales. As to you running up a small batch, that would be helpful, but for this project I will be coating a run of cable tens of thousands of miles long." There was silence at the other end and Tom was afraid the man might have hung up thinking Tom was some sort of crank.

Finally, Dr. Standeker let out a whistle and told him, "Well, I'm not able to do that much for you, but how about a five-gallon bucket of the stuff in about a week? As to the license fee, let's leave it at one thousand for now. If you think it is a viable product, then we can talk percentages, but I'm hopeless with that sort of thing."

"We are a fair company, sir. I can assure you that we will do what is right," Tom said before agreeing to have a courier— probably Bud, Tom thought—pick up the five gallons in a week.

During that week more and more items were coming together and more and more changes were being made. For one, Tom once again changed the dimensions of his proposed station cylinders. Now they would be about as wide as originally conceived, between six and eight hundred feet in diameter, but they were to be longer than before at eighteen hundred feet.

Tom completed the list and layout for every working and living space he wanted to build, and it all worked out to fit in one cylinder of this size.

One cylinder was almost exponentially easier that two or three cylinders that would need to be interconnected in about a hundred different ways. There would be no torque to worry about if one cylinder should get out of balance. Everything could be contained in the one space station piece, but it would not preclude future additions. That included one that Tom secretly hoped would be possible—a way in which the station could be self-powered to be used to explore the solar system. Not just in a ship like the *Challenger* with finite storage and limited operational ties, but years upon years of travel and study.

He sighed.

It was one of those "way in the future" things right now.

This was the time to concentrate on getting his space elevator built and in operation. Everything else depended on that.

He spent several days studying all of his designs. There were almost too many components and assemblies to count. Many heavily relied on the success and design of things that would come before them.

The cable depended on completion of the necessary equipment to be lifted and installed in the *Sutter*. But that depended on completing the mining operations to have the raw materials. And that had relied on ensuring they retrieved the right asteroid pieces. Fortunately all the materials Tom needed had been found, mined, processed, refined and were being used both in space and on the ground. Enough materials had already been processed to build at least a third of outer hull of the space station. By the time the *Sutter* finished making those panels another batch of asteroids would be in place and the process would continue.

In this manner Tom believed that he would be able to complete the station in twenty to twenty-two months.

The cable-extruding equipment was nearing completion at the Construction Company and would be able to go into space in about a week, The *Sutter* would be ready to receive it along with the spooling mechanism to wind the cable around.

The Attractatron mules were doing constant duty keeping everything in proper positions and he contemplated having a couple more built. That would take a month or more but he decided he would need them later on.

He meticulously went through all the designs for the elevator platforms. They would be the simplest items in the entire build. They were, after all, just platforms.

Even the central core they would attach to—positionable to meet different requirements—was not much of a technological stretch. It featured control and passenger cabins at both ends and wrapped around a central open space that would allow the anchor cable and the massive counterweight to pass straight through on the up and down journeys. Until the passing maneuvers, special arms would maintain an exact distance from the cable.

He was whistling to himself when he spotted a problem. Not with small letters, he realized. Screaming capital letters as in PROBLEM!

Where was he going to put the drive mechanism?

Tom felt a stab of frustration. Without realizing it he had put the proverbial cart before the horse. In this case he had okayed—and production had just completed on—the four outer casings that would form the counterweight shell for his space elevator. There could be no downsizing of the actual cable and there would barely be a ten millimeter gap between it and the case.

The cases had no extra room that wasn't going to be needed as fill space for the weight material. There were a series of protruding circular "pucks" on the inside that would be used to connect interior bracing during final assembly, but that was about it. Even they would be of little or no use.

He called Hank Sterling and asked him if they could meet at the Construction Company in a half hour.

Hank laughed in Tom's TeleVoc. "I'm already there, skipper," he told the inventor. "I'm in building three. As soon as you get here we can certainly meet."

Now Hank received Tom's laugh inside his head. "Guess what? I'm here in building one. I'll be over in five minutes."

When the inventor walked around the corner of the big, open sliding doors on the West end of the building he saw that Hank was there with Arv Hanson and a beautiful Asian woman. With a start, Tom realized that it was Linda Ming.

He had been so busy in the previous weeks since her return to Enterprises that he hadn't gone to say hello. She evidently felt no ill feelings as she came right up to him, gave him a big hug and told him, "Gosh, Tom. It's so great to see you. And I've got to say that in the past couple of years you've really outgrown the whole teenage genius look. I hear you're married to that Bashalli woman you used to date."

Tom smiled and told her how nice it was to see her. "Yes, we got married a year and a half ago."

"Well, whatever Bashalli is doing for you, good on her! Anyway, Hank tells us that you came over to talk to him. I guess Arv and I ought to leave."

Now, Tom shook his head. "The more the merrier for this one, Linda." He turned to the engineer. "Hank, I pulled a really bad goof. I'm hoping that you can soothe my nerves and tell me that everything will be okay." He described how he could not see any way to build a drive mechanism within the counterweight. "I can't do it in the platform core because that is too far away from the anchor cable.

"I know I can build a sort of pushme-pullyou affair like a little engine to haul freight cars around the switching yard, and that could be set up at both ends, but it will cause no end of troubles as the weight assembly slides through the center of the elevator platform. I'm afraid that we might need to pause things while the one about to impede travel is unhooked, the two big pieces slide past each other and then the drive gets hooked back in place."

Hank and Arv both nodded. It would be a messy way to handle things. The three men began an animated discussion about potential solutions. Five minutes later they all noticed that Linda had moved to one side and had not participated in the discussion. When Tom stopped and asked her if she had any input, she moved back to the small group.

"I've been thinking it over," she told them. "I see only one viable option. Repelatrons." They looked blankly at her. It was true that Tom's devices had many fine applications, but the inventor discounted them from the start as it might be impossible to assume that no cargo up or down might not have some of a targeted metal/element, and that could cause major problems.

"So," she continued ignoring the small, sad shake of his head

Tom had just given her, "that leaves us with a few choices. The whole twenty-mule team approach isn't going to work for the reasons I overheard you three discuss. I also don't think that having a giant array at the top and another at the bottom is viable either."

"Where does that leave us?" Hank inquired.

Linda had a delightful and almost melodic laugh and she favored them with it now. "Easy. Put it inside the counterweight!"

Tom shook his head again. "No room inside, Linda. And nearly all the outer skin is a tomasite and Durastress composite and harder than diamonds so we can't cut any panels out." He added the necessity for the total case volume to hold enough weight for things to work.

She pointed a thumb over her shoulder at one of the shell pieces that she and the two others had been admiring when Tom arrived.

"Unless Hank lied to me just to see if I could spot it, don't the internal mounting points pass all the way out of the shells?"

"Yes," Tom said warily.

"Well, they are a softer material so they can be heat welded to the braces once those get set inside. I say we pop those out, replace them with new and deeper ones that are hollowed out on the outside—pointing into the slot where the cable will run—and mount a series of small repelatrons in those new spaces."

She looked at them triumphantly and was smiling until she spotted Tom's look of consternation.

"What?"

"It's just this, Linda. We have eight sizes of repelatron emitters. The very smallest ones we've managed to build with any great power are used in our smaller model QuieTurbine jet engines. Even those are about twice as large as the space we might 'find' by doing it the way you suggested. I'm sorry, but I goofed so big I've probably jeopardized this project."

"Oh," she said. "Hmmmm? I suppose what you really need then is someone who specializes in miniaturization. Someone who could maybe design and build emitter and controller assemblies that *would* fit." She made a "tsk-tsk" sound. "Isn't it a shame you have *nobody* who fits that description?"

Tom turned beet red. He leaned forward toward the woman, his face turned down slightly.

"Go ahead," he urged her. "Slap me in the forehead because that's what I should be doing to myself about now." Linda laughed and declined to hit him "Can you forgive me for being a dunce about your skills?"

She smiled and nodded. "Yes, and I hope I can actually follow through and deliver on this. For now, I need some specifications." She turned to Hank and he nodded.

"Can do," he said.

Tom and Arv excused themselves leaving the other two to figure things out.

"Aren't you glad I let you talk me into hiring her again?" Arv asked.

Tom was still chuckling about it as he drove out the gate a few minutes later.

CHAPTER 16 /

AN U.N.-KIND CUT

THE DAY began with Tom, Damon, Anne, and Sandy, and all the executive staff at Enterprises being joined by nearly five hundred other Enterprises employees and city, county and state officials at the new auto plant. Only Bashalli had been unable to get any time off.

It was "Inflation Day" for the giant structure and also the official ribbon-cutting ceremony and dedication of the new facility.

A large platform had been erected to one side of the area now covered by most of the crowd. It was raised about five feet up from the ground and currently held the executives and twenty invited guests including the person who would, at least ceremonially, start the process of pumping the structure full of air and then the self-hardening foam that would keep it up and stable.

"Are we ready for this?" Damon asked Tom out of the side of his mouth.

"We sure are, Dad," the younger man answered.

Unlike the inflatable habitats on Mars or the Moon—that required many hours to inflate—sixteen high-powered fans would be able to get this building up in under twenty minutes. It could go faster but Tom wanted to take a slight pause after five minutes to do a check of the materials.

At eleven, the "zero hour," Damon stepped to the microphone and nodded to the video/audio team that would project his image on a pair of giant screens so those at the back of the crowd could see and hear the several speakers who would address them.

"Hello," he greeted them, waiting a few seconds for the last of the conversations to die away. "As you all *ought* to know, I am Damon Swift. With me today is my son, Tom, and a group of dignitaries." He pointed at them and named them all. "Our purpose is to puff up that giant mound of fabric and tubing you see over there—" he swept his left hand to point at the lumpy white pile standing a few hundred feet away, "—until it rises enough to have the bracing materials pumped in, and also to commemorate the process in much the same manner as when people launch ships."

He spent two minutes describing the process the crowd would only see the end results of, and then introduced the first of the speakers.

The Governor of New York stepped up. "Many thanks to you and your fine company, Mr. Swift," he began. "At one point in this state's glorious history we hosted more than twenty automobile factories. Some small and some not so small. Some came and went in months and some remained viable for years. And, while none of them might be considered part of the 'Big Four' manufacturers of today, for the most part they pioneered things that we see in today's automobiles.

"I believe we are about to see the launch, if I may borrow Damon Swift's term, of a new car company that will soon take its place among the top producers in not just America, but the world!"

He had to wait a full minute for the applause and cheering to die down. He spoke for another ten minutes of the ingenuity of the Swifts throughout the generations and their place in history. When he was finished he received enthusiastic applause and ceded the microphone the next speaker, the Mayor of Shopton.

Mayor Bartlett prefaced his talk by assuring the crowd he would be brief. His speech extolled the virtues of having Enterprises and the Construction Company as "cornerstones of commerce" in Shopton. He must have set a record by speaking for just three minutes, eleven seconds before smiling, nodding and motioning Tom to step forward.

If anything, he received a slightly longer and louder ovation.

Tom was even briefer.

"Thank you to our guests,, and I can think of nothing more to add except to tell you this will take twenty minutes once the big button gets pushed. Our own Chow Winkler can't be here to serve all of you hot and cold drinks and pastries today, but the staff of the Enterprises' Canteen is here and have set up ten stations for you. As inflation begins, please grab something and feel free to move up to the retaining ropes if you want a closer look. We'll call you back to your places when the next phase is about to start. Without ado, may I present the man who will get things going, the man who coined the term 'Marshmellers,' to describe this sort of building, Charles 'Chow' Winkler!"

The chef kissed his new bride and climbed the stairs. He proudly accepted the cheering of the audience before stepping to the special podium containing two very large buttons.

"I am mighty proud ta tell ya all that this here facility, ever'thing including this about-ta-be-blow'd up building, is hereforth to be known as the Swift MotorCar Company." He had to wait a minute for relative silence to return. "An, it's a pleasure an' a honor fer me ta press this big red button ta start things. I give you the Anne Swift Sub-Assembly Hall!"

Tom's mother turned to her husband and hissed something, but she looked extremely pleased by the honor.

Chow made a big show of pressing the button. Secretly, a technician watching from a nearby trailer pressed a key on his keyboard and the fans roared into operation.

Things progressed so well that the first of the upper materials began to rise within seconds. Most of the crowd was mesmerized watching for eight to ten minutes before wandering over for refreshments.

Tom, Bud, Hank Sterling and Marjorie Morning-Eagle slipped inside the now twelve to fifteen foot high space and did a quick check. Things looked perfect so they left through one of the temporary airlocks and Tom returned to the platform.

Everything went exactly as hoped and by the time the crowd dispersed forty minutes after the inflation started, all the structural tubes were filled with foam and it was on its way to hardening.

"Well, Son. It's up and we'll start to move in the equipment and supplies next week. I thank you deeply for getting us this far, but now I must tell you that I am relieving you of further responsibilities here. You have a space elevator to get built!"

"Thanks, Dad. It's actually been a lot of fun!"

As everything hardened only a single connection piece was found to have any problems and it was soon wrapped tightly to stop the small leak, a leak that would completely seal itself when the foam was set.

Tom and Bud had walked over using the new tunnel system. Most everyone had either walked or been driven over in one of several buses. When they came back up on the inside of the Enterprises' walls Bud headed for his office in one of the hangars while Tom went down to his underground office.

He was barely there five minutes when Munford Trent called.

"Tom. Your father would like to see you up in the office. Evidently there has been some sort of U.N. council meeting called regarding your current project and they are insisting that the two of you come to New York tomorrow. I don't have any other details, but he is waiting."

"Be there in five," Tom promised.

He walked into the large office and nodded to his father. "Trent told me something big is going on."

"Take a seat, Son. And Trent is right. We've been told in no uncertain terms to attend a full U.N. meeting tomorrow after lunch. Evidently Prime Minister Evelyn Estes has petitioned the U.N. for a couple things. She wants permanent sovereign nation status declared to keep Ecuador or any other Central or South American nation from trying to lay claims. Plus, I believe she has asked for the no-fly zone of perhaps as wide as one hundred miles be declared."

"Wow. That'd be great for us. I still haven't figured a way to keep stray aircraft from accidentally coming into contact with any cable system we put up. I can't do lights and it will be too narrow for RADAR reflectivity to be of much use."

"Well, we'll see what happens tomorrow. Unfortunately, this will not include Miss Estes, so I have a suspicion that it may not be the good news we hope for."

They flew one of Enterprises' Whirling Duck helicopters down to Manhattan and a heliport located just a handful of blocks from the large U.N. Building. As they came in for the landing both men could see the new U.N. complex being erected a few blocks from the famous tower, stretching from 36th to 41st streets. Like the original building it was situated to overlook the East River.

On their arrival by taxi they were taken to a special VIP elevator and whisked up to a waiting room. There, an aide informed them of an approximately thirty-minute wait before they would be escorted to the main hall.

This turned out to be nearly two hours and both men were about to get up and leave when a different aide came to get them. She, unlike the polite young man from before, was brusque and on the verge of being rude.

The main chamber was packed. In front of everyone stood the imposing golden wall with the United Nation's crest in the middle. In front of the raised dais with its three chairs was a simple table facing the two men and one woman sitting at the very front of the room. This table had two folding seats and a single microphone. It seemed calculated to put anyone sitting there at a disadvantage.

Tom and his father took the two seats but were asked to stand up and face the rest of the room. They were introduced by the Secretary General who also read a statement of purpose for their visit.

"The Swift organization of companies has embarked on a potentially dangerous endeavor. This being a new and unauthorized platform high in space for which they have provided no full accounting of their intent. Today they are here to answer this panel's questions. Be seated."

Both Tom and Damon had spoken to the assembled members

before. On those occasions things had rarely begun on pleasant terms but generally had swung in the Swift's favor.

The Secretary General addressed them.

"To the dismay of this body, several years ago you constructed a large wheel-shaped station in orbit. Many of our member nations feared at the time that this station would be used to either spy or to threaten them with weapons so that you might have control over world affairs. Do you deny that?"

Damon spoke. "Sirs and Madam. This body was fully briefed on the purpose and design of our current Outpost in Space. Many of your member nations still benefit on a daily basis from what we do up there. From the creation of our Solar Batteries to unique research opportunities to broadcasting television, data and radio that now circles the globe thanks in part to some of your members having launched repeater satellites. What we do is and has been proven to be totally beneficial to mankind. And to remind the body, the three official demands or requests you have made for inspections of our Outpost have been for a minimum of thirty individuals to be transported at our costs. Not only does the current station not have the capacity for even a third that number, other demands such as specialty gourmet meals, wines and other amenities are impossible to fulfill. You have been supplied with those reasons in writing each time."

"But we still have no idea what you have up there," insisted the woman sitting to the Secretary General's left.

"Actually, you do. You always have. Shortly after it was placed into operation we took a camera team up and videoed each and every compartment and space giving a non-stop running commentary on what you were seeing." Damon leaned over to Tom and whispered, "That should confuse them. It's their problem if nobody took the time to watch that video."

The trio at the dais went into conference. It lasted nearly five minutes and at one point it appeared that the second man was about ready to get up and leave. He did not appear to be happy.

"I have only now found out about such a video," the Secretary General told them. "It seems that my predecessor never shared it with more than a few members. We shall put that issue to one side for now. What is of utmost importance to this assembled body is the purpose for your very large new station, and what appears to be a dangerous physical connection it will have to the very ground below." He stared at the Swifts.

"Should I answer that, Dad?" Tom whispered after covering the microphone.

Damon nodded.

"May I address that, please?" Tom requested. "Although the design for the new station is different that our current wheel, and while it is to be more than ten times larger, it will serve most of the same functions." He took out his list of purposes, now sixty-three items long, and read them out. He also detailed the nature and need for the space elevator.

The other man on the dais slammed a fist down onto the desk, shouting, "You have no rights to put up a hidden military base to hang over us all like a Sword of Damocles! Deny that you intend to hold the world hostage to your whims!"

Tom couldn't stop himself. He slapped one hand over his mouth but his laughter came right out. Once he managed to gain control of himself, he tried to address the now very angry man.

"I am so sorry, sir. It is just that any public or private record will show that Swift Enterprises and each of our subsidiaries have *never* engaged in any sort of military or spy action. Other, that is, than building aircraft, ground vehicles and submarines. Nothing that leaves our assembly halls has a weapon in or on it. Governments the world over purchase our products and then turn them into weapons. Not us."

The Secretary General sought to regain control by stating, "But past history is no guarantee. Times change. People change. And so, the assembled nations of this body hereby decree that you must provide for a group of United Nations troops to be stationed in your new space habitat to ensure that you take no actions against those on the ground."

Tom shrugged, but answered, "If we do that for you, then other, non-UN nations will insist on the same thing. Can you guarantee it will never, ever escalate? If we do allow space and resources for your people, that will mean I need to go back and redesign everything to accommodate them. Meaning an even larger space station. If I do *that*, I will send the bill for all the additional materials and construction, plus transportation and housing cost to this body. If you do not pay immediately, your people will be sent back down and no other U.N. individual will ever be allowed at the station. And if they do not want to leave? Do they start shooting? Is that what this body is proposing?"

Damon added, "We have never given anyone cause to worry about what our peaceful intent is and has been. I must support my son. What you are asking is beyond reason." He pulled the letter from the Congresswoman Tom had once called a 'get-out-of-jail-free' card and handed it to an aide. "I would like to have you consider this official United States notification, please."

The three read it with varying degrees of surprise or anger. Another conference was started before the woman indicated that Tom and Damon should be escorted from the chamber. When they were allowed to return fifty minutes later, the Secretary General addressed them.

"The letter is of no interest to this body. Your refusal to open your space station to our members is both impudent and deceitful. And so, this body has passed a resolution barring any member nation from selling any materials to Swift Enterprises and all subsidiaries that might be used to construct this station. You may request a special hearing to review this in sixty days. That is all."

The trio rose from their seats and walked down a stairway at the back of the dais.

The Swifts left moments later but not before Tom faced the assembled members and scanned their faces. In the audience he spotted a mixture of anger, sadness and even a few who nodded to him but had to shrug as the vote had been out of their hands.

The flight back to Shopton was very quiet, but once on the ground Damon and Tom headed for the Legal department.

Jackson Rimmer listened to their recitation of the meeting with interest.

"There are two things you need to know," he told them. "First, as an international body the U.N. actually has no powers over commerce in any nation other than to declare sanctions against governments and entire countries. So, their declaration that you cannot purchase items is unenforceable. Secondly, senior Senator The Honorable Peter Quintana contacted me earlier today to say that he has, in his words, 'Swung the Government,' to be totally behind us."

Damon and Tom beamed broadly at the news.

"Does that mean the senator will be publicly supporting us, or will his assistance be behind the scenes?" Damon inquired.

"It would appear that he is intending to hold a press conference tomorrow to announce that the Government of the United States is behind you and fully recommends that the rest of the world jump on the bandwagon! I believe he will stress free trade, monetary aide programs and friendly cooperation for all mankind."

As they left to walk down to the office, Tom asked his father, "Does this mean it's full speed ahead?"

"I would really like to think so, but let's wait until we all see the reaction to Pete's news conference. It would really help our cause if the President were publicly behind this as well."

Thirty minutes later Trent buzzed Tom to say that a call was coming in from the United Nations in New York, "The caller doesn't sound very pleasant."

"I'll take it anyway. After what dad and I went through earlier today it can't be that bad." He picked up the receiver and said, "Hello."

"Is this Tom Swift? The one who wants to put that deadly monolith up through public airspace and try to bring down jetliners?" The voice had a European accent, possibly German or Austrian, and if Trent hadn't verified that the call was coming the switchboard at the United Nations building in New York, he might have thought it was Bud.

Carefully, Tom replied. "My name is Tom Swift and I am part of the ownership family of Swift Enterprises. As to your assertion or outright condemnation, I have to tell you that you seem to have your facts wrong, or are not in command of actual facts. Our space elevator system is no sort of monolith. It is a super-strong cable-based system designed to facilitate the construction of our forthcoming space station." He waited for the other man to say something.

Twenty seconds later, during which he caught bits and snatches of somebody translating his words, the man returned.

"I am Herr Schnitz and am the Secretary Vice General of the United Nations. You stood before us today. We have been brought to our attention that what you plan to do is detrimental to the welfare of one or more of our South American member nations. You will be stopping all development immediately. Ya?"

Tom was now fuming. "I will most certainly not be stopping anything, sir. As to your member nations, none of them will be the slightest inconvenienced unless they suddenly decide to invade the airspace of the independent nation of The Galapagos Islands. And those islands are their own sovereign territory having been rejected by Ecuador. No current airline routes within or outside of South America travels within three hundred miles of our forthcoming project. Besides, we have permission of the rightful government of the Galapagos Islands."

Again, there was a pause, this time almost a minute while the translator caught up to Tom's speech.

"Well, then I must inform you that the request from your company and from the Galapagos Islands to declare a safety zone around the islands is flatly rejected. What have you to say to that?"

CHAPTER 17 /

A PIECE OF THE SUN

TOM THOUGHT he was going to either be sick or explode in anger. Without replying he set the receiver back in its cradle, stood up and walked out of the office, down the stairs and out into the bright sunshine. Closing his eyes he leaned heavily against the wall of the building.

This is where Bud found him nine minutes later.

"Uh, skipper?" he asked tentatively. "You okay?"

Tom opened his eyes and looked at his friend. Right now he needed a friend. Desperately.

"Ah, Bud. It's all going down the drain," Tom said softly. At his friend's prompting they sat down on a nearby bench and Tom poured his heart out. All his joys bullied by the U.N. meeting and now this phone call.

Bud listened until Tom had no more to say. The inventor could barely breathe let alone talk any more. But, as soon as Bud sensed that Tom needed him to say something, he was ready.

He began by carefully choosing a swear word he knew would shock his best friend. He said it with vigor, and so much so that Tom gaped at him before bursting out in laughter. For nearly two entire minutes Tom laughed and laughed as the tears of frustration ran down his cheeks and dampened his collar. When he spoke again, the flyer used a much softer tone and offered his view.

"The way I see it, Tom, is that you've already had the legal word from this country that anything you can grab out in space is fair game. And, you've started to do that. You have companies and even some of the old U.N.'s countries waiting in line to get some of those rare earth metals. I can't see how the council managed to get the vote against you, but I think your old friendly United States Senator Peter Quintana might say a few things in a few individuals' ears along the lines of, 'Hey. Sorry that you voted against us as a body even if you may not have as a nation, but that's the way the old rare earth cookie crumbles. No precious metals for you!' If that doesn't get a lot of them back on your side, well... at least they won't get rewarded for being turncoats!"

The inventor shrugged. He couldn't find the words for what he felt. Anger, for certain. Deep friendship for Bud's support, a definite. He felt great uncertainty of both how to tell his father of this latest setback and of where this left his project; he was even uncertain if Enterprises should continue without international support for the no-fly zone.

Tom let Bud stand him up and they walked into the Administration building. Without looking where they were going, Tom was surprised when Bud eventually opened the door to the Legal department.

"Tom really needs to see Old Man Rimmer," Bud told the receptionist.

She was about to say something about whether Tom was expected, but a look at him and then at Bud's face told her that this was not the time to say anything other than, "Sure. Come on back."

Bud paused at the doorway thinking that Tom might wish to be alone, but the blond-haired young man grabbed his sleeve and dragged him along. To nobody's real surprise, Damon Swift sat in one of the visitor's chairs.

Tom sat down heavily in another chair and Bud stood behind his friend. The two older men looked at Tom but said nothing, preferring to wait until he had managed to compose himself.

The basic story of the U.N. meeting had obviously been covered by Mr. Swift, so Tom simply related the new phone call. Once he finished, Jackson Rimmer nodded at Damon.

"Son? I wish you'd come to me instead of beating yourself up over this. Probably half a minute after you hung up, the man who called you dialed my private number. I didn't know he had it and told him I wasn't happy. He informed me of what he had told you, so I informed him that I was registering an official complaint against him. I came right up here and Jackson and I just got off the phone with the Secretary General."

"Did it do any good?"

Damon and the lawyer smiled brightly. "Oh, absolutely. At least we both think so. For starters we were promised that a disciplinary hearing would be convened within twenty-four hours of receiving our complaint. Herr Schnitz broke U.N. regulations."

Jackson added, "In this country we have restraining orders when you don't wish to be in contact with someone. In the U.N. they have the *Mandaat van zijn mededeling* which is Dutch—for some unknown reason—for 'Do not communicate with this person.' The man who called will be served with such a mandate within the hour."

Tom took a deep breath before asking, "But is anything he said true? Can they refuse to grant the airspace safety zone? If they refuse, I can't imagine how I would feel if some unsuspecting airliner were to blunder into the cable, killing everyone onboard."

Mr. Rimmer shook his head. "By their own laws, the United Nations may do nothing that jeopardizes or might tend to jeopardize citizens of any nation not specifically under sanctions by or official condemnation of the U.N."

Damon turned to Tom and said, "In other words, they are breaking their own laws by refusing to grant the airspace exception. It might be in part of the Pacific Ocean, but it isn't international airspace."

Tom looked confused.

Jackson told him, "Once Ecuador gave up rights to the islands and Galapagos formed its own government, they—wait for the five-dollar legal words—*ipso facto* became a sovereign nation that must be honored as such by the world. Even if they are not a member of the U.N. they get all the privileges and protections the U.N. has to offer. And, they declared no-fly airspace so the U.N. is supposed to simply make it a done deal."

"See? I told this was going to work out," Bud told Tom patting him on the shoulder.

"It may take some time and an official reprimand from a friendly nation—perhaps even our own—but things will get turned in our favor," the lawyer assured them all.

As Tom and Bud were leaving the Administration building the flyer asked about the state of the space elevator.

"It's kind of in a state of flux, Bud. But, if you have a few minutes why don't we head over to Arv's workshop and have a chat with Linda Ming."

Bud blushed a little. It was something only known to Linda, Bud and Tom, but for a very brief period when the two young men were just nineteen, Linda had let the dark haired pilot know that she would not mind, at all, if he were to ask her on a date. There had even been a small kiss or two involved.

He hoped that she was over that or that she would not remember any of it.

Tom slapped him on the shoulder, saying, "She can't have been all that favorably inclined toward you. After all, when Arv rehired her she never said a word about picking up with you where the two of you left off." It was a tease and Bud knew it. He chose to say nothing.

Tom opened the door and they entered the rather large space that Arv preferred to use. He had an actual office in the building, but spent most of his time at one or another of the workbenches or computer stations that filled the room.

Arv greeted them with, "I think you must have some sort of second-sight, skipper. Linda just told me she was about ten minutes away from giving you a call. She has something figured out for the counterweight."

Seeing Tom and Bud, Linda came right over. "Wow. Talk about timing..." she said before noticing Bud's red face. "Don't worry, Bud. I won't bite. Any more." She gave him one of her delightful laughs and then seemed to forget about the entire episode. "I'm glad you're here, Tom. Arv probably mentioned that I believe I have solved things with the maneuvering of the counterweight."

"I have nothing but very high hopes, Linda," he told her. "It's been a day filled with potential set-backs and many antacid tablets. So, tell me what you've got."

She motioned for them to follow. By now, Bud had recovered and his curiosity overtook any anxiety about Linda.

Sitting at a computer station was what looked like a white hockey puck topped with a slightly curved dish. The dish was raised by about a half-inch from the top of the puck and appeared, as Tom looked it over, to be on a movable mount of some type.

"I've got to tell you both that it took a lot of computer time to figure this out. I can only heap praise on my very determined parents to turn me into a stereotypical Asian math whiz. The problem was in coming up with a repelatron system that is self-contained and flexible enough in settings to accommodate a wide array of loads."

Bud raised a hand. "I did not have the advantage of Asian parents, Linda. Small concepts?"

She patted his arm. "Okay. There are eighty-two cross braces that Hank has removed and recast giving me the room I need for these. Eventually these will be linked to a small computer by micro-wires that will provide both power and setting control." She picked the unit up and pointed to a thin connector port similar to ones used in a number of popular computer lines. "Power, control info and feedback. The wiring will run back up the inside of the wire guide tunnel and will take up two-thirds of one millimeter. Sorry, but that's the way it has to be. A dash of tomacoat will protect it."

She looked at Tom. He nodded. "We can live with that."

"Good. The controller box and the antenna sit so the antenna is recessed seven millimeters inside of the new indentations. That small extra space is needed to let the antenna swing up or down depending on direction of travel."

Tom frowned. "Are you saying that such a small angle can provide the necessary pushing forces?"

"I am. In fact as long as the total cargo load remains under two hundred-ninety thousand pounds these will do the trick. Remember. There are eighty-two of them."

"What if it is a lighter load?" Bud inquired.

"Good question. The reason for the computer link is that once the load, and the speed of travel, are determined—or adjusted— these can reduce or increase their push in a range of about twenty percent. If you need even less push, then some of these strategically turn off. For slowing and stopping, they change directions in appropriate numbers."

"What speed?" Tom needed to know.

"If Hank told me the truth, in atmosphere you have requested three hundred MPH. Out of atmosphere you want three thousand. Is that correct?" Her look told him she could likely give him a higher speed if he asked for it.

The inventor nodded. "Just the 3-K, please."

"You have it!" She paused and looked pensive.

"I sense a condition," Tom told her.

Nodding, Linda admitted, "It all depends on having the proper weight inside the case. I'm afraid that this all relies on you figuring out a way to make the counterweight at least seventy percent of the load on the platforms."

It was something Tom had expected. Even though the best he could locate on Earth would mean his load capacity was about half of the 290,00 pounds Linda had just mentioned, everything would still run, just with a lot less cargo.

*   *   *   *   *

The next day Bud stopped by Tom's underground office. He had tactfully decided to not ask any questions the previous day on seeing his friend's face.

After sitting down and telling Tom he felt bad for asking, he inquired, "How heavy does it have to be? The counterweight thing."

"Ideally it needs to be between about one hundred-eighty thousand and two hundred thousand pounds." He shook his head at the thought of that much concentrated weight.

"Oh. How much would lead weigh in that casing?"

"Barely half."

"Jetz! Say," he said brightening, "I just remembered about an old Army jet that used depleted uranium shells. Those were dense and heavy enough to go right through the thickest tank armor. What would that do?"

Tom shrugged. "If we had that much available, it would be about eighty-five percent of what I need. The thing is, it isn't available in that quantity. Plus, it isn't safe to handle. We could do it, but the public perception is already working against us, so that's out."

They were sitting quietly when a knock came on the door. Neither had heard Mr. Swift's footsteps outside.

"May I join you?"

"Hey, Mr. Swift. I've got no objections."

"Come on in, Dad. I was just telling Bud about the weight problems with the counterweight for my space elevator. Maybe you can come up with an idea."

"How heavy does it have to be?" his father asked.

Tom chuckled. "You and Bud, Dad. Same question and same answer." He told his father the figure he'd given Bud.

"You've considered a variety of weights that can be added or removed as needed?"

"Yes, and I dismissed it because of stability. With so many darned things going on I haven't spent enough time looking for what I needed. The total weight for any one load that I foresee is going to be about the weight of a jumbo jet aircraft. Empty. While we can purchase a surplus jet and even find a way to compact it down, that will still be far too bulky for our use. I have to find something heavier and smaller."

"Please tell me this isn't because I loaded you down with the auto plant assignment."

Tom smiled and shook his head. "Absolutely not. This came around after that. I just forgot to do my research into moving really heavy things."

Mr. Swift thought about this for a couple minutes. Twice he was about to speak when he stopped and went back to thinking about the problem.

"Depleted nuclear material," he said almost under his breath, but Tom caught it.

"I considered it, but where do I get it? I know the Citadel has a stockpile buried a couple thousand feet down. Heck, I dug the shaft with one of my earth blasters. But I don't recall them having even a quarter of that weight." He mentioned the public relations nightmare it might cause.

They both decided to think the matter over even before contacting their New Mexico facility.

When Tom's father left them, the flyer only had one idea to contribute.

"How about a piece of the sun?"

Tom shook his head. "Give me about three hundred years and I might find a way to get that close and contain that super-hot material, but it isn't going to be in our lifetimes."

Bud shook his head. "Sorry. I meant a piece of a spent sun. I read somewhere that a piece of a collapsed star the size of a pin head would be able to drag something toward it from fifty miles away and would weigh in at dozens of tons. Well, I may not have the exact numbers there, but you know what I mean."

Tom gave a resigned chuckle. "Yes. I do, but the same problems apply. It may be collapsed but it is still hot. Plus, if that small amount can attract something from a distance, can you imagine how hard it would yank you in if you got close to a whole Moon-size chunk of it?"

Bud now looked downcast. He had thought he might have a good idea. "Yeah. You could get close enough to go *splat* and never get back." He sighed. "Sorry. Is there anything really heavy here on Earth?"

"Oh, there are some of the heavy elements, but many of them are radioactive or have to be man-made, might last micro-seconds at that or just don't exist in any sort of quantity to be useful. If we could find a source of say, Mendelevium or better yet Nobelium then all I would need is a piece the size of a small school bus." Tom laughed at the notion. "That would be perfect if not in shape at least in volume."

"What makes the Nobelium better than the first one?" Bud asked, not understanding the ridiculousness of discussing something that could never be.

"Right. Okay. For starters Nobelium weighs more per cubic centimeter than Mendelevium. So we would need less of it. But the big one is radioactive half-life. Some isotopes of Nobelium have half-lives in the range of twenty two to twenty three seconds. They are a lot less dangerous than Mendelevium with its half life of nearly an hour and a quarter, and significantly less volatile than the heaviest of the metal elements, Lawrencium."

"Oh. And I'm getting the feeling you are about to tell me that there is something like one pound of these in the entire world."

"It's a bit better than that, Bud, but nowhere close to what we would need. Sorry, but it's a nice idea."

Bud looked discourage but rallied and asked. "So, everything else is working okay?"

Tom gave a small shake of his head. "Not really. I thought we had everything worked out with Linda Ming's new array of mini-repelatrons but I neglected to account of the passing of two cables that must slide through the L-Evator itself. Both the anchor and pulley cables are made of the same stuff the repelatrons will act against. If allowed to pass close by the top or bottom of the counterweight, the repelatrons will shove them together and could bring things to a grinding halt. When we get the counterweight all set and built, and up there," he pointed skyward, "it would be a miserable process to break it back apart and get it down here to be retrofitted with a channel down one side. Besides, that could put the narrow weight off balance."

"Well, it seems to me you have to work with what you still have down here. Right?"

Tom nodded, looking slightly defeated but almost immediately brightened. "That's it!" he shouted and clasped his friend by both shoulders. "I'll run the channel down the inside of the central core of the L-Evator. That will have the added benefit of keeping the two cables apart as much as possible. Great idea, Bud!"

Tom sat down at his computer to make the necessary changes to the design. He totally ignored the slightly bewildered, dark haired flyer who was later seen muttering to himself, "But I never gave him the idea. I didn't say a thing!" as he walked back across the hangar floor to the elevator.

None of the platform core assembly had been built so Tom was able to adjust the design allowing one cable to pass with enough leeway that there would be no problems.

He still needed the filling for the weight, but he felt confident that the final major "bug" had been eliminated.

A call came through the following morning and was answered by Damon Swift.

"Is this Tom Swift's father?" the slightly-accented female voice inquired.

"It is. And I believe I recognize your voice. Is this Madam Prime Minister?"

"Why, yes it is. I need to ask for your or Tom's help. We have been having daily overflights of jet aircraft. Military jets. They come from the direction of Ecuador but bear no markings. We have no defenses and I know of nowhere to turn."

Damon told her how to transmit a picture or video using the satellite system and suggested that she post someone to get the visual evidence.

"In the meantime I will have Tom fly down there immediately. I think one of our giant jets might put a bit of fear or respect into your, shall we say, unwanted visitors?"

She agreed, so Damon TeleVoc'd Tom and told him to drop everything.

The inventor called Bud, had the *Sky Queen* brought up to ground level and they took off just nineteen minutes after Evelyn Estes' call.

Tom and Bud had no sooner landed on the deck of the *Sea Charger* and climbed out of the *Sky Queen* than six fighter jet aircraft raced over them at less than two hundred feet. There had been no warning sounds from them indicating that they traveled at supersonic speeds.

This was verified a second later when the sonic boom hit them with a pressure wave that knocked them both over.

As Tom looked up at the receding aircraft he noticed they went into a tight turn and were swinging around and head back. When he raised himself to his knees he called out to Bud, "We've got to get inside. Come on!" there was no reply.

He heard a groan and saw his friend rising and staggering around holding his bleeding head. Bud was disoriented and began stumbling toward his left and the edge of the flight deck.

Horrified, Tom watched as the jets raced back over the deck and the pressure wave hit Bud, tossing him backward and over the edge!

CHAPTER 18 /

MOVING HOUSE

AS THE jets disappeared over the horizon heading back in the direction of land, Tom got up and ran to the edge fearing what he would find when he looked over. In spite of his fear he poked his face over the side. The distance to the water was something that not even an experienced high diver might attempt, much less a flailing body.

Bud was rubbing his head and looking at his bloody palm while sitting in the safety net that now encircled the *Sea Charger's* deck just five feet down.

"I forgot all about that," he called down to Bud feeling relieved. "Are you okay?"

"What's the saying? Bloodied but determined? Yeah. Just a little stunned. Whose were those?"

"Probably Ecuador like dad said. Also, no marking like Eva Estes described. On the positive side I noticed they carried no rockets under their wings. I think the intent was to scare, not harm."

Bud snorted and held up one reddened hand. "Does this look like scared to you?"

Tom helped his friend to climb back to the deck. Ten minutes later the medic had patched the cut on Bud's forehead and the two young men had headed to the radio room. Tom reported to his father about the flyover.

"Son, we have to face the most likely facts. That was an attack. Those pilots knew exactly what the effect would be of their sonic pressure waves. I'm calling Pete Quintana. And as much as I hate to admit, I think it is time to invite the U. S. Marines to visit the *Sea Charger* with some of their VTOL jet fighters. We'll call it a *courtesy visit*. I'll keep you posted. In the meantime, why don't you return the favor?"

After the call ended Bud asked Tom what that last bit meant.

Tom smiled. "Tomorrow, you will see."

They rolled the Skeeter—a miniature helicopter—out of the *Queen's* rear-facing hangar and took off for the capital.

Evelyn opened her front door when Tom knocked. "Did you call for a friendly pair of U.S. gentlemen, ma'am?" he asked is a phony southern drawl.

The strain on her face on seeing Bud's apparent injury melted into a smile and she invited them in. Over iced coffees Tom explained the possible arrival of a small attachment of Marine aircraft and that they would not touch down on anything other than the *Sea Charger*. He assured her they would not "patrol the skies" but would be on alert to take off at the first RADAR sign of incoming aircraft.

"Is it really necessary?" she asked. "We cannot have any fighting over our islands. The turtles..." She trailed off, looking sad.

"Dad thinks so and he is about the most reluctant person to ever involve the military. When we head home tomorrow Bud and I will leave their jets with a, hopefully, lasting memory of our visit."

The next day at dawn the *Sky Queen* lifted from the deck and headed almost due east. As they approached the coast at a very low altitude Bud finally realized Tom's intention. He checked a chart and suggested, "Fifteen degrees to port, skipper. Their air base will be eleven miles inland. Nothing around it for miles."

Three minutes later and at Mach 3, the *Sky Queen* screamed across the airfield at just fifty feet. By the time the first individual was able to get back up, the giant jet was twenty miles away and approaching eighteen thousand feet. A minute later and she was at sixty-two thousand feet and nearing the northern border.

In her wake were nearly a dozen fighter jets that had been picked up by the shockwave and slammed into the ground.

When the next day arrived and there had been no official complaint from Ecuador, Tom and his father agreed that their response had not backfired on them. And when three days went by with no further overflights of the Galapagos, they were certain the "message" had been received.

Over the following week Tom found it necessary to send the *Challenger* up to the staging area for the refined metals and rare earths. There were just too many of them and too much of most to be kept in place by the Attractatron mules. They had other functions requiring their attention, so he decided the excess had to come down.

Tom was awakened by a phone call at midnight. He groped for the receiver and cleared his throat before answering.

"Yeah," he croaked.

"Oh dear. Is this Tom Swift?" It was a woman's voice that he could almost place, but not quite. "I just realized that I figured the time difference the wrong direction. Oh, Tom, this is Eva Estes. The Galapagos?"

Tom was instantly awake. "Yes, Eva. It's Tom. It's about

midnight here. What time is it down there?" His brain wasn't completely engaged quite yet.

"I am so sorry. It is just ten here. But I had to talk to you. We have a problem brewing. At least, possibly."

"What is it?"

"I have received a communique from Ecuador. In spite of you chasing their Air Force away, their National Assembly just voted this evening to retake control of our island nation. I cannot think what to do."

"Do you believe they might use force?" Tom was now very worried about the safety, not only of his space L-Evator or the station, but of the peaceful people of the islands.

"I do not think so. I believe they simply intend to declare that our sovereignty is invalid and that they are resuming, as they put it, 'Management of the affairs of the Galapagos Islands.' Oh, Tom. I believe they also intend to take control of your *Sea Charger* and the space elevator project. What should I do? The Marines and their aircraft left us yesterday." She sounded stressed but nowhere close to tears.

Tom thought for a second. "Eva. I need to make a call to someone in Washington D.C. Fortunately he is a late night sort of man. I will try to call you back within the hour."

He broke the connection and then dialed a number he located in his tablet computer.

"Better be important," the voice at the other end answered. "Senators do not like to be rung after midnight. Interferes with our beauty sleep!"

"Senator Quintana. It's Tom Swift. I hate like the dickens to bother you this late, but..." He told the New Mexican politician about his call and the fear the situation was giving the Prime Minister down there.

Pete Quintana listened without interrupting the inventor. When Tom finished, his first comment was unprintable. But, a moment later he offered, "Give me ten minutes to get back into my jeans and I'll go hammer on the door of the Ecuadorian Embassy. While there is no love loss between our two countries, I know the Ambassador very well. The better part of this is that he knows me and he knows that if I say I'll reach down his throat and rip out his liver, that he had better close his mouth and clamp his teeth together."

It was arranged for Tom to call the senator's cell phone one hour later and then to bring Eva Estes' office in on a conference call.

While Tom waited Bashalli got up and made him some tea. She told him it had enough caffeine to keep him awake, but in truth it was decaffeinated. She hoped that he would remain awake only long enough to make the phone call and not be up all night.

Five minutes ahead of schedule Tom called the Galapagos. Eva answered. She sounded jittery and Tom commented on it.

"Too many cups of our coffee in the last two hours, Tom," she told him.

He explained the plan to bring her into the conversation but only in five or ten minutes. She offered to be put on hold, and that is what Tom did.

He called the senator. It rang just once.

"Tom? Pete. We might have a situation down there. Ecuador claims that they never cut the islands loose, that all they did was to offer to step back to see if they could manage themselves. Now the government is claiming that Miss Estes and her five ministers are about to do irreparable damage to the protected islands and species by letting you set up shop down there and so out of the goodness of their hearts, they will be stepping back into the picture. I told Santiago Carlos that I'd call up the Marines again, in full force, if they so much as cross their own ten-mile territorial waters and airspace with any sort of force, military or otherwise. Uh, should I wait on discussing all this until we get the Prime Minister on the line?"

"Hang on." Tom placed him on hold and brought Evelyn into the three-way connection, then reopened the line to the senator. After a brief introduction Pete Quintana reiterated what he has started to tell Tom and then told them what his next steps would be.

He also gave her his direct number. "If anyone other than Tom Swift appears over the horizon you call me. This line is always with me, even when I take a shower or am speaking on the floor of the Senate. I am not above excusing myself to take an important call."

"What will you do next, if I may ask," Evelyn inquired.

"Just what I told them I'd do. Call in the United States Marines again. Oorah!"

*   *   *   *   *

It was going to be one of the trickiest maneuvers in the history of space flight, and Tom knew it. There was no single spacecraft capable of lifting the enormous spool of the cable that would form the ground-to-space section of the spine of the L-Evator system. The *Challenger* had an auxiliary platform that could be mounted on its top—and had been used several times in the past—but even that could not hold the smallest spools necessary to carry a minimum of one hundred miles of cable... this is why the cable had been manufactured in space and would soon need to be eased down to the ground.

Two weeks had gone by and there had been no sign of anyone or any troops from Ecuador, but everyone was ready. Two U.S. Navy submarines now patrolled only a few miles off the coast of the island of Santiago.

The *USS Samoan Islands*, an amphibious assault carrier with thirty Marine VTOL fighters, and ship-to-air missile launchers, stood between the island group and the coast of Ecuador. Permission to fire warning shots *only* had been given, but if actively attacked they could fight back.

Everyone hoped they would not be needed at any point. They would remain in the area for the next several weeks or until Tom got the Space L-Evator in operation.

Months earlier Tom decided to start by hauling the components of the giant spool up and assembling them in orbit near the Outpost. He once anticipated that multiple spools might be required, but soon realized a much better method.

Hank Sterling's vacuum-form equipment was determined to be too small and so a new, special-use version was constructed. It could produce the hub to outer rim sections that would span three hundred feet in a single piece, and make six of them at a time. Forty-eight would eventually be required.

As the first sections came out, they were fed into a hardening oven. Rather than try to construct a giant box for that, Tom opted to make a small oven, open at both ends, which allowed beams to travel through on a conveyor belt. A wide-dispersal laser array provided the heat source. The material remained inside just long enough to cure and exited quickly enough that continuous strength was maintained.

Support beams of varying lengths were built and bundled up over the coming weeks. Once everything was complete, Tom and Bud took five loads up to the Outpost where things would get assembled. It would give the crew of the Outpost something new to do, and they set to completing the project with eagerness.

By the time Tom and Bud went up to the Outpost a few days before the cable drop operation, the giant spool had been built, wound with the initial one hundred miles of cable, and was floating in formation a thousand or so meters away from the outpost. The plan was to take the cable spool to a much lower orbit before the operation began. The cable, all thirty thousand miles of it, lay in a gigantic looping formation a fifty miles away from the Outpost.

"Now what?" Bud asked as they watched the start of the "Big Wind" as Bud called it.

"Now, once you and I get dirt-side and on the *Sea Charger*, one of the Attractatron mules takes the spool of cable to within ninety miles of the ground and holds it there. Another of the mules will be bringing down a sort of winch to control the unreeling. As soon as we signal that we have the cable attached, the empty spool and winch will be quickly hauled back to the outpost where the giant coil of cable sits. We'll be on the *Sea Charger* and use the *Challenger* to bring us the end of a cable as it gets lowered."

"And then up in space it's head 'em up and move 'em out?"

"Or, something like that. Yes," Tom replied giving Bud's shoulder a playful punch. "The mules will start maneuvering the giant coil of cable and move everything out to the end point."

After joining Ken Horton for an early lunch the two floated back to the *Challenger* and set a course for the *Sutter* and the mining operations on the sun side of the Earth's orbit. After producing the first batch of hull panels she had returned to her mining operations. They arrived nine hours later, in time to watch a shift change. But the sight that caught their eyes were the five asteroids flying is some soft of ghostly formation. Four of them formed a rectangle with the fifth one seeming to be stuck to the nose of the golden ship.

In reality the *Sutter* was attached to the asteroid and was drilling and coring, crushing and processing everything that could be extracted. The unusable parts were being streamed away from the ship in a continuous line that disappeared toward the sun.

Inside the golden ship they were met by her current captain and pilot, Red Jones. He and Art Wiltessa were on a two-week rotation with a crew of fourteen. It only required five people to operate the mining capabilities of the *Sutter* per shift, but they had brought a few extra to ensure the smooth running of the ship.

They dropped by the control room in the upper sail to say hello to Art before the three men headed down to the large common room to discuss how things were proceeding.

"Really amazingly well," Red told them looking over the top of his sippy cup of coffee. Even though the artificial gravity of the ship let people and solid objects stay rooted to the "ground," liquids were not affected and would float around if not contained. At first people felt a little silly using what was primarily a large version of what infants used, but they all soon forgot about it.

He described the typical day-to-day operations but his eyes lit up as he began to describe what they were finding in the current asteroidal chunk.

"Rare earths, skipper. And, lots of them. It's an incredible find and a lot higher levels than any of the other chunks so far."

"What sort of things?" Bud asked.

Red snorted. "Gosh, you name it. Scandium, Cerium, Neodynium, Samariium, Terbium, Ytterbium... at least twelve of the seventeen elements on the list. And where they might be found in concentrations of a kilogram per hundred tons of mined rock on Earth, we're finding that amount it perhaps a half-ton of crushed asteroid!"

They talked for another hour about anything that might be done from home to help. In the end Red had to say, "It is a logistical nightmare to be working a million miles away on *this* side of the planet and then have to periodically disconnect, travel that million plus the bit extra to get to the Outpost, and then to park our refined materials, load new containers and then come back and start over again. We lose three days out of ten this way." He looked helplessly at Tom.

Everyone knew that even with the safety factor of mining where they were, a small, rabble-rousing element on Earth kept trying to get public opinion and fear levels up by claiming that it was only a matter of time before things "crashed into the planet killing billions."

It was purely fear mongering and seemed to be concentrated among some of the more radical religious groups. Everyone found it to be annoying, and now it was hindering things.

"Let me talk this over with dad," Tom suggested. "I think it's time to move operations a bit closer and maybe put the Moon in between the operation and Earth."

Red smiled. "Boy, if you can get that to happen, I'd say we can nearly double our output. The only thing is—" and he bit his lip, looking worried, "right now we just shoot the smaller ejecta into the sun. What do we do with all that if we have the planet to worry about?"

Tom laughed. "Listen, you're not smelting out any more iron, right?" Red nodded. "So, we simply magnetize everything and let it compact back into a rough ball. I had always planned on putting as much back into the asteroid belt as possible, and this way we just move the packages to the L-1 Lagrange point for the time being and later take them back out there and let the natural attraction of the other asteroids gather up what we return."

Three days after returning to Shopton, Tom and his father made the decision to go ahead with Tom's plan. No announcement was made and no fanfare was even suggested. Over a one-week period the *Sutter* along with the Attractatron mules just quietly moved everything. There was, as expected, no public outcry.

It isn't even that it was hidden out of sight; a quiet word from Damon to several renown astronomers meant that nobody was told about the shift.

Using different pilots and crews to keep everyone fresh, the *Challenger* was kept busy ferrying down containers of valuable but unneeded metals and minerals. And again, without fanfare and only a cursory report to the U.S. Government regarding the downward shipments—something that Washington agreed they had no right to question or interfere with—nearly a hundred metric tons of such metals as pure aluminum, platinum, iron and copper went on the market.

As these had already been smelted and purified inside the *Sutter*, most were delivered at above 99% purity and so they fetched top prices. The first three shipments alone now covered a fifth of the costs incurred to date.

As is generally the case, with so much good news must come some bad, and it was a phone call from the Prime Minister of the Galapagos Islands that took some of the winds out of Tom's sails.

"Tom," she had begun, "I just came home from a requested appearance before the entire United Nations. I had petitioned, as your legal people suggested, to have both our territorial waters as well as a safety restricted air zone around the space elevator cables declared, but was practically booed off the podium at first."

"Yes, I recall that, and I am so sorry to put you in that position, Eva. Or, Madam Prime Minister if you are angry with me."

She laughed. "No, Tom. It is still Eva. I am only disappointed in all of those fat bureaucrats and their blindness. Things settled down once the Master at Arms threatened to remove some of the more vocal members. They sat there like spoiled children and scowled at me. I expected to see their stick their tongues out at me as well." She laughed again.

"How did things turn out?" Tom asked.

"In the end I received polite applause. I had fifty points to make and I made each and every one of them. Some members appeared to nod off so I began to yell and suggested their interpreters also yell. A lot of people suddenly straightened up and listened after that. It took me three hours without a break, and I have to admit I nearly fainted at the end, but I got through to them." She actually sounded less triumphant than sad to Tom.

"I'm not hearing intense happiness in your voice, Eva. What is the matter?"

She sighed, heavily. "In the end a motion was made and seconded and passed to table all discussion of my requests for thirty days. They want me back at that time and will, as they put it, decide whether to decide at that time. They might decide to delay it again, or they might decide to vote, or they might even decide to put off the vote for a specific period. Nobody knows! The one positive thing to come out of the meeting is that they voted to notify Ecuador to leave us alone. We shall see if that works."

Tom told her how proud he was of her. "I'm not anybody other than some kid who is trying to do a good thing here, but you and I are fairly close in age and it's difficult to get the world to take us seriously some times. You've made a stand and now it is time to let that sink in. Dad and I now have an old ace-in-the-hole back in Washington, so my next call is going to be to him. It's Senator Quintana and he still wants to champion our causes. You know the term 'a mover and a shaker?'" he asked.

"Of course I do. Remember… educated in Oregon?"

"Of course. Sorry. Well, that is Peter Quintana!—one of those but all in capital letters. With him behind us all, things ought to get moving. After all, he's the one who got the Marines and Navy involved!"

He wished her a pleasant evening and hung up.

Now, he thought, *I only hope that Pete Quintana can deliver on my promise!*

CHAPTER 19 /
PREPARATIONS AND FIDDLING LITTLE DETAILS

FIVE LONG weeks went by during which Tom and the Enterprises and Construction Company teams continued building everything needed to assemble the modular platforms and central drive system for the L-Evator. As each component was completed it was hauled out to Fearing Island and staged for the final trips down to the Galapagos Islands. Most of the actual platforms were simply grids of girders and attachment points that would be assembled on the *Sea Charger*. These would form geodesic shapes for maximum strength against any torque and also to hold large and heavy loads.

Back in her "construction" mode, the second mining phase having been completed for the time being, the *Sutter* had begun churning out flat panels. The first ones were assembled into cargo containers about 20 x 20 x 10 feet. It was in these the first of the rare earths were stowed and brought to Earth on the upper rack of the *Challenger*.

Mr. Swift had already been in contact with more than a dozen domestic companies and major corporations that were clamoring to buy practically everything Tom could get to them.

In other words, they were quite literally lined up at the gates of Enterprises on a Monday morning with cash in hand as the initial containers of six rare earths were put up for bid on the open market.

"We have discovered a trove of these metals and elements, gentlemen and lady, so today's amounts constitute about two percent of what you will be able to purchase during the coming six months. After that, well, we are still attempting to survey the possibilities." He handed out the spectrographic analysis reports on the purity for each of the metals.

The bidding had gone smoothly and quickly with the winners leaving with their purchases loaded into private armored trucks.

The "losers" were assured that they would have first pick of the next batch that would be brought down in two weeks time.

When he returned to the shared office, Tom was waiting. "How much did we make?"

Damon Swift smiled and came over to shake his son's hand.

"That first load has brought us enough to pay for at least half of the current unpaid expenses and the equipment you have commissioned for this project. Your earlier metals sale certainly helped. If we take into account what is sitting up in orbit, I estimate that the entire High Space L-Evator *and* the completed and manned space station can be paid in full if you can go back out and find an asteroid with another two or three tons of Lutetium, Promethium or Scandium."

Now Tom smiled. "I know of at least three bug chunks I can bring closer and mine. Once we have all the station's structural components built, of course."

"Of course." Damon turned serious. "What are you going to do about the counterweight?"

"I spoke with Art Wiltessa yesterday. He's up captaining the *Sutter* this week. They evidently mined out an odd conglomeration of metals that *Sutter* isn't able to separate out. He called it 'the great mass,' Anyway, I had him ship down a sample and it is being ferried over from Fearing today, It should be here in—" he glanced a the clock on the office wall, "—less than an hour. All I know is he tells me it is heavier than lead and very slightly radioactive."

The daily supply cargo jet returned to Enterprises, and Tom drove out to meet it.

He was standing by the jet as the side door opened and one of the crew hopped to the ground.

"Hi, skipper," he greeted the inventor. "I've got a special package for you, but... uh... well I hope you brought a forklift or something. It's kinda heavy."

Tom climbed into the jet and almost tripped over a small tomasite container. It was a one-foot cube and strapped down right at the center balance point of the entire jet. He nudged it with his foot; it didn't move. He sat down on his haunches and tried to give it a shove with his hands. Nothing.

It took more than an hour to get the proper equipment to the jet, unload the cube and deliver it to the elevator of the underground hangar.

But when they put it in, the "overweight" alarm went off. The elevator was rated to carry about 1,000 pounds, and this alarm brought to Tom's face, not a frown but a huge smile.

"Take it to the Barn and call Nuclear Engineering and ask them to bring a portable containment set-up," he requested.

An hour later Tom, in a radiation suit, opened the box that was now inside a makeshift tomasite-paneled room. He ran a Geiger counter over the dull metal contents. Yes, there was some radiation but as he watched the readout, it began to creep downward. Tom used a sharp tool and rubber mallet to pry off a small piece. Now when the counter was passed over the exposed spot, the reading went back up. A couple minutes later when he scanned the area again he was pleased to see that the counter was coming back down.

Tom's heart was racing with excitement. He only knew of a couple elements that lost radioactivity that quickly and that were already low on the danger scale to begin with.

And both were enormously heavy!

The piece Tom had pried off was very heavy for its size—another reason for his joy. He placed it into a smaller tomasite container, opened the inner door of the small room and stepped into the antechamber where he shed his radiation suit.

Outside he took in a few deep breaths of unprocessed air and thanked the technicians.

"Leave it set up for now," he requested. "I'll let you know what to do with the box in about an hour."

Tom went directly to the Metallurgy department. Once there he placed the small piece into one of their machines. The equipment clamped the piece tightly while a diamond-edged blade shaved off a thin piece and transferred it to the mass spectroscope. The vaporization and spectra-analysis process required ten minutes during which Tom could barely remain still.

His shouts of joy could be heard all over the building.

Mendelevium and Nobelium all held in a slurry of lead and gold.

After weighing the piece and using a scanning laser to determine the exact volume of the irregular chunk, Tom tried to remain calm as he placed a call to Communications. "Please connect me with the *Sutter*," he requested.

When Art came on the line Tom asked him how much of the material they had.

The reply nearly made him faint. "Keep it up there and don't let it get out of your sight!"

He thanked the man and cut the connection.

Tom had needed the counterweight to be at least 180,000 pounds and his calculations of the new metal mass told him he would be within about 7,000 pounds of that.

He could live with that slightly reduced lifting mass. He had never anticipated using the L-Evator at top capacity anyway. Overjoyed, he TeleVoc'd his father with the news.

That night Tom got the best night's sleep he'd had in more than a month.

*   *   *   *   *

Tom and Bud made five trips down in the *Super Queen* until all the components had been staged on the giant deck of the permanently-anchored *Sea Charger*. This did not include the shell for the two hundred-foot long, eight-foot wide counterweight. That would soon be taken up to the Lagrange L-5 point where the *Sutter* had parked the pelletized heavy elements mined from several of the asteroids.

Finally home for a week, their last job before taking everyone down to The Galapagos for the cable drop saw them out to Fearing Island.

Tom knew that the tons of materials inside the counterweight would not be sufficient on its own to balance the weight of materials either going up or coming down except in rare instances, and those probably by chance rather than design. But the addition of repelatron pushers tuned to only interact with the components of the heavy cable would do the rest of the heavy work.

(Damon Swift had suggested that Linda Ming be given the latest employee appreciation prize for her ingenious contribution. It would mean she received $20,000, something she could use to pay off her ex-husband's overdue bills!)

As he and Bud stood on the tarmac at Fearing watching the four shell quarters being lifted into position on the "roof rack"—as Bud called it—on top of the *Challenger*, Tom's TeleVoc beeped. When he responded it was to take a call from his father.

"Son? I have some great news. Pete Quintana is not just back as a member of the Senate as we already knew, he has taken the reigns of *all* of his old committees. Evidently, the replacement chairpersons were being overwhelmed and were quite ready to hand things back to him.

"That stick-in-the-mud senator from our old committee-attacks-the-Swifts visit was, to quote Pete, 'given the choice between censure over his conduct in that meeting, or stepping down from committee involvement.' He chose the latter."

"That's great, Dad. Does that mean our own government is fully behind us?"

"For now, that is exactly what it means. Pete is calling for a vote of confidence in the combined House and Senate tomorrow and expects it to pass nearly unanimously. He intends to take it for Presidential signature personally."

Tom asked if this also meant that the U.N. would stop trying to pressure Prime Minister Eva Estes over their hosting of the cable anchor point.

"That is uncertain, Son. On the positive side it has pretty much always been the case of what the United States wants gets highest priority at the U.N. So, if our ambassador is given the word that our government is backing us, it is at least an even bet the rest of the world will follow. Maybe not forever, but long enough for you to get that space station up, running, and for everyone to see that it is as benign as a butterfly."

Tom felt good for another two days leading up to the actual dropping of the cable from space. Word came through that the U.N. continued stalling on making the needed declaration of controlled airspace.

Even though the government of the Galapagos had declared it to be no-fly airspace, anyone could fly into the area, either by accident or on purpose, and find themselves on an unexpected collision course with the cable. Small planes would probably be damaged or destroyed, but a direct hit by an airliner might damage or sever even the super-strong cable leading to death and destruction!

By mid-morning the next day he was at the Construction Company supervising the last bit of work on a large piece of equipment. Bud, over there to ferry a new *Pigeon Commander* plane from the small airfield behind the construction buildings back to Enterprises happened to be walking past the open doors when he spotted his friend.

"Hey. I see you've got an even larger version of that aircraft fatigue scanner thing. What gives?"

Tom pointed at the two components being readied to get loaded into one of the cargo pods of the *Super Queen*. They were each nearly three times as large as the one Bud had seen months earlier. "That is going to be staged at Fearing until it can be transferred down to the *Sea Charger* and eventually sent up to the new station. As it continues being built I want to have each and every inch of each and every weld and seal on every hull plate fully inspected. There is no room to have even a few sloppy areas."

Bud nodded. "Good idea. I recall the couple times a pinhole meteorite hit the Outpost and what *that* little loss of air did. I can imagine if an entire panel broke away. Jetz!"

He watched as the unit was folded down and wrapped in a protective film.

When Tom turned around Bud was smiling at him. "Race you back to Enterprises? Me in a *Pigeon* and you in your car?"

"You're on!" Tom told him. Bud ran from the building and around the corner while Tom sauntered to his car waiting just fifty feet away.

Technically, Tom arrived back first coming through the executive gate a minute before the plane touched down but didn't make it to the taxiway before Bud landed and had the small plane sitting and waiting. They decided to call it a tie.

After having a late morning coffee together, they parted so that Bud could ready the new plane for its series of test flights before everybody headed South that evening. Tom went to the shared office and sat down and dismissed the screen saver intending to make some notes on his progress.

Instead, as the screen cleared, he could see that a small message was waiting for him. He had to smile to himself as he noted a large counter above the text that seemed to indicate the message sender had been waiting for at least twenty minutes.

A second later that disappeared and the message text size doubled.

> Your handling of the "Earth Belt" confrontation
> was unique to say the least. Bravo. We are very
> embarrassed that we gave no warning or
> had no ideas what our SA amigos had up
> their sleeves. Perhaps YTD not doing enough
> work. Apologies aplenty! And meant!

Tom typed:

> Any ideas on that nation's next move?

The answer came back:

> A little. Belligerent and hoping to turn this
> into financial gain, but ought to be made to
> behave if right pressure is put on them by
> the right int'l org. Comprende?

> Si. Is it going to work and come in time?

The answer came back almost immediately.

> Working on that... More later?

And, that was it for the time being. Or, so he thought. Just before he was ready to press the Return key to clear the messages, Collections came back.

> Forgot something. We're slipping. Embarrassment.
> You are about to be called to that Int'l Org's house
> for big news. Tread softly and you should find a
> rainbow after the storm.

Tom typed: Thanks! and started to go back to his original plan to make notes but his phone rang.

"It's the United Nations, Tom," Trend told him. "Line three."

Tom chuckled telling himself, *Some day I'm going to find out how they do that*. He took a deep breath, counted silently to ten, and pressed the indicated button on his phone.

The call was brief and was a relatively pleasant invitation to attend a special session in New York the following morning. Tom accepted knowing that he would be going alone. Damon Swift would be winging his way to the Citadel at that time.

He walked out from the waiting room and into the giant chamber. Before he scanned the audience he glanced up at the triumvirate on the raised dais. He noted with satisfaction that the second man, whom he now knew to be the Vice Secretary General, had been ordered to stay out of the chamber. Evidently the "restraining" order was still being enforced. Somebody he didn't recognize sat in his place.

Before taking his seat he looked out at the assembly. He saw a few sour faces but they were outnumbered by many more individuals either outright smiling or nodding encouragingly at him.

The meeting was brief with the Secretary General admitting that the assembly had overstepped their boundaries at the previous meeting. Their demand that no member nation sell anything to the Swifts was rescinded.

"I trust this makes you happy?"

"Sir and Madam and assembled delegates, it neither makes me happy nor unhappy. My father and I were disappointed when it happened and appreciate that you have made that decision null and void. I must tell you that we still will not allow a military contingency to come to the new space station once it has been built. However, we do wish to offer a small olive branch."

"I see. And that is?"

"Even with various space-capable nations attempting to reduce space debris there are thousands of pieces littering all around the first several hundred miles of space orbiting the Earth. We wish to offer our services, at no cost to any nation, to remove the outright junk from several satellite positioning lanes in space."

"Why?" the woman asked, sounding curious and not angered at the notion.

"Two-fold, ma'am. The first and totally selfish reason is to ensure that nothing will impact and damage our space elevator system. As it stands there are at least five hundred objects that could eventually be a danger. Not right away but we project the problems will begin in about three years. We wish to take care of that now."

"And, the second reason?"

Tom smiled. "We have been offered a contract by a consortium of fifteen of the member nations to periodically pick up, repair, refuel or just plain clean up, satellites of theirs that could have double or triple life spans, but only if serviced. To get to these and safely retrieve and then reposition them requires clear travel ways."

He also brought up the situation with Ecuador. The delegation from that nation started to protest but the Secretary General silenced them.

"That is our next order of business, Mr. Swift. Rest assured their stated intentions are not in keeping with the goals of this body."

An hour-long question and answer period followed. Generally Tom disliked these because of the often-inane questions asked. Today, however, the assembly seemed to be prepared and most questions were intelligent while only two might be termed, silly or uneducated.

"Why can you not just shoot everything you require into the sky? My country's scientists are perfecting an electrical method of pushing great weights into the sky. You could purchase that from us."

"Well, sir, I believe you speak of a rail gun. Is that correct."

"My belief is that is the terminology. Yes."

"Okay. Have your scientists told you of the great acceleration a rail gun can give?"

The man enthusiastically nodded and agreed.

"And have they told you that such acceleration would instantly kill anybody riding inside the capsule and crush anything not solid?"

Now, the man's face fell. This was new and disturbing information to him.

Tom explained, briefly, the issues, thanked the assembly, and then asked to be excused from the meeting. He left to applause from everyone, except for the delegation from Ecuador. They sat in angry silence.

After the weekend Bud knocked on the shared office door and

poked his head inside. "Oh, hi, Mr. Swift. Have you seen the skipper?"

"I believe he is next door in the big lab, Bud."

"Thanks!"

The flyer stepped back into the hallway and walked the fifty feet down to the next door. The DANGEROUS TEST IN PROGRESS sign was not lit so he opened the door without knocking. He stood quietly in the doorway for about twenty seconds.

"Now, correct me if I'm totally wrong about this, but I thought you had the whole cable thing finished. I mean, isn't it now siting in that giant coil out by the Outpost?"

Tom looked up at Bud. "No, you are not wrong and yes, it is now sitting there and just about ready to have the Earth end dropped."

"So why are you perched there watching a piece of that cable inside the test chamber?"

Tom was sitting at a control panel outside the chamber in his large lab. On the other side of the clear windows nothing appeared to be happening and yet Bud came into the room only to see Tom staring very intently at the five-foot length.

"I am testing that coating, the one you picked up from that small lab in Virginia. Remember?"

"Sure I do, but *what* are you testing? And, why only now?"

"Now because my original test cable has just finished a month in the aging chamber to make it act as if it has been in use for three years. Right now I am pumping about three hundred thousand volts through the aged cable to simulate a lightning strike. So far everything is holding. The great news is there has been no change from its pristine, new state. A strike at any point will only travel about three hundred yards before it just dampens out. I've already performed the same test at minus two hundred degrees and at plus five hundred degrees. If you had been here two hours ago you could have come with me to the wind tunnel. I was there I discovered that nearly ninety-two percent of the drag the cable had before the GreeS coating is now gone."

Bud gave an appreciative whistle. "How come the lightning just goes away?"

"It's a combination of having relatively little conductive metal in the cable and that incredible coating. Dad agrees that the Construction Company is going to license it and put it on the market. Three companies are ready to purchase it by the tanker load."

"That'll make that scientist guy, Sandeker, happy."

"I hope so. He ought to make a couple hundred thousand a year from it. On the practical side, that coating should make underground utility cables last decades instead of eight to ten years." Tom turned back to his control panel. "Come with me in a minute. I'll shut things down and then I need to ask dad something."

"Dad," Tom said as they entered the office, "I need to run an idea past you."

"Go ahead. I'm all yours for fifteen minutes," he said as he glanced at his watch, "before I need to leave for a meeting. What's on your mind?"

"Well, my visit to the U.N. didn't get any approval for our clearing the space junk, at least not yet. We're on a one-year 'consideration' moratorium. But as soon as the cable goes up I just know we're going to have some close calls. Do you think that a small self-powered robot scooting up and down the anchor cable armed with nothing other that an Attractatron to grab errant and useless junk might be okay?"

"To what end?"

"My thought is to have it travel autonomously when the L-Evator isn't in use and to pick up potential hazards and to bring them to the top of the atmosphere and sort of toss them to one side where they would burn up harmlessly. At least the small bits. Any large items would be taken back up to the station point where they can be gathered, possibly just shoved into the mining holes in the asteroid, and then sealed up never to darken anyone's spacial doorstep again. Or, to be brought back down and returned to their nations of origin."

Damon smiled at his son. "As long as it knows when to get out of the way of the L-Evator or counterweight. If you can make it smart enough to do that then I see no reason not to!"

CHAPTER 20 /

FIRST LOAD IN PLACE, MANY TO GO

BY THE morning of the cable drop, it became obvious that things had reached the boiling point. Even though Prime Minister Evelyn Estes had called the night before assuring Tom that their island anchorage was waiting and ready the fact that the U.N. still refused to clear the airspace and declare it out of bounds made him nervous.

But the Attractatron mule with the spool of cable couldn't remain in her low Earth orbit for more than twenty-four hours at a time before it would need to reel in the eighty miles of cable it had spooled out, move to a higher orbit and then spend another half day repositioning itself. Plus another six hours paying out the cable once again. There would be a swath of space junk and two low-orbit satellites to dodge around otherwise.

It had just arrived on station and was ready to lower the cable.

Tom was ready to depart from Shopton to where the giant *Sea Charger* was firmly anchored to the seabed via six monstrous cables and deep anchors. The single anchor point on her deck was ready and waiting; it was connected directly to the other anchors that would share all the stress load put on it without actually pulling at the ship herself. In fact, the multiple anchor cables ran through large-bore tubes so that the ship could rise and fall with the tide and not affect the cable to space.

He looked at his father. The older Swift smiled and nodded. "It's a 'go' from me, Son. As a wise man once said, there's no time like the present!"

Bashalli gave Tom's arm a squeeze. "I believe father Swift is correct, Tom. Get down there and make this a reality. Everything you have told me says that you are ready, that the ship up there is ready, and that the point in space where your counter weight is being held is ready." She kissed him on the cheek.

Tom nodded. He kissed his wife, shook his father's hand and climbed into the *Sky Queen's* lower hatch. Bud had already said his goodbye to Sandy and was waiting for him in the cockpit.

One minute later the giant aircraft lifted off from Enterprises and headed for the coast. They crossed the shoreline minutes later and turned South. Their course would take them down the East side of Florida and from there they would cross the lower portion of Mexico and head directly for the Galapagos Islands.

"What's your worry, skipper?' Bud asked as he watched Tom

chew tentatively on a fingernail.

Tom sighed. "I guess I'm still bothered by the whole 'We want to take all of your secrets' stuff a couple months ago, and now the Bravado and grumblings about reclaiming the islands as their territory by Ecuador. That may not be over."

"Eva Estes is a strong woman," Bud replied, "and her second speech to the United Nations, three weeks ago, was resoundingly and positively received. Ecuador has been put on notice as has the world. Besides," he said, grinning, "what with the incredible find of all those rare earth elements and your willingness to sell them to anyone in the free world, everybody except for the Chinese who have been hoarding what they have is very happy with the Swifts. That ought to count for something."

Tom had to agree, even though in the back of his mind he was wary that somebody might take exception.

They flew high and at supersonic speeds and reached the airspace of the Galapagos Islands six hours later. The *Sea Charger* responded to their radio call and relayed it to the Governmental residence.

"It is so good to hear your voice, Tom," Eva Estes told him. "I received a notice from your *Sea Charger* earlier today that a helicopter will pick me up in about... well, it looks to be in fifteen minutes. I will have to get dressed in my most fetching pair of overalls."

"Madam Prime Minister," Tom said as formally as he could, "I officially request landing permission on your islands with the intent of connecting our base ship with the High Space L-Evator cable that will be lowered in about two hours. Do I have your permission to proceed?"

With equal formality, although Tom could detect a hint of merriment in her tone, Eva Estes gave him official permission.

Ten minutes later he lowered the *Sky Queen* on her repelatron lifters and set down on the deck of the *Sea Charger*. As he and Bud left the aircraft a small team climbed back in and quickly flew off to land on the nearby island on a small pad build specifically for this. It was on land owned—but now rented to Enterprises—by Pepé, the man who had initially taken a shot at Tom's aircraft on their first visit. He was now a very proud man and had begun to share his new wealth with his family.

Almost as quickly as the giant jet left, her small, Skeeter, helicopter returned with a two-man crew.

Tom and Bud were now in the control room of the anchored vessel and just connecting with the *Challenger*.

"It appears that we are ready down here," Tom radioed the ship. "Where is the cable end right now?"

"Mule One has it hanging at an altitude of about twenty-five miles, skipper," came the reply. "We're having a small problem, though. While we can get your end down, the spool holding the rest of the initial length of the cable is jammed. I've had three people out there working on it for about half an hour and we're getting nowhere. What do you want us to do?"

Tom and Bud looked at each other. It would be impossible to bring the end down until the jam was cleared.

Tom considered his choices. "How long can you and your mule remain on station this go-around?"

The answer came back a minute later just as he was about to repeat the question. "On the safe side, thirteen hours. Stretching it, sixteen... maybe seventeen."

The inventor made a decision. "Okay. Stay there for no more than four hours. If things aren't freed by then, reel in—if you can— and go to higher orbit. Once there you might need to pop the entire spool apart to get things moving again. We'll wait for your call to let us know what you will be doing. Out."

Bud and Tom watched as the deck crew continued their preparations.

"Come on, skipper. Let's go below, wait for our guest and have some food and a cup of coffee, and cool down a little. It's really hot down here today and I'm starving and parched!"

It was almost as if Tom was coming out of a trance. He slowly turned his head, eyes not quite focusing on his friend, and then he shook his head and smiled. "It'll be another minute or so, flyboy. I think I know what's happening up there." He picked up his portable radio and pressed the call button.

"Tom here, *Challenger*. Come in, please."

"*Challenger* here. Go ahead."

"It just hit me that the main reason the spool might be a little stuck is that we never designed an accurate method to evenly wind the cable so we left the spool ends a little loose while it was being filled. Once that happened the ends were tightened. Check the operations notes and I think you'll find that little gem hidden way near the end. My goof. Go ahead and have your folks outside re-loosen the spool ends. If I'm correct, you can begin to lower the cable right away."

There was a pause and then, "Roger, skipper. We're looking. Hold a couple..." In about a minute he was back. "You're good, skipper! really good. It's right there where you said it would be.

We're resetting everything and will start the drop in five minutes. If you're ready for it."

"Believe me, we're ready." Turning to Bud he said, "Sorry, but you can go down. I don't have the time." He pointed to the approaching helicopter bearing the Prime Minster.

Bud gave him a sad grin and shake of the head. "Tom. You have time. They won't start for five minutes and then, what? six more hours to lower the cable? We have time to greet Eva, eat, drink, have a little nap, shave, eat some more and still get back out here with an hour to spare. Let the people up in orbit and the guys down here do their jobs without the overlord staring at everyone. Huh?"

In spite of the tenseness he felt in his gut, Tom had to laugh. "Right. As soon as Eva lands, let's go below."

She touched down moment slater and then escorted her to the Wardroom where the ship's serving team served them lunch.

Each hour brought a new status report, and everything was now on schedule. As the cable got closer and closer, the two men got into the Skeeter and headed for the landing pad for the *Sky Queen*. It would be necessary for the jet to go up and locate the end of the cable, and then to bring it down to the deck of the anchored ship. There was no other way as the position of the mule up in orbit might mean the end could be yards or miles away by the time it reached the surface.

The end sported both a large streamer in bright orange as well as a radio beacon, so locating it would be relatively easy. Bud suited up in a safety suit and climbed up the ladder to a hatch in the top of the *Queen*. Fifteen minutes of giving Tom maneuvering instructions while they slowly chased the wandering cable around, Bud was rewarded when he snagged it with a probe. It held hard and fast and was soon reeled in and attached to a mount that had been added to the hull of the jet.

"Let's take it to the *Charger*," Bud radioed as he was closing the hatch.

Tom radioed the *Challenger* telling them to have the mule give him about a thousand yards of slack, and then he began the slow flight back the half mile to the waiting ship.

It took nearly three hours to transfer the cable end from the *Queen* to its mount and then to totally secure it. There was a lot to do and the time went quickly. Soon, it was time for what Bud was calling "The tug test."

Tom radioed the *Challenger* and the mule locked down the mostly-empty spool for the downward cable. Next the remote control pilot, Zimby Cox, angled the maneuvering array downward and gave it a very short burst, designed to lift the small craft with its spool about one hundred feet higher. Once the cable went taut the mule poured on the lift.

It accomplished two things. First, the *Sea Charger* was lifted upward by about a foot. But the second one was the most important. It proved that the cable strength was more that adequate!

Zimby radioed down that they was about to leave orbit. "I've got the world on a string..." he sang out. Switching to his normal voice, he added, "At your command, skipper, we can head up and out. It's going to take a bit to get up to the top."

Tom grinned. "Yeah, Zim. Four weeks! Good luck. Bud and I will meet you at Fearing once you get that asteroid attached. *Bon voyage!*"

The actual flight time *could* be nearly a week less if there had been a single spool large enough to hold all the cable. As there was not, the formation of mules needed to work carefully so the giant coil of cable didn't kink as it played out the entire length of thirty thousand miles. They would accomplish this by locking their Attractatrons on each other and holding positions as they flew in formation.

That evening a huge dinner was put on by the chef of the *Sea Charger*. Eva Estes, her mother—of course—and all the islands' top ministers and leading citizens were helicoptered out for the affair. There were smiles and congratulations all around but it wasn't until Eva managed to get Tom to one side that the inventor felt his day had been a success.

"I wanted to tell you that I have been in contact with the government of Ecuador. They appear to be ready to sign a treaty with us to permanently leave us alone and to never try to interfere with our people."

"Wow," Tom told her, "that sounds great. I am happy for you."

"What is even better is that they seem willing to have free trade with us. As long as we can go get it, they will sell us whatever we might require." She looked at Tom to see if he had understood her hint."

He had.

"Then, it appears you are going to need some sort of cargo aircraft to be at your disposal," he told her, barely able to keep a straight face. All along he had planned to offer her one of the smallest Swift cargo jets as a thank you for her support and the use of Galapagos land.

"I just happen to have a jet capable of hauling about ten tons of supplies at a time. It needs no jet fuel as it uses my repelatron lifters and QuieTurbine engines. It is so quiet you could land it next to your house at three a.m. and not wake your mother!"

Eva laughed at the notion. "Ah, but Tom, my mother rises at three in the morning, and besides, she has a mother's instinct for when her daughter is sneaking back into the house. Oh, and I was asked to give this message to you. Your radioman handed it to me a few moments ago."

Tom unfolded the paper and read:

> Tom. Good news. The U.N. have voted to back off and support you. They will declare the airspace for fifty miles a hazard to navigation and require special permission and equipment for anyone needing to traverse within twenty miles of the cable. They also support a two hundred mile territorial water declaration by Galapagos to be "*enforceable*."
>
> ## Dad

Tom showed the note to Eva and she read it with obvious joy. She gave him a quick, congratulatory hug before they rejoined the rest of the party.

The following day a feast was declared and just about everyone from the major islands in the group was picked up and brought to the main island where many, many tables and chairs had been set up. Chow had flown down overnight in the *Super Queen* with both of her transport pods full of party supplies and food, along with one of the Swift's larger helicopters. By three that afternoon the party was in full swing with everyone enjoying—in most cases—their first taste of American cooking: barbecued chicken and ribs, hamburgers, sausages and even vegetarian patties.

Chow Winkler was in fine form raring to go. This party was just what he wanted and he was in his element as he dished up much of the food personally. He was even able to converse with many of the guests using a sort of pidgin Spanish he had picked up in his many years as a trail cook.

By the time everyone got back to Shopton, it was three days later. Tom and Bud went home to their wives and didn't go back to Enterprises until after the next weekend.

There was, of course, a lot to do in the coming weeks. For starters, all the various platforms and the central core of the L-Evator were completed and shipped to the *Sea Charger* for assembly. In the end it was decided that an overall length of two hundred feet was the maximum height for the L-Evator. Longer was possible but the loading and unloading back on Earth would be considerably more complex.

When the time arrived, Tom, Bud and a crew of thirty men and women crammed into the *Challenger* and headed to what was now referred to as OAP, the Outer Anchorage Point. EAP—Earth Anchorage Point—being the ground end. Both the large counter weight that would travel up and down the cable opposite the L-Evator as well as the anchor asteroid were being held in position by the two newest Attractatron space mules, just waiting.

Bud pointed at the anchor weight.

"Great idea to just use one of the asteroids, skipper. Stroke of genius, as they say."

Tom blushed a little as he replied, "Yeah, well I finally realized that as the station out here gets larger and heavier I needed a way to make the anchor weight smaller and lighter. This way we just carve off pieces as needed to keep things balanced. Plus, we can process what we remove for the rich veins of rare earths that asteroid contains."

"How long will it last?" one of the tech's asked.

Tom slightly shook his head. "I don't know, at least not exactly. But if you'll accept a round figure, two years. By that time the station will be complete and in full operation and with enough mass to no longer need the anchor. Also, by that time we will be finding it necessary to go out and grab more asteroid pieces to give us a continuing supply of metals to sell to keep this new station in operation."

The following day the approaching *Sutter* and the four mules and the last of the cable coil were near enough that they began to slow their rate of travel. One more day went by as they approached the anchor point and a further three hours were required for them to halt. The end of the anchor cable was attached to the asteroid and the pulley positioned for attachment.

The *Sutter* had earlier extruded the final cable, the one connecting the asteroid on one end and the pulley assembly on the other.

People and equipment went to work over the following five hours as the counterweight was first closed over the end of the anchor cable and the pulley cable was attached. Now the *Sutter* began to build the longer cable. It would temporarily be attached to the counterweight and lowered to the ground as that weight traveled back to Earth. After releasing that end—which would then be attached to the cargo platform core—the weight would go back up and be attached to the other end. Once that happened the L-Evator could begin operation.

It had been decided that two of the Attractatron mules would permanently be assigned to attach themselves to the anchor asteroid and used to keep it in both perfect position as well as taut. The other two would remain behind as well but to act as safety devices to keep any space debris from the area.

Tom sent word to the Construction Company to build replacements for these so they might resume their roles as protection devices for the planet below.

The final bit of work was to attach the special-purpose nuclear power supply to the counterweight where it became the upper sixteenth of the entire length. If was necessary to power the array of small repelatrons inside the weight continuously, providing the propelling force to move the entire L-Evator system. The L-Evator itself would have a similar arrangement and the two would work in concert.

With Zimby and his team piloting the *Sutter* for its next load, everyone else went home in the *Challenger*.

* * * * *

Tom, Bashalli, Bud, Sandy and Damon and Anne Swift were in attendance for the inaugural launch of Tom's High Space L-Evator. It really wasn't the first run as several test trips had been made to assure the smooth operation of everything, and one trip had brought down the latest load of rare earth elements, but it was to be the initial run carrying any cargo *into* space.

The first load consisted of several portable habitats for workers to relax in, plus food, water and other living supplies, along with three platforms filled with containers of tools. The assembly teams would be living inside of the *Sutter* but it had been decided that amenities should be stationed quite nearby the station.

As the platforms surrounding the central core began to rise from their anchorage point on the deck of the *Sea Charger*, Bashalli hugged Tom's arm even tighter. "You do know how very proud I am of you, don't you, Tom?" she said into his right ear.

Tom turned, smiled and was about to kiss her on the nose when something registered in his brain.

"Bash. You just used a contraction. You never use contractions. What gives?"

She smiled coyly. "Well, your sister has been working on me for a year or more. 'Why can you not...' sorry. 'Why *can't* you use contractions, Bashi.' I had no good answer for her. It has always been the way I speak, but I am trying to work a few into my conversations. You should have seen the people at work the first time I said 'won't' instead of will not." She giggled.

They both looked up in time to see the loaded platforms disappear through the cloud layer several miles up.

"Well," he told her taking her left hand in his right and turning toward the ship's island, "however you speak is fine with me. Do what feels good, they used to say."

As they walked toward the stairs to go below, she squeezed his hand and told him, "Being with you feels good. I'll do it forever!" When they got to the mess deck and crew lounge she took a seat while Tom went to get some refreshments. By the time he returned she was looking puzzled.

"What?"

"Well," she told him, "I was wondering what could be next."

He grinned. "That's just the first load with many, many more to go. Up *and* down. And with the deals Dad brokered for those rare earth metals we mined, every load down brings us more money than each upward load costs."

Bashalli shook her head. "No. I meant what is next for *you*. You never seem to sit still for very long, and I was hoping..."

When she didn't finish the sentence, he prompted her, "Hoping...?"

"Hoping that we might take a vacation. Maybe a cruise down in the Caribbean or up in Alaska?"

Tom nodded as he thought over the notion. It sounded like a nice way to relax. He could not know that their vacation would provide no long-lasting relaxation because a forthcoming deep sea mystery and a trip into the bowels of the planet were in store for him.

But, for now he just sat looking at his beautiful wife and trying to figure out what he should bring along to read on their trip.

<•>—< End of Book >—<•>

Manufactured by Amazon.ca
Bolton, ON

20380770R00113